T

MARBELLA PROJECT

by

Nigel James

ISBN: 978-1-291-49274-3

PublishNation, London
www.publishnation.co.uk

PROLOGUE

Cassie's mobile phone beeped and lit up, signifying a text message. She picked it up from the bar and read the message with irritation. *'Running late, will be another couple of hours'.* No apology. No explanation. Typical of Alexei, she thought. Why do I bother to get here on time when he is always late? But she knew the answer and she also knew why she would wait for him and not dump him for someone more considerate.

Alexei was rich, good looking and flashed his money around like there was no tomorrow. Despite her doubts about how he and his family made their money, he was the best thing that had happened to her since she had arrived on the Costa del Sol a few months earlier, looking for the glamorous lifestyle that she was hardly likely to get in her home town of Wigan. Then, she had been plain Sandra Wilson, check out girl by day and pole dancer by night. But on arrival in Marbella, she had re-invented herself as Cassandra Wilson or Cassie, as she now called herself.

Unfortunately, things had not progressed as well as she had hoped. Fame and fortune had eluded her. Good looking girls were two a penny.

To survive, she had taken a job as a salesgirl in a Puerto Banus boutique but the money was crap, despite the fact that she loved the atmosphere of Spain's flashiest port. She shared a rundown flat on the wrong side of Marbella with two other wannabe Brit chicks and the only men she had met had disappeared as soon as they had tired of screwing her. She had even contemplated advertising her services in the 'Adult Relaxation' section of the classifieds in the Sur, the local English language paper, but had been put off by girls she had met who had gone down that route. The economic climate had affected the sex industry and if she was going to be shagged by some smelly fat geezer, she would want more than sixty euros.

So Alexei was comfortably the best thing on offer and she could easily put up with his somewhat deviant behaviour in return for the goodies that came her way.

As she sat perched on the bar stool, she looked down admiringly at the three hundred euro shoes he had bought her with the ridiculously high spiked heels, wondering at the same time whether she should wait for Alexei or go back to her flat for an hour or so. The shoes made the decision for her. She could not walk far in them and a return taxi trip would cost her another thirty euros on top of the fifteen it had already cost to get to the bar back in Puerto Banus where they had arranged to meet. Perhaps one of the other girls would come down and keep her company...

As she pondered her options, she became conscious of someone standing quite close to her at the bar.

'Can I top up that drink for you?'

She looked up, opening her mouth to tell whoever it was to get lost but when she saw the smiling, handsome face looking down at her, different words came out.

'Why not?' she said. 'I'll have a vodka and tonic. No lemon.' She picked up her glass, finished her drink and handed the empty the glass to him.

She guessed that he was about the same age as her, around twenty, but he appeared to have the confidence of someone a lot older.

He caught the barman's attention and ordered a large vodka and tonic and a pint of lager. As the drinks were being poured, she noticed with amusement that he took a sidelong glance at her legs. Not surprising really given that her skirt barely covered her bottom and she had to keep her legs firmly crossed. She assumed that he had already noticed her cleavage and wondered whether she could persuade Alexei to stump up for a boob job to make them even more impressive.

He introduced himself as Tom and proved to be good company. He was there with two friends, whom he pointed out to her sitting at a table at the other end of the bar. They waved at him but she was glad that they did not come over and before long she noticed that they were chatting to two girls. She wondered what Alexei would have said if he had known she was being chatted up by a good looking English boy. But as the drinks flowed, Alexei faded from her mind. After about an hour, she excused herself and tottered on her high heels and under the influence of three or four double vodkas to the Ladies. She had two reasons for going there. First, she was absolutely bursting to pee, but also, she had decided to enjoy another of Alexei's goodies. She poured out a line of coke on the vanity unit and sniffed it up through a rolled up twenty euro note.

When she returned to the bar, she initially thought that Tom had gone and a wave of disappointment hit her. But then she saw that he was waving to her from a table at the back of the bar. She went over and sat next to him and saw that he had replenished her drink. She drank half of it and the effect of the drink and drugs immediately began to kick in. As always in that state, she began to feel very horny and when Tom put his hand on her thigh she looked around to see if people were watching.

As if reading her mind, Tom said, 'Don't worry. No one can see what we get up to under the table.'

4

Cassie smiled. 'You've planned this, haven't you?'

She uncrossed her legs and opened her thighs slightly. Tom needed no second invitation. His fingers slid between her legs, under her knickers and straight inside her. She moaned and reached out and felt his hardness underneath his jeans.

'Why don't we finish these drinks and take a walk?' Tom said.

This time, it was Cassie who needed no second invitation. They drank up and left the bar arm in arm. Their walk turned out to be a trip down the first deserted alleyway they found. Tom pushed Cassie against the wall, pulled down her low cut T-shirt and took out her breasts. While he fondled them, Cassie undid the buckle on his jeans and pushed his jeans and boxer shorts down. She then pushed him away for a moment as she stepped out of her knickers. Tom then hoisted up her skirt, pushed her against the wall, lifted up one of her legs and entered her. Within moments, Cassie screamed and they were both spent.

As Tom pulled up his trousers and pants and Cassie stepped back into her knickers, the fresh air seemed to sober her up a bit. She looked at her watch and saw that she still had another half an hour until Alexei was due.

'Tom, don't take this the wrong way, but I'm meeting someone in the bar in about half an hour and he wouldn't be happy if he saw us together!'

She need not have worried. Tom had had his fun and was happy to go back to his friends.

'OK, no problem. I'll go back and join my friends. You follow on in a couple of minutes and we will ignore each other completely if that's what you want.'

'Great. Thanks,' Cassie said. Tom kissed her and then made his way back to the bar.

Cassie lingered a bit longer, touching up her makeup in her vanity mirror, before she left the alley and walked down the road back to the bar. Serve Alexei right, she thought, smiling to herself. That will teach him to leave me on my own!

As she walked along, a car drew up beside her and stopped. She looked up and was shocked to see that it was Alexei's black chauffeur driven limousine. The rear window descended and Alexei called out to her.

'Cassie, what the hell are you doing out here?'

'I...er wanted a bit of fresh air before you arrived. I thought you said a couple of hours?'

'It was a family meeting chaired by my father, so I had to attend. Fortunately it ended earlier than I expected.'

The rear door opened.

'Come on, Cassie, get in the car!'

Cassie had no choice but to get in. Alexei made room for her and she closed the door behind her. She noticed that he was drinking champagne.

'Want a glass before we go to the bar?'

'We're only a couple of minutes away,' Cassie replied.

'No hurry,' Alexei said, eyeing Cassie up and down. 'Nice shoes!'

Cassie realised that the car was remaining stationary. She wanted to get to the bar and visit the Ladies again before Alexei started pawing her but to her dismay he pressed the button which closed the screen between the rear of the car and the driver and bodyguard in the front.

'Here,' said Alexei, passing her a glass of champagne. 'It's been a very boring day and I've amused myself by imagining what we are going to get up to!'

Cassie forced a smile. 'There's plenty of time for that. Why don't we give the bar a miss and go straight to a club?'

'Fine by me. But it's a little early for a club. You know no one arrives till after midnight. But if you don't want to go back to the bar, I'm sure we can amuse ourselves here.'

Alexei put his right arm around Cassie and put his left hand on her thigh. Instinctively, she moved it off with her free hand.

'What's the matter? Playing hard to get for the first time in your life?' Alexei's tone had changed. He was not used to anyone saying no to him, let alone Cassie who from the first time they had met had shown herself game for almost anything.

'I'm just not in the mood at the moment, Alexei,' she said in as appealing a tone as she could muster. 'I'll be fine later.'

'Well, I'm in the mood now,' Alexei said and took hold of one of her breasts.

'Stop it, you're hurting me,' Cassie exclaimed and grabbed his wrist and tried to push him away.

Alexei pulled his hand free of hers and then slapped Cassie hard across her face, causing her to squeal and drop her glass of champagne, spilling it all over her top.

'You'll do what I want, when I want,' he shouted, 'and if that means I have to get rough then so be it. It's all the same to me!'

With that, he forced his left hand between her legs, up her skirt and ripped her knickers down. He then put his hand back up between his legs.

'You're soaking!' he exclaimed. 'So you do like it rough after all!'

But after a few moments, he withdrew his hand, a look of shock on his face.

'You can't be that wet already!' He looked at his hand, then picked up her knickers from the floor and looked at them closely. He then sniffed his hand and her knickers. Recognition dawned and his response was immediate. He smashed his fist into Cassie's face again and again.

'Filthy whore! You're just like all the other English sluts down here.' He then pulled her down so that her head was flat on the seat facing upwards. Then kneeling on the floor with one hand round her throat, he smashed a champagne glass in her face and dragged the broken remains down the side of her face. Oblivious to the blood pouring over the leather seat, he screamed 'Tell me who it was or I will rip your face off bit by bit!'

'It was this guy,' Cassie sobbed, 'he made me do it!'

Alexei jammed the broken stalk into Cassie's cheek and twisted it. 'Don't lie to me! He didn't make you do it. One more chance. Who was it?'

'It was a guy called Tom. He's back in the bar now! Please don't hurt me anymore!'

'Describe him!'

'Dark hair, jeans, white T-shirt!'

Alexei pressed the intercom button.

'Drive to the bar now!' he shouted.

Alexei dragged the whimpering Cassie back into a sitting position. He then leaned across her, opened the car door and kicked her out of the moving vehicle.

Alexei walked into the bar, followed by Dmitry and Ivan. He had used champagne to wash the blood off his hands and was still in a raging temper. Dmitry and Ivan did not know exactly what had happened but they had seen Cassie in their wing mirrors rolling down the road after being thrown from the car so they had a pretty good idea as to what had occurred given that Alexei was clearly looking for someone. They had tried to advise caution but he wouldn't hear of it. They felt conspicuous in their black suits in a bar full of youngsters dressed in jeans and other casual clothing.

It did not take Alexei long to identify Tom. He was at a table with two other men and two girls and, so it appeared, telling them something that caused them great amusement. In Alexei's rage, he assumed that he was bragging about his conquest.

Alexei strode up to the table and knocked Tom's drink over so it spilt all over the table and down his jeans. Tom jumped up and faced Alexei. Alexei turned round to Dmitry and Ivan.

'Just stay back and make sure no one interferes,' he said in Russian. Dmitry and Ivan looked at each other and shrugged.

Alexei turned back to Tom.

'So, English boy, do I have your attention?'

'I don't know what your problem is, Boris, but why don't you and your two goons just fuck off!' Tom replied.

'You fuck my girlfriend and then you treat me with disrespect? I will teach you some manners!' With that, Alexei produced something from his pocket and there was a gasp from onlookers as he clicked open the blade of a flick knife. The others at the table then all stood up and backed away. Alexei lunged forward with the knife but Tom ducked out of the way, grabbed Alexei's arm and twisted it, causing the knife to clatter to the floor. He then pulled Alexei towards him and headbutted him with a sickening crack so that Alexei's nose exploded and he collapsed on his back.

All this happened in seconds. Dmitry and Ivan then charged towards Tom but were restrained by bouncers who had arrived at that precise moment. The two huge Russians would have fancied their chances against the bouncers but realised that getting involved in a mass brawl would not please Alexei's father. The bouncers quickly found out that Alexei had started the fight and pulled a knife and the three Russians were unceremoniously escorted to the door and thrown out.

When they reached the car, Alexei told Dmitry to drive back to the house. They drove up into the hills to Alexei's family home, a huge fortified

11

villa with electronic security gates. Dmitry and Ivan thought that their evening was over and were worried how Alexei's father would react to his son's squashed and bloody nose when they were supposed to be looking after him. However, when the car stopped, Alexei got out and told them to stay in the car, while he went into the house. A few minutes later, he came back and when Dmitry saw what he was carrying, he jumped out of the car.

'I can't let you do this, Alexei!' he said. 'It's crazy! Just let it go! Your father will go mad!'

'My father will go mad if I tell him you failed to protect me!'

Dmitry hesitated and looked at Ivan through the windscreen. Ivan shrugged. Dmitry reluctantly opened the rear door for Alexei. They then drove back to the bar and parked along the road. Ivan was sent to check that Tom was still in the bar. They then waited. An hour later, after Alexei had snorted two lines of coke, Tom and his two friends left the bar and started to walk along the road. The black limo slowly caught them up. They turned and saw it.

'Jesus,' one of Tom's friends said, 'who the hell is this trailing us?'

'It could be those Russians again, waiting for us!' Tom said.

'What do you think we should do?'

'Run!' said Tom.

At that, they all started to run but the car speeded up. Tom then made a fatal error. He turned off down a side road. This played right into the Russians' hands. They followed Tom, ignoring the other two, in whom they were not interested anyway. The car overtook Tom and cut in front of him blocking his path. Ivan jumped out and grabbed Tom. He punched Ivan in the face but it had no effect. The big Russian just grinned. Ignoring Tom's flailing arms, he hit Tom just once in the stomach causing him to double over. He then kneed him in the head and threw him in the back of the car semi-conscious. They then drove slowly until they found a deserted alley, unbeknown to any of them the same one that Tom and Cassie had been in earlier.

Tom was hauled out of the car. Dmitry went to the end of the alley to ensure no one would be passing. He gave the thumbs up. Tom was then thrown over the corner of a skip with his face towards the ground. Alexei went back to the car and fetched the object he had taken from the house and returned to the skip where Tom was groaning.

'No one makes a fool of me, Englishman!' The reflection of a street light caused the blade of the machete to flash as Alexei brought it down.

An hour later, Alexei, Dmitry and Ivan stood in front of a large antique desk behind which sat a huge and clearly furious man, Alexei's father, Viktor Durchenko. On one side of Viktor stood one of Alexei's older brothers, Georgy, and on the other, Viktor's long time friend and chief of staff, Vitaly Petrov. None of them were smiling.

On returning to the house, Dmitry had reported what had happened to Petrov, his immediate boss, as he had known that it would be all over the papers the next day and there would be a full police investigation. Petrov had exploded in fury and woken up up Viktor.

Dmitry had just explained to Viktor exactly what he had told Petrov. Viktor glared at the three of them. There was a moment of silence and then Viktor crashed both his massive fists down on the desk so hard that the whole room seemed to shake.

Viktor then got up and walked round to the front of the desk.

'How could this have happened?' he shouted. 'Have you taken leave of your senses? A dispute over some English slut and you decide to execute a tourist? A method of execution that points directly at us and will bring the whole family under scrutiny?'

No one spoke.

'I'm waiting for an answer!' Viktor roared.

'We tried to dissuade Alexei but he was very angry and insisted,' Dmitry stammered.

Viktor put all his force into a backhanded blow across Dmitry's face. Any normal man would have been knocked unconscious but Dmitry's head barely moved and he did not dare put his hand up to the vicious welt on his face caused by Viktor's ring.

'My son Alexei is a fool! A young hothead!' Viktor shouted. 'You tried to *dissuade* him? You should have told him not to be such an idiot and told Vitaly or myself what he planned. Are you two as thick as you look?'

'No one makes a fool of our family, father! You said that yourself!' Alexei said.

'You don't need anyone to make a fool out of you, Alexei! You already are one!'

Alexei's surly face infuriated Viktor and he grabbed his son by the throat. At that, Georgy stepped forward and put a restraining hand on his father's arm.

'Why couldn't you just have asked Dmitry and Ivan to rough him up a bit, maybe break a few bones? The police would barely have been interested.' Georgy said. He then looked more closely into Alexei's eyes. 'You've been on the coke haven't you? I can see it in your eyes. That's what has caused all this. When will you learn? We may sell it but we don't use it.'

Viktor released Alexei and waved them all away. 'Get out of my sight. All three of you!'

When they had gone, Viktor said more to himself than to Georgy and Petrov, 'I love that boy but he is becoming a liability!'

'He's only twenty one,' Georgy said.

'Pah!' Viktor retorted. 'By that age, I'd removed most of my opposition in Moscow and ran over fifty girls!' He then turned to Petrov. 'Damage assessment, Vitaly?'

'We'll be OK. I have already been in touch with our police contacts. There were witnesses to the fight in the bar but no clear identification and anyway, they were all tourists not wanting to get involved. There were no witnesses to what happened later. A few vague sitings of a black limo but so what? We can provide all three of them with cast iron alibis.'

'So we've got away with it?'

'Yes, I'm confident there will be no comeback.'

Chapter One

The alarm sounded at 6.30am, as it did every day. The fact that it was a Saturday made no difference to Dan Green. He was a creature of habit, used to routine. He got up immediately and pulled on a T shirt, shorts and trainers and took the lift down to the gym. After a vigorous half hour workout, he returned to his flat and put some coffee on to brew while he took a shower.

After putting on a polo shirt and some tracksuit bottoms, he took his coffee out on to the balcony overlooking the river Thames and downloaded the Times on to his iPad. London was in the middle of a heatwave and even at that time of the morning, it was hot enough to sit outside.

Dan was looking forward to the day. He was a big cricket fan and had a ticket for the test match at Lords against the West Indies. He had arranged to meet up with some friends for a bacon sandwich at the open air cafe adjacent to the members' stand an hour before play started at 11.00am. He had already worked out that if he walked the short distance to Canary Wharf from his docklands flat, he could take a Jubilee line train all the way to St John's Wood station, about five minutes' walk from the ground.

After drinking his coffee and flicking through the day's news, he went back inside and began to get ready for the day ahead. Shortly before nine, he was ready to leave, having dressed in lightweight clothes and packed a bag containing a hat, his binoculars and most importantly a few cans of lager and some food for sharing with his friends.

As he was carrying out a final check before leaving, the doorbell rang. Puzzled as to who it could be, Dan pressed the button for the video answerphone and picked up the handset. To his surprise, he saw that there were two uniformed police officers, a policeman and a policewoman, waiting by the doorbells outside the foyer.

'Hello. Can I help you?' Dan asked, wondering if they had pressed the wrong bell.

The intercom crackled into life.

'Mr Green?' the male police officer asked.

'Yes?' Dan replied, anxious as to why the police should be calling on him at this time on a Saturday morning.

'I wonder if we could come up? We need to talk to you.'

'OK,' Dan replied hesitantly. 'Flat 126 on the 12th floor.'

Dan pushed the entry button and waited at the the door until he saw the police officers come round the corner from the lift. He stood back to let them in and showed them into the living room. The male officer was probably in his forties but the female officer was much younger and looked very uncomfortable. They both had their hats tucked under their arms and as with all visitors to the apartment, their attention was drawn to the view over the Thames.

'Nice view,' the male officer said, somewhat awkwardly.

'Please,' said Dan, 'sit down. What's this all about? Is it something to do with my work?'

Dan worked as a security consultant in a partnership with some of his former army colleagues and it had occurred to him that perhaps the visit was connected with one of their clients.

The two officers sat on the sofa but perched on the edge.

'No, sir, it's nothing like that. It's...er...about your son.'

Dan went cold. He suddenly recognised all the signs. In his army days, he had had to make a number of visits to relatives after soldiers had been killed in action. But surely, he must be mistaken. Tom wasn't in the army. He wasn't even in the country. He was on holiday in Spain!

'What about my son?' he said quickly.

'You're Thomas Green's father?' the officer replied.

'Yes, but he's in Spain on holiday.'

The two officers looked at each other.

'Yes, Puerto Banus,' the male officer said. There was then a pause. 'I'm afraid there's no easy way to tell you this, sir. Your son has been killed.'

'Killed?' Dan blurted out. 'What do you mean, *killed*? There must be some mistake.'

Even at that moment, it occurred to Dan that his reaction was just the same as all the people he had visited in similar circumstances but he still wanted to cling to the hope that there had been some sort of mistake.

'I'm afraid not, sir. That's your son, isn't it?' the officer said, pointing to a picture of Tom on the sideboard.

'Yes,' Dan said with a croak.

The officer handed Dan a piece of paper. Dan saw that it was a photocopy of the page of Tom's passport, naming Dan as the next of kin to be contacted in the event of an emergency.

'The Spanish police faxed that to us. And your son's friends have identified him.'

Dan felt the blood draining from his face. There was no mistake.

'How was he killed? A car accident?'

'I'm sorry, sir. I know how difficult this must be for you. I'm afraid your son was murdered.'

'Murdered!' Dan shouted. 'How? Who by?'

'I'm afraid I don't have all the details, sir. But I do have the details of the Spanish police officer handling the case.' The officer handed Dan a piece of paper. 'I assume you will want to fly out to Spain to make the necessary arrangements. I suggest you get in contact with the Spanish police before you leave and arrange to see the officer in charge.' After a short pause, the officer continued, 'Is there anyone else who should be notified about this?'

'If you mean Tom's mother,' Dan replied, 'we divorced years ago. Although I am the next of kin on his passport, Tom lives...lived with his mother and stepfather in Leicestershire.'

'I see. Do you want us to inform them?'

'No. Leave it to me. I will drive up there as soon as you leave.'

The two police officers looked at each other. 'Are you sure that's wise, sir, setting off on a fairly lengthy drive after such a shock?'

'I'll be fine. The least I can do is tell them personally.'

With that, the officers rose to leave and after expressing their condolences left Dan on his own. Dan went out on to the balcony for a few moments but for once he did not take in the view. Having worked out what needed to be done, he went back inside.

First, he phoned one of the friends he had planned to meet at Lords and, trying to keep his voice as normal as possible, explained that a crisis at work had occurred and he could no longer attend the match.

Next, he phoned his ex-wife's home. Tom's stepfather, Richard, answered the phone.

Once again, Dan tried to keep his voice as normal as possible. 'Hi Richard, it's Dan here.'

'Hi Dan, how are you?' Richard replied.

'Er, not too bad...Richard, are you and Carol going to be in in at about twelve? I'm going to be in the area and thought I might call in.'

'Yes, we will be here,' Richard replied. 'There's nothing wrong, is there?'

Dan wondered if Richard had detected something about his voice and dodged the question.

'There's something I need to discuss with you and Carol, so I thought I would come round and do it in person.'

'OK, fine. We will look forward to seeing you then.'

Dan ended the conversation, feeling guilty that Carol and Richard might actually be looking forward to his visit. Dan and Carol had been childhood sweethearts and had only been eighteen when Carol had fallen pregnant with Tom. Dan was about to join the army and getting married and having a baby had certainly not been in their plans at that time. However, they decided to make the best of it and Dan started his career as a married man with a pregnant wife.

Unfortunately, things had not worked out. Dan had wanted to join the army since he had been a young boy. Carol on the other hand was not cut out to be a soldier's wife. They had separated within two years. Nevertheless, they had remained friends for Tom's sake and Dan had never shirked his responsibilities as a father, visiting whenever his duties permitted.

While Dan had gone on to have a successful army career, fulfilling his ambition to join the SAS, Carol had married Richard, a young country solicitor, and ended up with the lifestyle that she had always wanted. She had had two other children, Alan and Vanessa, with Richard, who had treated his stepson no differently from his own children. Dan became a regular visitor to their home and had even become a godfather to the other children.

After ending the conversation with Richard, Dan started up his laptop and booked a late afternoon flight from Luton Airport to Malaga. He worked out that he would have time to visit Carol and Richard and then cut across to the M1 which would take him straight to the airport.

He then telephoned the number on the piece of paper handed to him and was put through to an Inspector Valdez, who fortunately spoke fluent English. Valdez said that he had been expecting a call and expressed his condolences. He was not prepared to say much over the phone but said that he was happy to meet Dan that evening and would send a car to pick Dan up at Malaga Airport.

Lastly, Dan packed a carry on bag with enough clothes for a few days and then took the lift down to the underground car park.

Fortunately, the traffic was not heavy on a Saturday and Dan made good time. He followed the Satnav in his Audi like an automaton, his mind elsewhere, as he skirted around north east London before speeding up the A1 and turning off towards Melton Mowbray. When he pulled into the sweeping gravel drive of the house in a pretty village outside of the town, he still hadn't decided how he was going to break the news. As he got out of the car, the front door opened and Carol and Richard stood there smiling. The smiles did not last long. They could see from Dan's grim face that he was not bringing good news.

As he approached them, Carol solved the problem as to how to start the conversation.

'It's Tom, isn't it? Has something happened to Tom?' she asked, putting her hand to her face.

'Let's go inside,' Dan said.

After he had broken the terrible news to them, he waited while Richard tried to comfort Carol who was sobbing uncontrollably. Dan then told them that he was booked on a flight to Spain later that afternoon and had arranged to meet the officer in charge of the investigation into Tom's murder.

'We should come with you to Spain,' Richard said.

'Perhaps, but let me fly out today and maybe you can join me in a couple of days. I have got to go straight to the airport. In the meantime, there are people to be told, his grandparents, Alan and Vanessa and his friends,' Dan replied. 'Also, there are funeral arrangements to consider. I don't know whether the Spanish police will release the body yet. Hopefully I will find out this evening.'

'Yes, of course,' Richard said. 'I can do the phoning. But how I'm going to break the news to Alan and Vanessa, I don't know. They worshipped him as you know. Vanessa is upstairs in her room now and Alan is round at a friend's house.'

Dan felt relieved that Richard was taking over the task of telling people what had happened. He realised how awful it would be to have to contact so many people and give them such terrible news and then listen to their reaction.

Dan left it that he would would ring Richard as soon as he had any news from the Spanish police and Richard said that he would break the news to as many people as possible and make tentative enquiries as to when a funeral might take place assuming the Spanish police were happy to release Tom's body.

Chapter Two

Dan was met at Malaga Airport by a young police officer whose limited English precluded any meaningful conversation in the drive to Marbella and as Dan was not in the mood for small talk and the officer doubtless knew Dan's situation, the journey passed in silence. Dan was vaguely conscious of huge roadside billboards proclaiming Andalucia as Europe's California and advertising such things as luxury properties and breast enhancement operations, but otherwise took no note of his surroundings, still trying to come to terms with the loss of his son and still harbouring the forlorn hope even then that some huge mistake had been made.

The journey from the airport took about half an hour and on arrival at the Police headquarters in Marbella, Dan was taken straight up to an office on the third floor where Inspector Valdez was waiting for him.

Valdez was a small, smartly dressed man in his mid forties. He stood up and walked round his desk to shake hands with Dan.

'Senor Green,' he said, 'Once again, I'm so sorry for your loss. Please, take a seat.'

'Thank you for seeing me on a Saturday evening,' Dan replied.

Valdez shrugged as he sat at his desk. 'This is a terrible crime, Senor. I can't pretend that we don't have our problems with crime in this area but nothing like this...'

'Can you tell me what happened?'

Valdez shrugged again. 'It's still early days. What I can tell you is that your son's body was found in an alley off one of the main streets in Puerto Banus by a cleaner in the early hours of this morning. Fortunately, he was carrying his passport. That enabled us to trace the hotel where he and his friends were staying. Although we have not yet ascertained the precise time of death, the police doctor called to the scene estimates that your son died between midnight and 2.00am.'

'How did he die?' Dan asked.

Valdez hesitated. 'That's what's so terrible, Senor Green. I'm so sorry to have to tell you this, but he was beheaded.'

For the second time that day, Dan felt the blood drain from his face.

'Why...how, who would do such a thing?'

Valdez did not reply. He stood up and poured a glass of water from a jug on a table beside the desk. He handed it to Dan.

'But surely there must have been witnesses?' Dan asked after taking a drink.

'There were. Not to the incident itself but your son's friends have given us a full description of the events leading up to the assault. I can tell you that we already have a man in custody.'

'So you've got him?'

Again, the shrug. 'We think so, but there are several lines of inquiry we still need to pursue.'

'So, you must be able to tell me why my son was killed in such a barbaric fashion?'

'I'd prefer not to speculate at this stage, senor. I am hopeful that we will complete our inquiries tomorrow and I will be able to tell you more.'

Dan continue to question the inspector but it was clear that he was not prepared to say more that evening. Valdez suggested that Dan return the following day at 2.00pm and Dan reluctantly agreed.

'Do you have a room booked for tonight?' Valdez asked.

'No I don't,' Dan replied. 'I should have thought of that.'

'Don't worry,' Valdez said, picking up the phone, 'I will get a room booked in a hotel for you and arrange for you to be taken there.'

After he had made the arrangements, Valdez stood up to show Dan out.

'One final thing, senor,' he said, 'the murder of a tourist like this will be headline news here. I suspect it will also be a major news item in the British press. You may wish to warn those who were close to your son that this is likely to feature prominently in the papers and maybe in the television news.'

'Yes, of course. I will warn Tom's mother to expect a lot of press coverage. I expect they will try to contact her,' Dan replied.

Dan was taken by a police car to a medium grade hotel at one end of the main promenade. The fact that the people in and around the hotel all appeared to be happy holidaymakers made him feel even worse and he was glad to reach his room where he could be alone.

The first thing that he did was to phone Carol and Richard. Carol answered the phone but Dan couldn't bring himself to tell her how Tom had died and insisted on speaking to Richard.

Not surprisingly, Richard was stunned and horrified by the news. He said that he would tell Carol and try to prepare her for the following day's papers and the fact that the house could be besieged by journalists and perhaps even TV cameras that day. He was pleased to hear though that someone had been arrested and Dan promised to ring him again after he had seen Valdez the following day.

Just as he was about to end the conversation, a thought occurred to Dan.

'Richard, do you know which friends Tom had come down here with?'

'Yes, Charlie and Joe. Why?'

'Well, I imagine they are still here and won't return until Valdez is satisfied they can't assist further in the investigation. You don't have their mobile numbers do you?'

'No, I don't. But I know Charlie's parents. I could ring them and ask for his number. They will know what's happened by now.'

'Could you? I'd like to speak to them if possible before I see Valdez later.'

'Will Valdez approve of you speaking to material witnesses in the middle of his investigation?'

'I don't see why not. I'm not going to sleep much tonight and I just want something to do tomorrow morning or I'll go mad!'

'OK. Leave it with me and I will phone you back.'

In fact, it took Richard an hour to phone back as he had had to explain things to Carol, who was devastated to hear how Tom died and then to Charlie's father who was also shocked as to what had happened.

Chapter Three

Dan found it almost impossible to sleep and even
when he did doze off, he was then woken up by
the sound of happy holidaymakers returning to
their rooms after a night out. After no more than a
couple of hours sleep, Dan was the first down to
an empty restaurant when it opened for breakfast
at 7.30. He did not feel particularly hungry but
forced down a croissant and a cup of coffee as he
had not eaten the previous evening and knew that
he had to eat something.

At 8 o'clock, he phoned Charlie's mobile
number. Charlie answered immediately. He was
only too happy to talk to Dan. He said that he and
Joe had been told to stay at their hotel as they
might be required for some sort identity parade
that morning but they were hoping to return to
England later that day. He gave Dan the name
and address of their hotel just outside Puerto
Banus on the beach.

Dan then took a taxi to their hotel where
Charlie and Joe were waiting for him in the foyer.

They went up to Charlie's room and the two
boys told Dan what had happened, how Tom had
chatted up a girl, how they had left the bar for
about half an hour, how Tom had come back

alone. They then told him about the fight between Tom and a Russian boy who had two minders or bodyguards with him. Finally, they recounted the events when they eventually left the bar much later at about 1.30am.

'Why didn't you stay together?' Dan asked.

'We thought we were together.' Joe replied. 'We all ran down the road back towards our hotel. It was only when we were sure the car was no longer following us that we stopped and realised that Tom wasn't with us. We went back but couldn't find him so we assumed that he had taken a different route. When he didn't come back, we got really worried and called the police.'

'You called the police?'

'Yes. But they weren't particularly interested. They said if he wasn't back by the following morning, we should phone again. But before we did, they came here and we found out what had happened.'

'Maybe the police could have done something,' Charlie said.

Dan thought about it for a moment. 'I doubt it,' he said. 'By the time you'd got back to the hotel and waited before calling the police, it would have already happened.'

'We're so sorry, Mr Green,' Charlie said. 'We should have done something earlier.'

'No', Dan replied firmly, 'you're not to blame yourselves. No one would have acted any differently and anything you might have done would not have made any difference. And anyway, how were you to know these people were such animals? At least they appear to have caught the guy who did it!'

'Really?' Joe said. 'That's news to us!'

Dan told them about his meeting with Valdez the previous evening.

'That's why we might have to attend an identity parade!' Charlie said.

'Presumably,' Dan replied. 'You will be able to identify this Russian and the other two, won't you?'

Charlie and Joe looked at each other.

'To be honest, I'm not sure.' Joe said. 'It all happened very quickly and it was pretty dark in that bar. And we had had quite a bit to drink. I know the younger Russian who had the fight with Tom was dark and medium build and height but that's about all I can say.'

'If they were to put him in a line with other dark haired men of roughly the same age and build like in a British ID parade, I don't think I could pick him out,' Charlie added. 'I hope the whole case doesn't depend on us identifying him. There were loads of other people in the bar. Surely the staff will remember him. I doubt it was his first time there.'

'Well just do your best,' Dan said. 'Don't worry if you can't pick him out. As you say, the staff may know him.'

He then produced a street map of Puerto Banus that he had picked up at his hotel and asked the boys to show him where the bar was and in which direction they had run.

Dan then walked into the centre of Puerto Banus and it did not take him long to find the bar and the alley further down the road which was cordoned off with police tape. As he looked down the alley, he could feel fury rising within him as he saw where his son had been brutally slain.

The time until his meeting with Valdez dragged. He phoned Richard but could not get through as the line was engaged. He eventually got him on his mobile and Richard told him that he and Carol had been inundated with calls, mostly from the press, so he had unplugged the landline. There were journalists camped outside the house as well as TV vans. He had made a short statement but it had not deterred them.

Dan arrived for his meeting with Valdez half an hour early but was shown straight to his office. Valdez did not look happy.

'So what's the news?' Dan immediately asked after they had shaken hands.

'Not good, I'm afraid.' Valdez replied. 'We have had to release the suspect.'

'*What*?' Dan exclaimed. 'You seemed so confident yesterday that you had got the right man!'

'I'm still confident I had got the right man. But proving it is something else. With your background as a security consultant, you will know that.'

'You've been checking up on me?'

Valdez spread his hands. 'I like to know who I'm dealing with. And 'checking up' is putting it a bit strongly. A couple of clicks on the internet and your firm came up.'

'Well never mind that. Tell me what the problem is.'

'The problem is quite simply this. The only witnesses who have made statements are your son's friends and they haven't been able to identify the suspect. The other customers in the bar were all tourists and can't be traced. The bar staff on duty at the time all claim that they could not describe any of the three Russians involved. There is no evidence at all linking what happened in the bar to your son's murder some two hours later. Further, even if your son's friends had identified the suspect, his lawyers have produced numerous sworn statements to the effect that he was elsewhere at the time. Any half decent lawyer would have been able to discredit an identification in a dark bar carried out by people

36

who if not drunk were well on the way to being drunk.'

'I see. Do you believe the bar staff?'

'Certainly not. The suspect was a regular at that bar. It is inconceivable that they don't know who he is. I haven't the slightest doubt that they have been...how do you say it in English...*got at.*'

'Who the hell are these people?'

Valdez paused before replying.

'The reason that I made the arrest in the first place was that in my opinion only one person could have committed this crime. The description of a black limousine, a young Russian with bodyguards and the mode of execution pointed in one direction only.'

'And that is?'

Valdez paused again.

'OK. Because of your loss and the horrific nature of this crime, I will tell you. A few years ago, a notorious Russian gangster moved down here with his family. Far from retiring here as so many foreign criminals do, within eighteen months he had wiped out or scared off his opposition and he now controls most of the brothels between Torrelominos and Estepona. He is also the biggest drug dealer and extortionist on the Costa del Sol. He relies on extreme violence, bribery or anything which achieves his aims. As we found out from our colleagues in Moscow, he sometimes executes his business rivals by

37

beheading them. He knows that this sort of ritualistic assassination sends out a message to those who might stand in his way. However, to my knowledge, he has only used this method of killing once down here when he first arrived and an Albanian crime boss stood up to him.'

'So why now, on Tom?'

'I'm coming to that. When I heard about the mode of execution, I asked the same question. In my opinion, there is no way that he would have sanctioned the murder of a tourist in this way. Not only does it have no benefit to his business but more importantly it shines a spotlight on his family and their dealings. I confess there are people who are content for him to control major crime down here either because they have been bribed or because they take the view that it is better to have one gang in control than several in competition with each other. So, he can keep a low profile. I think he will be furious about this. If he'd wanted your son dead, he would have manufactured a street fight and had him knifed or something like that.

But, he has three sons, the youngest of which, Alexei, is only twenty one, some ten years younger than his older brothers. By all accounts, he is a hothead and has not been allowed to take control of any part of the business. But Viktor, the father, dotes on him and he is extremely spoilt. He fits the description given by Tom's friends. I think what happened is this. I think your son picked up one of Alexei's girls and Alexei, emboldened by a flick knife and a couple of his father's thugs, decided to challenge Tom but was then humiliated in front of the whole bar. I can tell you that Tom made quite a mess of Alexei's nose! Then, in a rage, Alexei decided to take revenge on Tom in what in his warped mind was the family method.'

'So what now?'

Valdez looked embarrassed.

'I have no other suspects and have no way of proving Alexei was responsible.'

'Surely there must be other avenues to pursue? Can't you grill the bar staff again?'

'I'm sorry. I've been told by my superiors to wind down the investigation.'

'*What*?' Dan shouted. 'After only two days?'

'There's nothing I can do. I have already gone out on a limb by arresting a member of this family. I should not be telling you this but I am in no doubt that this family's influence stretches to this building too.'

'I can't accept this!' Dan exclaimed. 'This isn't finished! I will have justice for Tom!'

Dan stood up angrily, knocking over his chair.

'If you won't help me, I will find someone who will!'

Valdez hesitated then took out his pen and scribbled something on a piece of paper. He handed it to Dan.

'You never received this from me. Agreed?'

Dan looked at the piece of paper and saw that there was a number on it.

'OK. What is it?'

'This is the number of a man who may be able to help you. Tell him that you would like to talk to him about the Durchenkos. He knows more than anyone about them.'

'And what about Tom's body?' Dan asked. 'Can I take it back to England?'

'Of course,' Valdez replied. 'I promise I will not officially close the investigation but we have no reason to prevent your son from being buried.'

Chapter Four

Dan was furious when he left the police station. He had been consoled by the knowledge that the police had arrested Tom's murderer and now it looked as if he was going to get away with it due to a combination of witness intimidation and corruption. He walked aimlessly for about ten minutes and then sat down at a table outside a bar and ordered a coffee. He looked at the piece of paper that Valdez had given him. There was a single number on it which Dan presumed to be a Spanish mobile number. He took out his own mobile and, remembering to add the Spanish prefix 0034, dialled the number.

'Hola', said a gruff voice after the phone was answered.

'Hello,' Dan replied. 'Er... do you speak English?'

'Si, Senor Green, I speak English.'

'You know who I am?' Dan said, surprised.

'Of course. Jose told me to expect your call.'

'Jose?'

'Jose Valdez. I know he told you not to mention his name, but he thought he had better warn me to expect your call. He phoned me as soon as you left his office.'

'I see. So you know what I want?'

'I know you want to talk about the Durchenkos. By the way, I am very sorry about your son.'

'So was Valdez but it didn't help bring his killer to justice.'

'Don't be too hard on Jose. It took courage just to arrest a Durchenko.'

'How do you know so much about them?'

'I prefer not to talk about this on the telephone.'

'Can we meet then?'

'Where are you now?'

'I'm about ten minutes walk from the police headquarters.'

'OK. You know how to get to the main promenade on the waterfront, the Paseo Maritimo?'

'Yes.'

'When you reach the Paseo Maritimo from where you are, turn right and you will come to the Alhambra Bar on your right. I will see you there at three.'

'How will I know you?'

There was laughter on the other end of the phone.

'I will undoubtedly be the fattest man in the bar and of course will be sitting alone.'

'OK, I will see you at three.'

'One more thing, Senor Green. Please make sure you aren't followed.'

'Followed? Why should I be followed?'

'I'm not saying you will be followed. I am simply saying it is a possibility. You have a lot to learn about the Durchenkos. They will be monitoring the investigation into your son's murder closely. They will know that you have arrived from England. They have eyes and ears everywhere.'

'Including police headquarters?'

'Regrettably, yes. I will see you at three.'

Dan had no trouble finding the bar. The outside tables were mainly occupied with tourists and locals enjoying the fine June weather. When he went inside, he had no difficulty identifying the man he had come to meet. He was indeed the fattest man in the bar. In fact, he was the only man sitting inside. He was a large man, probably in his mid sixties, with thinning dark hair and a bushy, drooping moustache. His large brown eyes gave him a lugubrious countenance as he looked up from the plate of paella he was eating and beckoned Dan over.

The man wiped his hand on his napkin before offering it to Dan to shake.

'Senor Green, please, sit down. I'm Luis Mendez.'

Dan sat down at the table.

'I thought it would be more private in here. Not many people sit inside in this weather,' the man continued. 'Have you eaten?'

It occurred to Dan that he had not eaten anything since his modest early breakfast.

'No, I haven't,' he replied.

'I can recommend the paella.'

A waiter came over and Dan had a quick look at the menu.

'I'll have a toasted cheese and ham sandwich and a sparkling water,' Dan told the waiter.

'So', Dan said, after the waiter had gone, 'how do you know Valdez?'

Mendez laughed.

'I used to be his boss!'

'You were in the police?'

'For over forty years. I retired last year. I have known Jose for over twenty years. He is a fine officer but powerless to act against the Durchenkos. By the way, I take it you were not followed?'

'No. I almost wish I had been. The mood I'm in I would gladly have broken the neck of anyone I had detected following me!'

Mendez looked Dan up and down. He saw a broad shouldered fit man of about forty, about six feet tall with not an ounce of fat on him. There was something about the square set of his jaw and the close cropped dark hair which gave him a military bearing.

'And you would know if someone was following you?' he asked.

'Oh yes. I would know,' Dan replied. 'You can be sure of that.'

'Jose said you are a security consultant. What does that entail?'

'Are we here to talk about my CV or the people who killed my son?'

'Humour me, Senor Green. I will happily tell you about the people who killed your son. But I'd like to know that you are not the sort of man who is simply going to naively stir things up and get himself killed.'

'OK, fair enough. My firm advises companies and wealthy individuals on all aspects of security.'

'And your qualification to do such work? What did you do before that?'

'I was in the army for fourteen years.'

'OK. But that doesn't necessarily qualify you for security work.'

Dan sighed.

'I was in the SAS for several years. Does that answer your question? So, yes, I would know if I was being followed and although I may not be as fit as I once was, I know how to handle myself!'

At that point, the waiter brought Dan's sandwich and drink.

'I understand your anger.' Mendez said after the waiter had gone. 'I share your anger. Not because I have lost a son but because of the cancer the Durchenkos have brought to this beautiful part of Spain. I spent the last few years of my career trying to bring them down. I failed. Whenever I found a witness, they either disappeared or were intimidated into changing their story. It was as if they knew every move I made. I was obstructed by my superiors who had been leant on by local politicians. In the end, the only way I could continue was in my own time. Jose Valdez was one of the few officers I could trust. I can tell you that when your son's body was found, Jose rang me and we knew immediately that this was the work of the Durchenkos. When he found out about the fight in the bar, he arrested Alexei. I don't know if any other officer would have had the courage to do that. But once again, the Durchenkos wriggled free as they always do.'

'So, tell me about them. Valdez told me they control most of the brothels down here and are into drugs and and extortion.'

'What he may not have told you is how the brothels are run. I'm not a prude, Senor Green. I have no problem with brothels providing the girls are not exploited and they are run as a proper business, but most of the girls working for the Durchenkos have been trafficked into the country illegally from Eastern Europe or Africa in lorryloads. They are no better than slaves. They are either promised decent work here or have simply been kidnapped off the streets. On arrival they are drugged, raped and beaten until they are completely subservient and then put to work. If they step out of line at all, they are severely beaten or, if of no further use, killed. One girl who became pregnant and was afraid to tell anyone was found on a rubbish dump with an iron spike through her and the foetus. I tell you this because you must understand that these are the most vicious criminals I have ever come across in a lifetime of policing.'

'I get the point, Senor Mendez. But can you give more specific information about their personnel and whereabouts?'

'Please, call me Luis.' Mendez looked at Dan for a few moments as if assessing him. 'OK, come with me and I will tell you everything I can about them. Though how it will help you, I do not know.'

Mendez called over the waiter and they paid the bill.

'Where are we going?' Dan asked as they left the bar.

'To my apartment. It's in that block there.' Mendez pointed to a high rise block only a few yards from the bar. It was a fairly old block but in a prime position right on the seafront.

They took the lift to the seventh floor and entered a flat which had a stunning view out over the sea. It reminded Dan in some ways of his own flat though this flat was not so modern and not kept nearly so tidy.

'Please excuse the mess, senor,' Luis said as if reading Dan's mind. 'My wife died a couple of years ago and I'm not very domesticated.'

'I'm sorry to hear that....about your wife I mean!'

Luis laughed.

'And you can forget the 'senors'. I'm Dan,' Dan added, warming to this overweight but sad looking retired policeman.

Luis went into the kitchen and returned with two bottles of cold beer.

'Here,' he said, handing Dan a bottle. 'If you want to know about the Durchenkos, you have a long afternoon ahead of you. Come with me.'

He led Dan into the corridor and to a door further down.

'This is my office. As you will see, it no longer serves as a second bedroom.'

Dan was astonished when he entered the room. It was set up more as the incident room of an ongoing inquiry. The walls were covered with photos of men with their names underneath. There were photos of what were obviously crime scenes. There were maps with pins sticking into them. There were lists of names and locations pinned to a board. There were boxes of papers all over the floor. There was a table or desk with a computer, a photocopier and a phone, as well as numerous files.

Dan walked over and looked at the photos on the wall. At the very top was a photo of an aggressive looking bull of a man and underneath the name, Viktor Durchenko. Next to that photo was one of a hard faced woman with dyed blond hair in her fifties. Irina Durchenko. The photos were clearly surveillance photos. Nevertheless they were of good quality. In the row beneath were three younger men and a younger woman. It was the furthest to the right which attracted Dan's attention. Alexei Durchenko. Then beneath that row was a single photo of a cruel looking man with a shaven head and beneath that a long row of tough looking men all with Russian names.

'What do think?' Luis asked.

'I'm amazed,' Dan said. 'I thought you'd retired!'

'I have. But I told you I was forced to continue my investigations into the Durchenkos in my own time. So I set up my own headquarters here and built up a huge collection of photos and information. I have just continued it since I retired.'

'You wife didn't mind?'

'No. She knew I was obsessed with them and she wanted them brought down too.'

So how did you keep it going after you retired?' But Dan already knew the answer. 'Valdez?'

'Yes. Jose comes to visit me and helps me keep things up to date. Everything is here. Photos of the family and the main people in the organisation. Details of most of the brothels. Lists of the drug dealers they sell to. Copies of the files relating to crimes we know were committed by the gang.'

'Who is Vitaly Petrov and why does he have a row all to himself beneath the family?' Dan asked.

'Probably the most dangerous of them all, after Viktor,' Luis replied. 'Ex KGB, he joined Viktor about thirty years ago. They have been inseparable ever since. He is Viktor's only real friend, his right hand man and the only man he really trusts. Probably more so than his own sons. Well, certainly more than Alexei, who he doesn't trust at all!'

'And the other sons?'

'Georgy and Sergei. Ten and twelve years older than Alexei. Georgy is a thug but an intelligent thug. He works closely with Petrov who he looks up to. Sergei is the family's money man. He trained as an accountant. He must have a first class honours degree in money laundering!'

'And the girl?' Dan asked pointing to the photo of a stunningly attractive woman with high cheek bones between the photos of Georgy and Alexei.

'Natalya. The daughter. Thirty years of age. I don't know too much about her. So far as I'm aware, she has nothing to do with the family business. I believe she lives in London.'

'And this guy set apart from the others? Arkady Durchenko?' Dan pointed to a photo on the same row as Viktor and Irina but set well apart.

'That's Victor's younger brother. Half brother to be accurate. He's ten years younger than Victor and looks after Viktor's Moscow interests now that Viktor has moved down here.'

'Isn't Viktor worried he will take over things for himself?'

Luis laughed.

'He wouldn't dare! He'd be dead within hours if he tried anything! Besides, Arkady has everything he wants. No one dares touch him in Moscow. If anyone tried anything, heads would quite literally roll down the streets of Moscow...I'm sorry. That was a tactless remark.'

After a pause, Luis continued. 'So, Dan, is this what you wanted?'

'I didn't expect this but this is exactly what I want!'

Luis picked up a lever arch file and handed it to Dan.

'OK. Let's make up a dossier for you.'

Two hours later, Dan left the flat with a full file of photos, maps and information, promising to keep in touch with Luis. He had not yet made up his mind what he was going to do with all the information but he was certain of one thing. The Durchenkos were going to pay for what they had done.

Chapter Five

On the following day, Carol and Richard flew out. Not surprisingly, they were very upset to hear that the man in custody had been released and that the police investigation was seemingly going no further. They wanted to go and see Valdez themselves and demand an explanation but Dan persuaded them that it would do no good and that it was not Valdez who was the problem.

Dan did not mention his meeting with Luis Mendez nor the dossier that he had compiled. He merely said somewhat cryptically that as far as he was concerned, the matter was not over.

'What does that mean?' Carol asked. 'I know that look on your face. Have you got something in mind?'

'Not at the moment, no. But do you really expect me simply to accept that the man who killed our son should get away with it?' Dan replied.

'We can talk about that later,' Richard said. 'In the meantime, Carol, we have arrangements to make. But I'm sure we will support Dan in whatever course he chooses to take.'

Maybe, maybe not, thought Dan.

Against the advice of both Dan and Richard, Carol insisted on seeing Tom's body. Inspector Valdez said that he would arrange it and accompanied them to the mortuary. Dan was relieved that the sheet was only pulled back sufficiently far for Tom's head to be revealed. Carol broke down but the sight of his son's face hardened Dan's resolve to wreak a terrible revenge on those responsible, not just those who had committed the murder but also those who had covered it up afterwards so as to prevent justice being done.

Afterwards, out of earshot of Carol and Richard, Dan thanked Valdez for putting him in touch with Luis Mendez.

'I don't know how it's going to help but at least you now know what we are up against,' Valdez replied. 'By the way, there is something I've discovered which might interest you. Is there any chance you could come to the station later?'

'Of course,' Dan replied.

Later on, Dan told Carol and Richard that he was going for a walk as he wanted to be alone for a while. Fortunately, Richard seemed happy to make all the necessary arrangements to take Tom's body home. Dan was grateful for that as he had other things on his mind.

Once again, on arrival at the police headquarters, he was shown straight up to Valdez's office.

Dan got straight to the point.

'So what have you discovered?' he asked.

'At about the time of the fight between Tom and the young Russian, whom I assume to be Alexei Durchenko, and about two hours or so before we believe Tom was killed, a young woman was admitted to the Costa del Sol Hospital suffering from serious injuries. She had been found in a street not far from the bar where the fight took place and the alley where Tom was found. At first it was thought that she had been the victim of a hit and run accident but her injuries are not consistent with that. She had a broken arm, a dislocated shoulder and multiple abrasions all of which could have been caused by being struck by a car but it was the injuries to her face that are unusual. She had abrasions to her head consistent with striking the tarmac but down one side of her face were deep ragged lacerations. It is difficult to see how those injuries could have been caused by being run down. I have seen such injuries many times before. They are the sort of injuries you get from a broken glass or bottle.'

'You mean from a fight in a bar?'

'Exactly.'

'Did you interview her?'

'I didn't, no. But other officers did. A member of the public found the girl in the road and telephoned for an ambulance. Officers subsequently attended at the hospital to find out what had happened.'

'And?'

'And nothing. The girl refused to say anything. I have spoken to the officers and they say she seemed terrified.'

'What connection do you think this has with Tom's death?'

'Well, you remember I speculated that the fight in the bar was about a girl. We know Tom had spent time with a girl in the bar and left with her for about half an hour before returning. What if this was the girl and Alexei had already taken his revenge on her before going after Tom? It seems too much of a coincidence that this girl appears to have been severely assaulted in the same area and at the same time by someone she is too terrified to talk about.'

'I agree,' said Dan. 'Did the officers get her name?'

'Sanda Wilson. They also got her address. I phoned the hospital and discovered that she had discharged herself this morning, so I visited her address. She had been sharing a small flat with two other English girls. One of them was there and told me that Sandra had turned up early this morning looking terrible with her arm in a sling and dressings covering one side of her face. Apparently she was in a real state and insisted on packing immediately. The other girl helped her to pack and she then took a taxi to the airport.'

'Did you have her stopped at the airport?'

'Of course not! Her flight had probably gone and anyway, she has committed no crime. I have no authority to detain her!'

'So why are you telling me this? There must be hundreds of Sandra Wilsons in England. We will never trace her now.'

'The other girl gave me one other piece of information. Sandra worked in a boutique in Puerto Banus. It's not much I know but maybe someone there could help trace her.'

'So are you following this up?'

'No.'

'Why not?'

Valdez shrugged.

'On what basis can I justify trawling round the boutiques in Puerto Banus to locate a girl who does not want to press charges against anyone, has not committed a crime in this country, who has in all probability left the country....and who is not part of any ongoing investigation?'

Valdez looked at Dan and raised his eyebrows.

'You expect me to do it?'

'I don't *expect* you to do it, Senor Green. But I have heard about your meeting with Luis. It is an avenue of inquiry. I say no more than that.'

'May I ask you a question?'

'Please do. I can't guarantee to answer it though.'

'How certain are you that Alexei Durchenko and his men murdered my son?'

'There is no direct evidence linking him to the murder but I would say I am 90% certain. If you find the girl and she confirms that Alexei assaulted her and then went after Tom, then I would say 99%. For 100%, I would require witnesses to the actual murder or a confession but it is surely inconceivable that total strangers with no connection to the earlier incident chased these three boys down the street and singled one out to brutally murder him.'

Chapter Six

Puerto Banus has dozens of boutiques and Dan did not know where to start. He found that the most expensive boutiques selling the top designer clothes were mainly situated along the eastern part of the waterfront but he decided not to start there, guessing that Sandra Wilson was more likely to have worked in a less exclusive establishment.

He therefore started with the boutiques in the road just behind the western part of the waterfront. No one had heard of Sandra Wilson.

He then walked back into the centre of the town where there was a square with boutiques down one side and a small shopping centre containing mainly clothes shops. He tried there and then the boutiques to the side of the square. Then he found another side street leading towards the port.

The third boutique he tried seemed to specialise in black leather clothing with studs of one form or another. It was called 'Goth Heaven'. There was only one girl working there, wearing tight black leather studded trousers and high heels and a black T shirt with some sort of purple graphics on it, matching her purple lipstick and thick eye shadow. Her pale arms, blue eyes and swept back bleached blond hair did not suggest that she was Hispanic in origin.

'Can I 'elp you, darling?' she said in what Dan immediately recognised as an Essex accent. He imagined that she was wondering what someone as old as him was doing in a boutique like that.

'Maybe,' he said. 'I'm looking for someone who works in this area in a boutique. Her name's Sandra Wilson.'

'Good luck to you,' the girl replied. 'I wish I knew where the little cow is! She didn't come in Saturday or today, so I guess I won't be seeing 'er again.'

Dan breathed a sigh of relief.

'So she does work here then?'

'Did! If she shows 'er face here again, she can piss off! She begged me to give 'er a job and I felt sorry for 'er. She was usually late and now she's left me on my own 'ere without even a phone call to explain why! I expect she's found some bloke. That's all she was looking for. She said 'er name was Cassie, short for Cassandra. Probably thought it sounded more exotic. But 'er real name's Sandra.'

'She told you that?'

'Nah! I saw it on 'er passport. I took a photocopy of 'er passport when I gave 'er the job. I didn't want no trouble with the authorities down 'ere and wanted to be able to show she weren't no illegal.'

'Have you still got the photocopy?' Dan asked, a little too eagerly.

'I might have,' the girl replied, hands on hips looking him up and down. 'What's it to you?'

'Can I look at it?' Dan asked.

'Why? What's in it for me?

'Oh...er, of course,' Dan said, and got out his wallet.

The girl laughed.

'I'm only teasing. I don't want your money. But if you're free later, maybe we can 'ave a drink and some fun.'

The girl looked at the wall and Dan followed her gaze. On the wall was a selection of leather whips.

'I... er...'

Once again the girl laughed.

'Only teasing again. You may look a tough guy but I'd have you for breakfast! Just wait 'ere.'

The girl disappeared into the back of the shop and re-appeared a couple of minutes later with a sheet of A4 paper.

'Ere you are,' she said, handing it to him.

Dan looked at the photocopy and noted the photo of a pretty teenage girl, probably taken a few years previously.

'Looks proper innocent, don't she. Don't be fooled. She's a right little slapper!' the girl said.

'Really? You didn't meet any of her boyfriends, did you?'

'Nah, she never brought them here but she'd spend all day bragging about them.'

'Did she mention anyone special recently?'

'Yeah, as a matter of fact she did. She said he was loaded and she was planning to hang on to him despite his kinky habits in bed.'

'Did she say anything else about him?'

'Only that he was foreign. Russian, I think.'

Dan noticed that beneath the photo, Sandra Wilson's mother was named as the person to be contacted in the event of an emergency and there was an address in Wigan given.

'You couldn't copy this for me, could you?' he asked.

'Keep it. I don't need it no more,' the girl replied.

'Thanks,' Dan said. 'You've been really helpful.'

'Why are you looking for her?'

'Oh..er, I've been hired to trace her by her family.'

'You don't look like a private investigator to me.'

'What did you expect? A dirty mac and a comb over?'

'Yeah, something like that.'

As was leaving, the girl called after him, 'I meant it about the drink, you know. I promise not to bring any whips.'

'Another time, maybe.'

'Here, take my card. Give me a call if you're coming back to the area.'

Dan took the card. It was black on both sides with the name of the shop and the girl's name, Dana Martin, described as the proprietress, in white. He put it in his pocket.

'One last thing...' Dan said.

'Yeah, what?'

'Don't be too sure you'd have me for breakfast!'

They both laughed and Dan realised that it was first time he had either smiled or laughed since he had first been told about Tom's death.

Chapter Seven

On his return home, Dan felt overwhelmed by a sense of loss. At least in Spain, he had had something to do, although what he was going to do with the information that he had acquired there, he did not yet know. Back in England, it really dawned on him that life would never be the same again without Tom. Dan had had no other relatives apart from Tom.

Although Tom had lived with his mother, he had been a frequent visitor to Dan's flat, usually combining a visit with a trip to Upton Park to watch their beloved West Ham. They had both understood the pain and disappointment that went with being West Ham fans. They had been more like friends than father and son. Tom had regularly rung or texted Dan and kept him up to date on what he had been doing.

In the days leading up to the funeral, Dan spent most of his time sitting in his flat alone studying the file that Luis Mendez had provided him with and gradually a plan began to take shape. He decided that not only would he seek justice for his son but he would also ensure that Tom had not died in vain. He resolved to do what Mendez and Valdez had failed to do.

He realised that he could not do what he had in mind without help so he phoned one of his partners at his security firm and asked him to trace two men.

On the morning after the funeral, Dan headed north. It took him longer than he had anticipated to reach Wigan and he arrived at about lunch time. The Satnav then took him to a rundown area of the town and a street consisting of terraced houses, some of which were boarded up. The summer drizzle added to the depressing nature of the area. He was able to park quite close to his destination, number 23, and as he locked his car, it occurred to him that his new Audi seemed out of place in such a location. He wondered whether it would be on bricks when he returned.

He rang the doorbell and waited. There was no answer. He rang it again but just as he was about to return to his car, he saw a curtain flickering. There was someone in. Dan was not in the mood to give up. He put his finger back on the bell and kept ringing. Eventually, he heard movement in the house. He then heard a bolt being slid back and the door opened on its security chain.

'What do you want?' asked a woman aggressively in a broad Liverpool accent.

Dan wondered whether he had the right house. The woman was small and slim. She had long straw coloured hair but the last few inches had been dyed black. Her face was a peculiar orange colour suggesting that she had spent too long under a sunlamp or had caked it in false tan. From Dan's view through the crack in the door, she could have been anything from twenty to fifty.

'I'm sorry to bother you,' Dan said politely, 'but I'm looking for Sandra Wilson.'

'There's no one here of that name,' the woman replied quickly. A little too quickly, Dan thought.

'Um, would you be Mrs. Wilson?' Dan asked.

'No, I'm not,' the woman replied. 'What business of yours is it who I am?'

'Look, it's really important I speak to Sandra Wilson,' Dan said. 'This is the address she gave on her passport of her mother's house. I can assure you I mean her no harm.'

'She doesn't live here any longer.'

'Who? Sandra or her mother?'

'Don't you get clever with me. She's not here so just fuck off!'

'OK. I'll go back to my car and wait there a few minutes. But please tell Sandra I'm Tom's father. I can understand why she doesn't want to see anyone.'

At that, Dan started to back away from the door but as he did so, he heard another voice from further inside the house.

'It's OK, mum. I'll see him.'

The door closed. But after about half a minute, it opened again and the chain was removed.

'OK, you can come in,' the woman whom Dan assumed was Sandra's mother said. He could now see that she was nearer fifty but dressed as if she was twenty. 'But if you upset her at all, I want you out. Do you understand?'

'Perfectly, Mrs Wilson. I have no intention of upsetting your daughter.'

'It's McMahon, not Wilson,' the woman said, standing aside to let Dan in.

Dan entered a small hallway and was shown into the front room. A nervous looking young woman was sitting curled up on the sofa. She was dressed in a black track suit. She was sitting sideways on to Dan and after briefly glancing at him, she turned away as if she didn't want any eye contact with him. Dan noticed that in contrast to her mother she wasn't wearing any make up and her hair was unkempt.

Dan sat down in a chair opposite her. Her mother remained by the door leaning against the wall with her arms folded.

'It's OK, mum,' the girl said again. 'I'll be all right. You can leave us alone.'

Mrs McMahon was clearly not happy with that, but said 'Only if you're sure. I'll be right outside if you need me.'

'Thank you for agreeing to see me, Sandra,' Dan said after Mrs McMahon had closed the door.

'You're Tom's father?'

'Yes.'

Sandra started to sob.

'I was so upset when I read in the papers what had happened to Tom. He seemed a really nice boy.'

'So you did meet Tom that evening?'

'If I tell you what happened, do you promise not to tell anyone that I told you?'

'You have my word. I'm just trying to find out what happened. As any father would.'

There was a pause. Then Sandra told Dan about how she'd met Tom in the bar and how they had gone outside for a kiss and a cuddle. But when she got to the bit about what had happened in Alexei's car, she broke down and that brought her mother rushing back in again.

'Right, you, *out*!' she screamed. 'I told you not to upset her!'

'He hasn't upset me, mum,' Sandra said tearfully. 'I'm just telling him what happened. Please, mum, he needs to know. I'm fine.'

Mrs McMahon withdrew again, somewhat reluctantly. After she had gone, Sandra turned round and faced Dan for the first time.

'That's what the bastard did to me!' she said, pointing to the side of her face that she had kept hidden from Dan till then.

Dan saw that that side of her face was deeply scarred from her forehead down to her chin. He had known about the scarring from Valdez but was shocked at how bad it was.

'I've seen fresh scars before,' he said. 'They will fade in time. And surely there is some fantastic plastic surgery available these days.'

'Not on the National Health! To make any real difference would cost thousands!'

Dan reached inside his jacket. He pulled out one of the photos that he had got from Luis Mendez.

'Is this the man who did this to you?' he asked.

Sandra looked at the photo.

'Yes! That's the bastard! That's Alexei!'

Dan took a deep breath. So there it was. The final piece of evidence that he needed to justify the plan that he had formed.

'I understand how terrifying this may have been. But you're home now. Safe. He can't harm you again.'

'It's not just Alexei!' Sandra replied.

'What do you mean?'

'It's what happened at the hospital that was almost worse!'

'Why? What happened?'

69

'It was the next morning. I had just woken up. This man came to see me. I thought he was a policeman. He pulled the curtains around my bed and then walked straight up to me and put his hand around my throat. I thought I was going to die. He kept squeezing. I couldn't breathe. I could feel myself passing out and then he released me. He leant down so his face was only about six inches from mine and said if I ever told anyone what had happened the night before, he would find me wherever I was and kill me as well as all my family. That's why when the police turned up I said nothing and got out as soon as I could!'

'Can you describe this man?'

'Definitely Russian. He had the same sort of accent as Alexei. Big, with a shaven head.'

Petrov, thought Dan. Or some other Durchenko thug. But most likely Petrov as protecting one of Viktor's sons would warrant the involvement of someone very senior in the organisation.

There was no more that Sandra could tell Dan but before he left, he made her a promise that he was determined to keep, namely that not only would there be retribution for what had happened to her and Tom, but also that she would soon have no reason to live in fear.

Dan left the house grim faced even more determined than he had been before speaking to Sandra. He saw that a group of youths had formed by his car and they appeared to be waiting for him. The obvious leader of this group was a large skinhead with heavily tattooed arms. He was leaning against the driver's door of Dan's car.

'Can I help you?' Dan asked.

'Can I help you?' the skinhead mimicked. 'What were you doing visiting Sandra?'

'What business is that of yours?' Dan asked.

'Sandra's very popular round here. We look after our own.'

'Glad to hear it. Now would you mind getting out of my way?'

'Make me.'

Dan smiled.

'You really don't want to be doing this,' he said. 'I'm not in the mood for this so back off, sonny, before you get hurt.'

As soon as he said that, Dan realised that there could only be one outcome to this confrontation as the other man could hardly back down in front of his friends. He saw hesitation in the skinhead's eyes and he glanced quickly at his friends then back to Dan. He was obviously used to people backing down to him, not openly challenging him and showing him a lack of respect.

After a pause, the skinhead kicked back with his heel, denting Dan's car door.

'Nice car,' he smirked.

Something snapped in Dan. Maybe it was all the pent up rage he had felt since he had heard of Tom's death.

'If you like it so much why don't you take a closer look?' he said.

Before the other man had a chance to react, Dan grabbed him and twisted him round so that he was facing the car. He put one hand on the back of the man's head and smashed his face into the door frame of the car. Then he did it again and again and again until he regained control. He let the man go and he slid semi-conscious to the ground, his face a bloody, swollen mess.

Dan looked at the others who had backed away and clearly had no intention of intervening.

'Pick him up and take him home,' Dan said.

Two men shuffled forward and helped their friend to his feet. Dan got in his car and drove away. After about a mile he stopped. He was still shaking. He realised that he had no chance of succeeding in his plan if he lost control. In the past, he had been doing his job. Now it was personal and that made things very different.

Chapter Eight

On arriving back at his flat, Dan checked his emails. His colleague had traced both the men that Dan had asked him to find and provided addresses and brief details of their circumstances.

On the following morning, Dan telephoned his colleague and thanked him. He could have done that by email but the real purpose of the call was to explain that he would not be in to work for a while and ask whether his partners could cover for him in his absence.

'That's no problem', his colleague replied. 'Take as much time as you need, Dan. You do what you've got to do. If you need any more help, just let us know.'

The colleague knew better than to ask Dan what he was planning. Dan's partners were all ex military. He knew that he could rely on them for information but there was no way that he could involve them in any other way in his plans. They were all family men and to do so would put their lives at risk and jeopardise their freedom and the future of the firm which provided employment for numerous ex servicemen.

Dan then packed a bag and headed north again on a journey which took him a long way further than Wigan. After only a couple of stops for petrol and a sandwich, Dan arrived in the highlands of Scotland by late afternoon and it was nearly six by the time he pulled up at an isolated cottage on the moors on the edge of a large estate.

Before Dan had knocked on the door, it opened and Alan Campbell's large frame filled the doorway. Dan had not seen him for nearly fifteen years but he had not changed at all. He had to be nearly sixty but looked as fit as he had been when he had been Dan's fitness instructor in the Regiment. Maybe there was a touch of grey in the red hair but his craggy features and piercing blue eyes were just the same.

For a moment, the two men just looked at each other. Then Alan stepped forward and enveloped Dan in his huge arms.

'I was so sorry to read about your boy, Dan.' Alan said.

'That's why I'm here, Jock. I need your help.' Alan had somewhat unimaginatively been known as 'Jock' in the Regiment and Dan had never addressed him as anything else.

Alan laughed.

'It's a long time since anyone called me that!' he said. 'Up here, you'd have to call everyone Jock! Now, come in and tell me how I can help you.'

Alan led Dan into a spartanly furnished living room.

'You look as if you could do with a drink,' he said.

'It's been a long drive,' Dan replied.

Alan poured two generous glasses of malt whisky and handed one to Dan.

'How did you find me?'

Dan explained briefly about his work and how they were used to tracing people and that he had found out that Alan was working as a gamekeeper on a large estate.

'So why come all the way up here? What can I do to help you?'

'I want you to get me fit.'

'You look in pretty good shape to me.'

'Well, I work out in the gym. But that's not the same. I want to get back to the same sort of fitness I had back in the day.' Dan paused. 'I'd also like to refresh my combat skills.'

Dan knew very well that taking on what he had in mind was somewhat different from getting the better of a skinhead barely out of his teens.

'And why would you want to do that?' Alan asked.

So Dan told him everything, the gruesome details of what had happened to Tom, how the Spanish police had been unable to act, the meetings with Luis Mendez and Sandra Wilson and finally, what he planned to do.

'So there's no point in me trying to talk you out of it?' Alan said after Dan had finished. 'Or pointing out to you that you are likely to end up dead or in prison?'

'None whatsoever.'

'Good. Because I have no intention of trying. I'd do the same in your shoes. What I will do though is get you in the best possible shape I can so you won't fail for any shortcoming on my part. But I warn you it won't be easy!'

Alan was as good as his word. He kicked Dan out of bed at five thirty the following morning and twenty minutes later, they were standing out in the yard with Dan dressed in just a vest and shorts.

'OK. Let's see how good your reflexes are,' Alan said, and almost before he had finished speaking, Dan had to block a chopping blow aimed at his neck. More blows followed which Dan managed to block and then Dan tried to take the offensive by spinning round and kicking out at Alan. He missed by a mile as Alan avoided the kick easily and span round and elbowed Dan in the stomach. Dan managed to recover but after the two men had exchanged a few more blows, Alan feinted to the left before hooking Dan's legs and dumping him on his back.

'Not bad,' Alan said, looking down at a shaken Dan. 'But you've a long way to go!'

'Maybe I'm still tired after the long drive!' Dan replied, smiling.

For the next week, Alan put Dan through hell. While Alan attended to his duties on the estate driving a battered old Land Rover, Dan had to keep up, running with a heavy pack on his back, up and down hills, through streams and over whatever terrain they encountered. Whenever Alan stopped to mend a fence or carry out some similar job, Dan was made to do press ups, sit ups or whatever Alan barked at him.

At the beginning and end of each day, there was combat training, both unarmed and with knives.

There was no more malt whisky and Dan was kept to a strict diet.

At the end of the week, they had their final session of unarmed combat. Neither man held back, and, to Alan's satisfaction, it was he who found himself on his back, shaking his head to get rid of the stars.

'I think you're ready!' he said.

That night, the malt whisky re-appeared and the two men talked over Dan's plans. They were necessarily fluid because Dan did not know how things would develop in Spain. Alan was more concerned with Dan's first choice as his partner in the venture. Dan had explained that he could not do the job on his own but on the other hand, he did not want a whole team. Given that very few people would agree to embark on such a dangerous, not to mention illegal, operation, Dan had decided that he wanted one person who would not only be willing to join him but on whom he could rely on totally. He had identified that person as the second man whom his colleague had traced.

'Aren't you worried that he's a bit of a psycho?' Alan asked. 'I know you all got a buzz out of what you did, but he really enjoyed it. Too much, in my view!'

'I know what you mean. But he was in my team and never let me down.'

'How do you know he'll be up to it? A long time has passed.'

'I don't. But I will when I meet him. If he's not up to it, I'll have to think again.'

'If he is up to it and willing to take part, do you want to send him up here for some of what you've been through?'

'It's kind of you to offer. I'll see how he seems. But whereas I've been basically doing a desk job, from what we have found out he's been on some dodgy overseas ventures as a mercenary so seems to have kept his hand in.'

'Now why doesn't that surprise me?'

Chapter Nine

On the following day, Dan headed south again, timing his journey so that he arrived in Coventry at about ten in the evening.

He managed to park diagonally across the street from the Movers and Shakers nightclub in a space not lit up by a street light. Things looked fairly quiet at that time and Dan supposed that the club did not get busy until the pubs started to empty. Dan waited about half an hour and saw a few people enter the club through the large chrome door underneath the neon lighting. There was one bouncer outside the door, a huge black man dressed in a dark suit but as more and more people started to arrive, he was joined by two others.

Dan recognised Jimmy Johnson immediately. He lifted his binoculars and studied his former corporal. He was no more than average height and though stockily built was dwarfed by his two fellow bouncers. However, Dan was in no doubt as to whom he would rather have beside him in a fight. Whereas the other two were bigger, they looked slow and flabby in comparison with Jimmy, and Dan was sure that Jimmy could have taken out the other two together with very little effort.

Dan sat and watched as very soon a queue formed for entry to the club. The three bouncers seemed to get on well with each other and the customers as they slowly admitted people to the club. However, after a few minutes, a group of about four young men reached the front of the queue. Their body language suggested that they had been drinking and the progress of the queue halted. It was obvious that the group was being refused admittance. Dan put his window down and could hear the men shouting and demanding to be let in. There was some pushing and shoving as one of the larger bouncers tried to move the men on but it was not until Jimmy stepped forward that the situation was defused. He stood close to the group facing them with a deadpan expression and although Dan could not hear what he said, whatever it was caused the men to back away and beat a hasty retreat.

By about eleven thirty, the queue had disappeared. Dan decided that it was time to make his move. He got out of his car and walked across the road. As he approached the club, Jimmy recognised him.

'I don't believe it! Captain Green!'

'At ease, corporal', Dan replied. 'And from now on, it's just Dan, OK?'

The two men shook hands and then embraced.

'I was so sorry to hear about Tom,' Jimmy said. 'I know he meant the world to you. Have they got the bastards who did it yet?'

'Well, actually, that's why I've tracked you down.'

'Really? Tell me more!'

'When do you get off?'

'Not till about three! But I can sneak off for a bit now we've got the main crowd in. There's not usually any trouble here but if there is, it won't be till people have had a few more drinks.'

'My car's just over the road. We could go there.'

Jimmy then introduced Dan to the other two bouncers. Dan shook hands with them.

'Look guys,' Jimmy said to them, 'I haven't seen this guy in years. Do you mind if we go and have a chat in his car over the road for a bit?'

'No, go ahead,' one of them replied with a smile. 'If it all kicks off, we'll come and get you so you can sort it out!'

'As I usually do!' Jimmy said.

'You look in good shape.' Jimmy said when they had got in the car.

'I should do!' Dan replied, and told Jimmy about his week with 'Jock'.

'Bloody hell! What was all that for?'

So Dan told Jimmy everything, as he had with Alan.

'So you intend to take on the biggest and meanest organised crime gang on the Costa del Sol?' Jimmy asked.

Dan did not reply.

'And let me guess. You want me to join you in this crazy venture?'

'It probably is crazy and I'd quite understand if you're not interested.'

'Don't be daft. 'Cause I'm fucking interested. Sounds like the most fun I've had in years!'

'Jimmy, this isn't some mercenary op in some third world country. This is in an EU country and highly illegal.'

'So we could end up dead or in jail? Dead's dead wherever you are and jail in Spain is probably better than jail in some third world country. When do you want to leave?'

Dan told him about Alan's offer.

'Don't worry about me. I'm pretty fit.'

'I'd heard you'd kept your hand in.'

'Yeah. I've been to Africa a few times and worked for some dodgy security firms in the Middle East. Always on the side of the good guys, of course!'

'I'll pay you the going rate.'

'Forget it. I don't want your money. We've both saved each other's lives. If you want my help for personal reasons, you have it. Unconditionally. Well, perhaps not unconditionally...'

'Go ahead.'

'As I said, this is personal and that makes things different. I could tell how this has affected you as you were telling me what had happened. That can affect judgement. It's your show and I know you were the captain when I was only a lowly corporal, but all I ask is that we both have an equal say in what goes down and how we do it.'

'I have no problem with that,' Dan said, remembering how he had lost control in Wigan.

He put out his hand. Jimmy took it.

'I will finance the op though,' Dan said.

'I'm sure we'll get your expenses back and some remuneration as well,' Jimmy replied.

'How do you work that out?'

'We're taking on a crime family right? What's their prime motivation? Money! And they deal a lot in cash. Unless we fall at the first hurdle, I'm sure we'll pick up some readies as we go along!'

'Maybe. We'll see. But what about your job?'

'A poxy job as a bouncer? I'm only doing it because I've nothing else at the moment. I'll just tell the agency that I've found something else.'

'OK, great. I suggest you come and stay at my flat for a couple of days when we can go through things and work out our strategy and then we can fly out.'

'Suits me. But what are we going to do about equipment when we get there? We'll need to get tooled up. We can hardly take on the Russian mafia with a couple of kitchen knives we've bought from a hardware shop!'

'Yes. That could be a problem. But there's nothing we can do about it till we get there.'

'You got any contacts out there?'

Dan thought about Luis Mendez.

'Maybe. There's a former police officer who might be able to help. He's been trying to bring the Durchenkos down for years.'

'And failed apparently.'

'Not for want of trying.'

'We'd better show him how to do it then!'

After discussing matters for a few more minutes, Dan gave Jimmy his address and the two men swapped mobile numbers. Jimmy went back to the club and Dan headed home.

Chapter Ten

Two days later, Jimmy arrived at Dan's flat and they spent the rest of the day and the whole of the next day studying Dan's file on the Durchenko family and familiarising themselves with the area with the aid of maps, Google Earth and any other information they could find on the internet.

After debating whether they should find a base in the centre of a busy town such as Marbella or Puerto Banus or somewhere quieter a little further out, they opted for the latter. They knew that once they had made their first move the family would try to hunt them down and they figured that although there would be more people in the towns to lose themselves in, there would also be more eyes and ears to report back to the family. They worked out that east of Marbella, there were some upmarket urbanisations catering mainly for tourists and the ex-pat community where according to Mendez's files, the Durchenkos had no regular presence.

On the following morning, they caught an early flight to Malaga and after collecting their bags and hiring a car they headed east and about five miles from Marbella turned off at an urbanisation known as Elviria.

In the small development of shops, bars and restaurants just to the right of the turn off from the N340, there were a number of estate agents and as Dan had already ascertained on the internet, they all had dozens of properties on their books available for rent.

They picked the largest and, posing as a couple of golfers hoping to enjoy a month playing the various courses in the area, found an enthusiastic response from the young German estate agent only too glad to get one of the numerous properties on his books occupied. A letting for a month was not to be turned away outside the school holidays and he offered to show Dan and Jimmy some properties immediately. They specified that they wanted somewhere quiet and the agent recommended that as they were golfers, one of the developments on a golf course might be appropriate. These developments were largely unoccupied as the golf season was coming to an end with the warmer weather and holidaymakers who had no interest in golf preferred the more family orientated developments nearer the beach.

Dan said that that would be just fine and after looking at the particulars of a number of properties, they selected a few and set off in the agent's car to view them.

In fact, the agent found that he had to work harder for his commission than he had anticipated. The process took the whole afternoon as Dan and Jimmy deemed one property after another unsuitable. The agent could not help noting that while he was showing Dan round the inside of the properties, Jimmy spent all his time checking the outside, not so much the view but such things as means of access and the precise position of the apartment in the block.

Eventually, they arrived at an apartment in a block adjacent to a fairway on the Santa Clara golf course, about two miles closer to Marbella and about three miles from the town centre. Access to the apartment was up some steps from the car park and then along an external walkway at first floor level to the apartment at the end of the walkway. Because the land was lower on the car park side, on the other side it was at ground floor level with patio doors leading to the communal gardens separating the block from the golf course.

Jimmy led Dan out into the garden while the agent hovered hopefully in the apartment.

'This looks fine,' Jimmy said. 'It's at the end of the walkway so no one has to walk past to get to their property and on this side, there is access to the golf course if we have to leave in a hurry.'

'What about the wire fence?' Dan asked.

'That's no problem. If we get some wire cutters from that hardware shop back by the estate agents, I can sneak out here when it's dark and make a couple of snips by that post so we can raise a flap in the fence should we need to. No one will notice and besides, I reckon there are only a couple of flats occupied in the whole block.'

Dan nodded and went back inside to tell the relieved agent that they would take the apartment and would pay a month's rent plus a deposit in cash when they returned to the shop to sort out the paperwork.

After they had completed the formalities and been handed the keys, they went straight to the hardware shop and bought wire cutters and some other equipment that Jimmy insisted might come in handy. They then went to the Supersol supermarket in the same development and stocked up on groceries. Before they returned to the apartment, they drove to a large shopping centre just outside Marbella to the north of the bypass. Dan had already found out on the internet that this was the nearest place where they could buy mobile phones. The shopping centre had three mobile phone shops. So as not to arouse suspicion, Dan and Jimmy each bought separately a pay as you go phone in each of the shops.

Back at the apartment, Jimmy spent about an hour rigging up a makeshift security system with some of the equipment that they had bought at the hardware shop.

Dan made the first call from one of the new phones.

'Hola', the gruff voice said at the other end of the line.

'Luis?'

'Si.'

'Luis, it's Dan Green here.'

'Ah, Senor Green. Dan . What can I do for you?'

'I've got something I need to ask you. Something you may not be able to help me with. Or may not be willing to help me with.'

'OK. Well there's no harm in asking, is there? Is this something you can ask over the phone or would you prefer to meet? I assume you are in Spain?'

'I am in Spain and no, it's not something I want to ask over the phone.'

'Where are you?'

'About twenty minutes from your apartment.'

'I see. Do you want to come over?'

'If I could. We could be there in about half an hour.'

'We?'

'Yes. I have a colleague with me. If it's ok with you, I'd like to bring him along. I'd like you to meet him.'

'Ok. I will expect you in half an hour.'

Chapter Eleven

Mendez was waiting by his door after he had buzzed Dan and Jimmy into the block. Dan shook hands with him and introduced Jimmy.

'Pleased to meet you, sir,' Jimmy said.

'Please, er...Jimmy, call me Luis. Dan and I dispensed with the formalities when we met before,' Mendez replied. 'Come in and have a beer.'

They entered the living room and Mendez fetched three bottles of beer from the kitchen.

'So, Dan, what brings you back to Spain?'

'I think you know that, Luis.'

There was a pause. Luis looked at Jimmy.

'I take it you are a former colleague of Dan's from his army days?' he asked.

'We've been through a lot together,' Jimmy replied.

'I'm sure you have!'

'Do you have any further news for me?' Dan asked.

'I'm afraid not,' Luis replied. 'As Jose explained to you, the investigation is over.'

'So it's business as usual for the Durchenkos?'

'Regrettably, yes.'

'Not for much longer.' Dan said.

He told Luis about Sandra Wilson and how he had managed to trace her. When he dealt with the incident in the hospital, Luis immediately interrupted and said that the man involved must have been Petrov.

'That's what I figured,' Dan replied.

'So what is your plan?' Luis asked.

'To put the Durchenkos out of business. Permanently.'

'And how do you propose to do that?'

'Can we trust you, Luis?'

'What do you mean by that?'

'Supposing we were planning to take action against the Durchenkos which would involve us committing crimes in your country? Would you report us to Valdez so that we are arrested and deported or even imprisoned?'

There was another pause.

'Everything you tell me will remain confidential.' Luis replied eventually.

'Ok. Since the police force and justice system seem powerless to bring down the Durchenkos, we intend to do it by the only alternative. To kill them.'

'Just the two of you against a small army?'

'We aren't amateurs. We are as you know ex special forces. To put it bluntly, we are trained killers. To begin with we will have the element of surprise and at the very least we will do them serious damage even if ultimately we fail.'

'You mean if you are killed.'

'Yes, but that's a risk we are prepared to take. We've been up against superior numbers before. It was part of the job.'

Luis looked at Jimmy, who simply nodded.

'So what is it you have come here to ask me?' Luis asked.

'We need weapons. We don't know how to obtain them.'

'And you think I do?'

'I thought you might be able to point us in the right direction.'

Luis chuckled.

'I suppose my old service revolver won't be enough?'

'Hardly. We need specialist equipment.'

'Asking me to keep your confidence is one thing but now you are asking me to help you obtain weapons which you clearly intend to use. How do I know this won't lead to innocent civilians being caught in the crossfire? Your own country has the strictest arms control laws in the world for just that reason.'

'We propose targeted strikes against the Durchenkos and their interests, not gun battles in the streets.'

'Even so, you cannot eliminate all risk. And if, as is inevitable, the Durchenkos come after you, they will not be so concerned about innocent bystanders.'

'We accept that. There can never be any guarantees. But we are used to working in situations where priority is given to ensuring the safety of the public.'

Luis sighed.

'I can see you intend to pursue this with or without my help and I suppose I encouraged you by giving you access to my files. I can give you the name of a man who might be able to provide the sort of equipment you require. But I have not heard of him since I retired. For all I know he is no longer in business. He had a reputation as being the main armourer for the underworld on this coast. I'm afraid he was another of my failures as we never managed to charge him with anything. He was always very cautious. I heard a rumour that he did some business with the Durchenkos when they first moved down here but they then froze him out when they found an alternative method of smuggling arms into the country and have taken over much of the market in illegal weapons.'

'So this guy may be only too pleased to see us hit the Russians?' Jimmy said.

'Yes. If he's still around. For all I know, they may have already killed him or frightened him off,' Luis replied.

'So who is he and where can we find him?' Dan asked.

'His name is Fernando Ortega. As to where to find him, I can only give you one lead. You could try the Bar Felipe in Malaga. It's in a rough area down by the docks. You won't find any tourists in that area and it's not the sort of bar which welcomes strangers.'

Luis then got out a map of Malaga and marked on it the approximate location of the bar.

'Malaga is about half an hour from here,' he said. 'You drive back past the airport.'

'OK, thanks, Luis.' Dan looked at his watch. 'Much as I want to get on with things, it's probably a bit late to go there now and it's been a long day.'

'Have you eaten?' Luis asked.

'That was the first thing you asked me when we met before!' Dan said.

'Well as you can see, food plays a big part in my life! Come, I will take you to one of my favourite restaurants. You may as well enjoy yourselves now as I suspect there won't be much opportunity to relax soon.'

'Eat, drink and be merry for tomorrow we die?' Jimmy said.

'Yes, something like that,' Luis replied.

Luis took them to a rather shabby looking restaurant a few minutes walk from his apartment. But what the restaurant lacked in style, it certainly made up for it with the quality of its food. In contrast to Jimmy, who seemed relaxed

94

and shared a bottle of red wine with Luis, Dan
found it difficult to switch off and was content to
let the other two dominate the conversation which
covered the usual topics when men go out
together such as football and women. Dan had
always envied Jimmy's apparent ability to enjoy
himself as if he didn't have a care in the world
and then be ready for the most dangerous of
missions the following day. Dan had a couple of
beers and joined in from time to time but his
mind was really on the days ahead.

Chapter Twelve

The Bar Felipe was just as Luis had described. They arrived there at about 8pm the following day. While Jimmy had spent most of the day lounging around the pool in the communal garden and swimming, Dan had used the time going through his file yet again and checking things on the internet. One feature of the block which had been a pre-requisite was that it had Wi-Fi.

By the time they had found the bar, the journey had taken them nearly an hour. They parked the car in a nearby street and approached the tatty looking bar with subdued red lighting near the waterfront.

When they entered the bar, two things occurred to Dan immediately. First, it appeared that any regulations in Spain banning smoking inside did not apply to this bar. Secondly, and more significantly, the noise level dropped considerably as seemingly everyone in the bar turned and looked at them as they walked towards the bar.

The barman was a large man with a shaven head and eyes which disconcertingly looked in different directions. He simply glared at them with what Dan presumed was his good eye as they approached the bar.

'Do you speak English?' Dan asked.

There was no response.

'Ingles?' Dan tried again.

The barman just stared at him.

Dan pointed to some bottles of San Miguel on the shelf behind the barman.

'Dos. Por favor,' he said.

Eventually, the barman reluctantly opened two bottles and pushed them towards Dan.

'Cinco euros,' he growled.

Dan handed over the money.

'Gracias,' he said, and then in a voice loud enough to be heard by a number of the customers standing nearby, 'Busco Fernando Ortega.' Dan had some basic Spanish and knew enough to say he was looking for Ortega.

The barman looked at him for a moment and then just moved down the bar to serve another customer.

'What do we do now?' Jimmy asked.

'We wait,' Dan replied. 'Enough people heard that. We just have to hope that eventually someone will approach us.'

'And if they don't?'

'We come back tomorrow.'

Dan looked around the bar and spotted a free table. They took their drinks and sat down. By now, the novelty of two foreign strangers appeared to have worn off and the noise levels increased. Nevertheless, Dan had the impression that they were still being watched. It was still early and as time passed, the bar began to fill up. Virtually everyone who came in seemed to have a good look at Dan and Jimmy and when they met up with their friends the group would turn and look at them, no doubt because the newcomer had asked 'who the hell are they?' or whatever the Spanish equivalent was.

There were few women in the bar and it was clear that those who were there were hookers and seemed to be well known by the male clientele. Dan noticed that a couple of times, one of them would disappear with one of the men through a door behind the bar.

Jimmy had also spotted this.

'Jesus,' he said, 'Those women are older than us! Who the hell would pay to have sex with them?'

'Dockers, sailors and petty criminals,' Dan replied. 'This place is hardly likely to attract high class hookers!'

By ten o'clock and after the surly barman had reluctantly served them with three more rounds of beer, it seemed that they were wasting their time.

'Let's give it till we've finished these beers then call it a day,' Dan said.

No sooner had he said that than a large, swarthy man dressed in an ill fitting brown suit sat down at their table.

'I hear you ask for Fernando Ortega. Why you want him?' he asked in a thick accent.

'We hope to do some business with him,' Dan replied.

'What sort of business?'

'The business we hear he specialises in.'

'He has many businesses.'

'Are you Fernando Ortega?'

The man laughed.

'No. I not Fernando Ortega.'

'But you know him?'

'Maybe.'

'Well, could you tell Senor Ortega that I am keen to do some business with him?'

The man looked at both Dan and Jimmy and then seemed to make up his mind.

'Wait here,' he said, and with that he got up and left the bar.

Chapter Thirteen

Time passed and Dan began to wonder if they had failed whatever test had been set for them. However, after about half an hour the man returned.

'You come,' he said and without waiting for a reply headed back towards the door.

Dan and Jimmy glanced at each other, then pushed back their chairs and followed him. The man set a brisk pace down the road and then turned into a side road leading away from the waterfront. No sooner had Dan and Jimmy followed him around the corner than four other men appeared out of the shadows. Two of them seized Dan and two Jimmy. They were pushed from the back roughly against the wall. Dan managed to turn his head towards Jimmy.

'Easy,' he mouthed, worried that Jimmy might resist.

As Dan suspected, the men simply wanted to search them. It proved to be a very thorough search and included in Dan's estimation a check to see if either man was fitted with a wire. Eventually they were released and at that precise moment a black Mercedes S Class glided to a halt across the junction. The man who had approached

Dan and Jimmy in the bar opened the back door of the car and beckoned to Dan to get in. Jimmy tried to follow Dan but the the other men held him back.

'You wait here,' he was told.

Dan got into the back of the car and found himself sitting next to a slim neatly dressed man of about fifty with a moustache and slicked back black hair.

'You must excuse the way you have been treated, senor,' the man said, smiling, and in perfect English. 'But in my business I have to be very cautious.'

'Fernando Ortega, I presume?' Dan replied.

The man nodded.

'And you are?'

'John Smith.'

'Of course you are. Anyway, you do not appear to be from the police.'

'You must have known we were British, so we were hardly likely to be police.'

Ortega shrugged. 'Why not? Our police help yours to arrest your criminals down here so maybe you were returning the favour.' He paused. 'So why are you so keen to meet me? I was intrigued by your perseverance when I heard you were still in the bar after two hours. You don't look the sort of man who would normally spend an evening in such an establishment.'

'I was hoping we could do some business.'

'And what do you know of my business?'

'That you might be able to help me.'

'And who told you this?'

'Someone I met in a bar in Marbella who gave me your name and where I might find you for a hundred euros.'

'Really? That sounds most unlikely. But never mind. What do you want?'

Dan took a piece of paper out of his pocket and handed it to Ortega.

'Well,' Ortega said, after he had read through the list, 'I thought you might want a couple of handguns but this is very serious stuff. Are you planning to start a war or something?'

'Maybe,' Dan replied. 'Can you get it all?'

'Of course. The guns are no problem but some of this stuff will take time.'

'How long?'

'A week. Maybe more, maybe less.'

'How much will it cost?'

Ortega took out a calculator and did some sums.

'The total comes to 27800 euros.'

Dan winced.

'Shall we say 25000?'

'No, senor. We shall say 30000. I do not keep this equipment in my backyard. Some of it I will have to bring in from abroad. I don't know who you are or how reliable you are. No one buys this sort of stuff unless they intend to use it which means a lot of questions will be asked as to how you got it whether you are caught or not. All this increases the risk and adds a premium to the price. Besides, I doubt you will get it anywhere else.'

Dan knew he had no choice.

'OK. Cash on delivery?'

'Of course. Give me your number. I will phone you when I have it and tell you the handover arrangements.'

Dan gave Ortega the number of one of his new mobiles. They shook hands and Dan got out of the car. The car immediately drove off and the five men left with Jimmy melted away.

'Well?' Jimmy asked.

'He can get it all.' Dan replied. 'It could take a week or so. He's going to phone us.'

Chapter 14

Dan and Jimmy spent the next few days checking out various locations listed in the Mendez files and watching the movements of the family. The huge villa where the family and their entourage were based was high in the hills behind Marbella at the end of a private road. Any car approaching the villa along the road could be seen from the villa so the only way that Dan and Jimmy could get a good look at the villa was to leave their car at the bottom of the hill and climb it on foot until they reached a ridge from which they could observe the villa through binoculars. Using rocks and brush they built a concealed hideaway from which they could watch the villa lying on their stomachs. The villa was surrounded by a large wall which was almost certainly alarmed and entry was through electric gates guarded by at least two men based in a small gatehouse just inside the gates.

On the first day, they both watched the villa all day and when darkness fell, they could hear in the distance the faint sound of dogs barking from time to time signifying the presence of guard dogs.

So as to monitor the movements of the family, they decided to maintain a vigil on the premises and worked out a system whereby one man would watch the villa and the other would remain in the car at the bottom of the hill. If someone left the villa, the man keeping watch would phone the man in the car who would then follow the vehicle to see where it went. Obviously, with only the two of them, it was not possible for every vehicle to be followed but fortunately the volume of traffic from the villa was not high and a pattern soon emerged.

So far as Dan and Jimmy could work out, Viktor Durchenko himself did not leave the villa at all during the period of reconnaisance, but during the day Georgy Durchenko and Petrov made regular visits to various premises such as brothels, nightclubs and restaurants owned by the family. At night, Alexei would visit the bars and clubs of Puerto Banus always accompanied by the same two bodyguards.

On one evening, it was Dan's turn to do the following and it took great restraint on his part not to take them on by himself. Alexei's evening seemed to follow a familiar pattern. He would visit a bar where his willingness to flash his money around and buy everyone champagne ensured an entourage of hangers on, both male and female. He would then move on to one of the nightclubs, usually one owned by his father according to Mendez's files, either with a girl he had picked up in the bar or with a group of people. He would then leave the club in the early hours with a girl and either take her back to her place in his limousine or simply drive around for about half an hour before dropping the girl off. Dan noted that he did not take girls back to the villa. If the girl did not have a convenient place to go where the bodyguards could wait outside, Dan assumed that the driving around was to enable him to have sex in the back of the car.

Later that night, Jimmy told Dan that while he had been following Alexei, a car had turned up at the villa and from what Jimmy could see while the car was being checked over by the guards at the gate, it was full of women. The car had then left about three hours later.

'Interesting,' Dan said. 'Hookers for the troops?'

'That's what I thought,' Jimmy replied.

After they had kept observation on the villa for five days, Jimmy suggested that he should carry out a reconnaissance at the first target that they had identified, a high class brothel in an upmarket residential area.

'Purely for the purposes of sussing the place out,' he said.

'Yeah, right,' Dan replied. 'And how would you propose doing that?'

'Well, I'd have to go as a regular punter, wouldn't I? Anything else would look suspicious!'

'I guess so. But don't forget why you're there!'

Dan gave Jimmy some cash.

'Thanks,' Jimmy said. 'I'll try not to enjoy myself too much.'

Jimmy returned about three hours later with a big grin on his face.

'Well?' Dan asked.

'Oh yes, I'm absolutely fine,' Jimmy replied.

'I'm sure you are! But that's not what I meant.'

'Only kidding. It's quite a place. You pay an entrance fee when you go in and then the downstairs consists of a bar and open plan sitting areas where you can meet the girls. Out the back is a swimming pool and loungers. When you decide on a girl you go upstairs to the first or second floors where all the bedrooms are and pay her separately for whatever you want.'

'Security?'

'Very discreet. In fact, I wouldn't have noticed it at all if I hadn't deliberately caused a fuss. Apart from the woman on the door and the girls, I saw no men at all. The girls even served the drinks. I suppose it's all to put the punters at their ease. So I decided to do a little test. This guy was just about to go upstairs with a girl. I'd talked to her earlier so I accused him of nicking the girl I wanted. There was a bit of an argument and these two heavies soon appeared. Big guys. Probably Russians or Eastern Europeans of some sort. I put my hands up and said everything was cool and shook the hand of the guy I'd been arguing with and they just melted away again.'

'Do you think they were armed?'

'My guess would be yes. It was hot. The girls had virtually nothing on and the punters were all in T shirts or lightweight shirts. These guys had loose fitting jackets. I reckon they were carrying.'

'Probably. Did you go upstairs?'

'Of course. But only in the interests of reconnaissance! I only went in one room but I would imagine they were all the same. A small double bedroom with ensuite shower and toilet.'

'OK. That's helpful. Do I get any change?'

'Er, no. I spent the lot!'

Chapter Fifteen

Ortega rang on the seventh day after their meeting.

'John Smith?'

'Yes,' Dan replied. 'You have my gear?'

'Yes. You have the money?'

'Yes. How do you want to do this?'

'You know the turn off for Elviria?'

'Yes.'

'A couple of minutes drive inland is the Santa Maria golf course. I will see you in the car park there at 10.00am tomorrow.'

That afternoon, Dan and Jimmy visited the golf club. They drove in through the gate and found that the car park consisted of two lines of cars, one on each side of the road which bent round to the right to the clubhouse and pro shop. The car park was nearly full and there were people either unloading golf equipment from their cars or loading it back in after their games. There was a ramp and steps to the left leading to a higher level where the first tee was situated and a restaurant and bar which overlooked the car park.

'Looks a strange place to hand over the equipment we've asked for,' Dan commented.

'Maybe we're just starting here, then moving on somewhere else,' Jimmy said.

Dan looked around. To the left there was an apartment block overlooking the area.

'Easy to stake out,' he said. 'I'll drop you a few minutes walk from the club at about nine so you can arrive early and check things out. You can have a coffee up there overlooking the car park. I'll arrive at ten. I'll have my earpiece in and you can phone me and tell me if you've spotted anything iffy.'

Dan drove into the car park the next day at two minutes to ten. He had the cash in a small canvas bag. He had known that the equipment would be expensive and had brought cash out from England in anticipation. However, the thirty thousand euros were virtually cleaning him out.

Jimmy spotted the car and phoned Dan from the bar above the car park.

'I've seen one of the men who searched us outside the bar hanging around the pro shop. I also think someone's watching from one of the flats in the block overlooking the course. Three times I've caught a glint of what I believe to be binoculars reflecting in the sun.'

'Can't really blame them,' Dan replied. 'They don't know us. I'd be equally cautious.'

'Let's hope it's just binoculars and not telescopic sights!'

At that moment, a grey VW 4 by 4 came around the corner and parked about four spaces away from Dan. Dan recognised Ortega as the passenger and the man who had first approached them in the bar as the driver.

Ortega got out of the car and had clearly dressed for the location. He was wearing a peach coloured polo shirt and a pair of check shorts down to his knees. On his head he had a sunhat of the sort favoured by golfers set at a jaunty angle. His large companion had also tried to blend in with the surroundings but in Dan's view had failed as he looked out of place in his baggy shorts and overtight polo shirt revealing tattoos of the type not commonly seen on golf courses.

Dan walked over to them.

'Senor *Smith*,' Ortega said smiling, emphasising the name. 'Good to see you again. Do you play?'

'No, do you?' Dan replied.

'Of course!'

'Lucky you. I've got other things on my mind.'

'You should take up golf. It is very relaxing. The golf courses down here are some of the best in the world!'

'Well, perhaps you'll excuse me if I don't join you for a round. Do you have the gear?'

'I do. And I take it that's the money?'

Ortega pointed to the bag in Dan's hand.

111

Dan nodded whereupon Ortega opened the rear door of the VW and the other man unloaded two large golf bags containing what appeared to Dan to be far less than a full set of clubs. The bags were set down on their ends and Ortega gestured to them. Dan took a couple of steps over to them and looked inside. The dividers which are in larger bags to separate the clubs had been removed and as Dan looked down he could see the barrel of an AK 47 pointing upwards in each bag.

'It's all here?' he asked.

'Of course. Spare magazines and ammo in the bottom of the bags and the rest of the equipment in various pockets and compartments. Please, have a quick look.'

Dan opened the zipped pocket on the side of one of the bags and saw two Glock pistols. He put his hand down inside and felt two silencers. He opened a couple of further zips on each bag and realised that the bags were indeed crammed with the equipment he had ordered.

'You see,' Ortega said. 'I am a man who delivers what he promises. I would not cheat you. And you can tell your man he can come down from the bar, where he's been for the last hour. Now if you give me the money, you can load the bags into your car and our business is concluded.'

Dan handed over the bag. Ortega looked inside it briefly and tossed it to his companion.

'Aren't you going to count it?' Dan asked.

'I trust you, senor. Anyway, I now have enough pictures of both you and your companion which would make it very unwise for you to cheat me. But don't worry. I will have them deleted from the camera as soon as our business is over.'

Dan nodded and picked up the first bag and lifted it over to the boot of his car. Ortega's man carried over the other.

'One last thing, senor,' Ortega said. 'I can only think of one reason you might require such equipment in this area. If I am right I wish you the very best of luck! You will certainly need it.'

With that, Ortega and his companion got back in their car and drove away. A minute later, Jimmy joined Dan.

'Neat way to hand over the stuff,' Jimmy said.

'Yes, he's no fool. I think he knows exactly what we want it for too.'

'Is that a problem?'

No, I don't think so. According to Luis, he'd be only too happy to see the Russians taken down.'

Chapter 16

'There are lights coming down the hill,' Jimmy said.

They waited in their hire car in a spot they had found just off the road halfway down the hill which led to the private road leading to the villa. There were no lights on and no one coming down the hill could see their car unless they happened to look directly to their left as they passed. Even if they did, Dan and Jimmy would not have been visible.

The car was a red sports car. It was the third car that had passed in the half hour that they had been waiting and must have come from one of the villas further up the hill and past the turn off to the Durchenkos' villa.

Dan checked his watch yet again.

'It's still only half past ten,' he said.

They continued to sit there in the dark in silence.

Ten minutes later, another car swept by. This time, a big black limousine.

'We're in business!' Jimmy said.

Dan started the engine and waited a full thirty seconds before pulling out. He knew that it would take the black car at least two minutes to get down the rest of the hill and on to a well lit road so following the car without being close behind it would be easy. Anyway, he was fairly sure of the direction that the car would be taking.

When they reached a busier road, Dan kept his car at least two cars behind the car he was following and as anticipated followed it into Puerto Banus. The car continued down to the port and parked in a prominent position on the waterfront in the only space available, which appeared to have been reserved. They passed the car and in his mirror Dan saw Alexei Durchenko and his usual two minders get out. Fortunately he knew where they would be heading, to the bars in the street just behind the waterfront, where the places preferred by the younger crowd were situated.

Parking presented a problem. They had to have a space near the limousine. It was no good them parking in one of the underground car parks further back in the town where most people parked. It was mainly the flashy cars whose owners wanted to show off which were parked on the waterfront and spaces were hard to come by. In the event, Dan had to drive around the block several times before eventually he nabbed a space vacated by a BMW M Class, about ten cars away from Alexei's limousine.

They found Alexei in the first bar they tried. His minders had taken a table in a corner where they could see everything and Alexei was already presiding over a large table of young men and women, with others standing around nearby. There were half a dozen open bottles of champagne on the table and it wasn't long before Alexei was waving over to the bar for more.

Dan and Jimmy stood by the bar watching until a table became vacant. It was not long before the drink started to take effect on Alexei and his hangers on. At one point, Alexei went to the Gents and Dan was tempted to follow him in and break his neck there and then. When Alexei returned, he turned his attention to the nubile young blond beside him and started caressing her thigh. As Dan was thinking about Tom and Sandra Wilson, Jimmy nudged him and he saw that one of the minders was heading to the Gents.

Jimmy finished his beer and got up.

'Let's just see what they're made of,' he said, and before Dan could stop him, he followed the Russian into the Gents.

Ivan was bored. Ever since the incident involving the English boy, he and Dmitry had been given nothing to do other than babysit Alexei. Although he would never have told anyone, he loathed Alexei, whom he considered to be a spoilt brat and he was fed up with doing nothing other than ferry him around and clean up the car after he'd been carousing with some young tart in the back.

He was therefore not in a good mood as he stood urinating in the Gents. He was also less than pleased when a seemingly drunk man came and stood at the next urinal when there were plenty of others free. The man then barged into him causing him to lose his balance and pee all over his shoes. Ivan swore in Russian and swung his right fist at the drunk's head. However, to his surprise the drunk managed to duck out of the way of the blow and and then hit him so hard in his ribs that he was driven back on to the wall beside the urinals. Ivan roared with rage and with his penis still hanging out of his trousers launched himself across the room towards Jimmy. Jimmy span round and kicked the Russian in the stomach and then elbowed him in the throat. Ivan collapsed gasping for air and Jimmy simply left him there. Jimmy could easily have killed him by crushing his windpipe but that was not in the plan at that stage.

Dan saw Jimmy leave the Gents and walk over.

'Jesus, what have you done?' he asked.

'Nothing much. But I suggest we retreat back there where I can't be seen from where they're sitting,' Jimmy replied.

It was another five minutes before Ivan appeared. He did not look happy and was still rubbing his neck. He certainly had no intention of telling Dmitry that some drunk had got the better of him.

'Where the hell have you been?' Dmitry demanded when he got back to the table. 'I was going to come and look for you but couldn't leave wonder boy on his own. You don't look too good.'

'I must have eaten something bad,' Ivan replied sheepishly. 'I've been on the toilet.'

He had a furtive glace around the bar but Jimmy was tucked away out of sight by then.

Chapter Seventeen

About an hour later, Alexei and his friends left the bar with Alexei clutching an open bottle of champagne in one hand and with his other arm around the blonde. Ivan and Dmitry followed at a discreet distance and Dan and Jimmy followed a little further back. Dan assumed that they were heading to a club but after a while, the girl whispered something in Alexei's ear and giggled. Alexei smiled wolfishly and shouted something to the others. He then headed off back towards the port with the girl while the rest of the crowd continued.

'Result!' Jimmy said. 'We won't have to wait in some noisy nightclub for the next few hours. He's obviously had an invitation and he's going to give her one now!'

'Yes. But where?'

'Either in the car or at her place,' Jimmy replied.

They hurried back to their car by a different cut through to the port and got there before the Russians as Alexei kept stopping for a snog.

When they set off it seemed to Dan that the limousine was headed for somewhere definite rather than driving around aimlessly. They ended up outside an apartment block in San Pedro, a resort just a few minutes away. Dan kept the car a discreet distance away and he and Jimmy watched Alexei and the girl get out of the car and enter the block.

'Unless he's going to bang her in the hall and then dump her, I reckon we've got at least half an hour!' Jimmy said.

'Plan A then?' Dan asked.

'Yes, but you'll have to play the drunk this time. One of them has already seen me.'

They checked the silenced Glocks which they had left in the car while they had been in the bar. Dan took off his lightweight jacket and got out of the car with the jacket covering his weapon. They had assumed that the glass in the car was bullet proof so needed a distraction.

Dan started staggering towards the limousine and Jimmy approached less obviously from the other side of the road.

When Dan reached the car he deliberately fell against the back of it.

'What the fuck?' Dmitry shouted. He had watched the drunk approaching in his wing mirror.

'Some arsehole has just lurched into the car. He had better not have scratched it! Shit, he's going to have a piss against the car!'

Dmitry threw open the passenger door and turned towards Dan. He never heard the loud crack as the bullet struck him between the eyes.

Ivan was looking sideways from the driver's seat. He saw Dmitry fall backwards and a spray of blood from his head and knew exactly what had happened even before the crack from the silenced gun registered with him. He seized his own gun from the pocket in the door beside him and flung the door open hoping the car would give him cover from Dmitry's assailant. As he dived out of the car he looked up and saw someone else in front of him. 'It's that bastard from the bar' he thought. It was his last thought. Jimmy smiled and put a bullet through Ivan's right eye.

Chapter Eighteen

Alexei left the apartment block still on a high. He'd taken some more coke before he and the girl had had sex and, without the drink and drugs, may have been more restrained but the incident with Cassie had given him a taste for the rough stuff. He'd left the girl bloodied and bruised, sobbing on her bedroom floor.

As he approached car, his mood changed when no one got out to open the door for him. 'Lazy bastards,' he thought. 'They had better not have fallen asleep. Petrov is going to hear about this.'

He wrenched open the back door, ready to bawl out Dmitry and Ivan and sobered up very quickly when he saw Dan sitting on the other side of the car pointing a silenced gun at him.

'Get in,' Dan ordered.

Alexei froze but was shoved into the rear of the car by Jimmy. Jimmy then got into the driver's seat and drove away.

Dan looked at Alexei with contempt.

'If you're wondering where your bodyguards are, they're not far away but they won't be much help to you. They're in the boot. Dead.'

'Who are you?' Alexei stammered.

Dan did not reply.

'Do you know who I am?' Alexei blurted out. 'When my father finds out who you are...'

'Your father will soon know who I am. In fact I'm going to tell him myself.'

'You're kidnappers?'

'I suppose this a kidnapping. But we haven't done it for money. You asked who I am. Do you remember murdering a young English boy by beheading him?'

Alexei did not reply.

Dan grabbed him by the throat.

'Answer the question!'

'I didn't...'

Dan smacked the gun across his face, splitting it open.

'Don't lie to me!'

'It was them, not me!'

'What? The bodyguards?'

'Yes, yes,' Alexei squealed.

'So at least you admit you were there. But I know it was you.'

Alexei sobbed.

'I'm the boy's father,' Dan continued.

Alexei gasped and lost control of his bladder.

'Jesus,' Dan said. 'Hurry up, Jimmy. It stinks in here!'

Jimmy drove the car up into the mountains on the Ronda road to a spot that they had identified the day before. Concealed off the road was a car that they had 'borrowed' and left there. Jimmy came round and hauled Alexei out. Dan followed him out of the same side of the car and immediately shot him in the back of the head.

Dan went over to the other car.

'Are you sure you want to do this?' Jimmy asked.

'Of course.'

Ten minutes later, they turned the limousine so that it was facing towards the gorge. Jimmy released the hand brake and they pushed it over the side. They heard it crashing down but were unable to see that the boot popped open and two of the three bodies in the car flew out.

They then drove back to where they had left their car outside the girl's block, abandoned the 'borrowed' car and drove back to their apartment.

Chapter Nineteen

Viktor Durchenko sat behind his desk drumming his fingers impatiently. His wife, Irina, and his other two sons, Sergei and Georgy, sat on the sofas around the coffee table in the middle of the room. None of them said anything. Earlier that morning, Petrov had reported to Viktor that Alexei had not returned to the villa since going out the previous evening. There had been no word from Alexei, nor from his bodyguards, Ivan and Dmitry. It was not unusual for Alexei to stay out until the early hours of the morning but this was unheard of.

'Maybe he's spent the night with some whore,' had been Viktor's first reaction.

'That doesn't explain the lack of contact from Ivan and Dmitry. They would have rung the gatehouse to tell them what was happening and I would have been informed first thing in the morning,' had been Petrov's reply.

'Maybe they ended up at some party and they all got stoned,' Georgy had offered.

'Impossible,' Petrov had said. 'Ivan and Dmitry wouldn't dare. Particularly after the last fiasco.'

'If that's the explanation, I will personally cut their throats!' Viktor had added.

Petrov had then gone off to investigate.

'Well?' Viktor demanded, as soon as Petrov reappeared.

'I traced the bar he'd been in. One of the bar staff said he'd left with a group of people at about midnight. None of the clubs he frequents are open but I tried the bars and restaurants where the car would have been parked. I got lucky. At one restaurant a waiter had just arrived for his shift and had been on duty the previous evening. He remembered the car and says that shortly after midnight when they were packing up, four people got in the car and drove away. He described Alexei, Ivan and Dmitry. The fourth person was a girl, who was all over Alexei.'

'And then?' Viktor demanded.

Petrov shrugged.

'Nothing,' he said. 'We can only assume they went back to the girl's place. Ivan and Dmitry would have waited outside. We have no way of finding out where she lived.'

'So what now?'

'I have men out trawling the streets looking for the car and I have spoken to our contacts in the police and asked them to let me know if they hear anything.'

'You don't think he could have been kidnapped?' Sergei said.

Viktor snorted. 'Who by? We've neutralised all the opposition down here!'

'Maybe it's someone who doesn't know who we are. Someone who's seen him flashing his money around.'

'What? Someone capable of hijacking a bullet proof car and taking out two armed bodyguards! That's hardly likely!' Georgy said.

'I agree,' Petrov said. 'Ivan and Dimitry may not be the brightest men but as soldiers they are second to none.'

The guard in the gatehouse watched the approaching motorcyclist through his binoculars as he rode up the private road to the villa. He certainly did not look a threat. He looked like a skinny teenager with a crash helmet perched on his head and his shirt tails flapping behind him. The guard was fed up. He still had an hour to go until the end of his shift. It was already very hot and he cursed Petrov's insistence that they should all wear black suits whatever the weather. He had taken his jacket off in the gatehouse but knew that he would have to put it back on to go out and meet the motorcyclist and see what he wanted. Still, at least it was a small break from the tedium. He was aware that Alexei's car had not returned from the night before and in his view Ivan and Dmitry would be in big trouble when they eventually returned.

The guard was waiting behind the gate for the motorcyclist when he arrived. The boy took off his helmet and placed it on the handlebars. He then said something in Spanish to the guard. The only words that the guard understood were 'Senor Durchenko'.

'English? Ingles?' the guard shouted.

The boy shrugged. 'Little,' he said.

There then followed one of those conversations where both parties have limited knowledge of a third language but the guard understood that the boy had a delivery for Viktor, not least because he pointed to a cardboard box strapped to the rear of the motorcycle on which the words 'Viktor Durchenko' were written.

Given the continuing absence of Alexei, the guard was under instructions to report anything remotely unusual direct to Petrov, and this was definitely unusual.

He therefore took out his phone and phoned him. Petrov answered immediately.

'Vitaly, this is Boris at the gate. There's a young boy on a motorcycle here who says he's got a parcel for Viktor. It's a cardboard box about the size of a crate of wine.'

'Who's it from?'

'I don't know.'

'Well ask him, idiot!'

'I'll ring you back in a moment. His English is poor.'

'So is yours! Ok. Ring me back immediately.'

Ten minutes later, Boris rang him back.

'Two men, probably English, paid him a hundred euros to make the delivery.'

'Can he describe them?'

'Not really. I gather they had hats and sunglasses on. He reckons they are about forty, one a bit bigger than the other, dressed like tourists.'

'OK. Take the package and send him away. I'll send someone down to collect it.'

'Are you expecting a delivery?' Irina asked.

'Of course not!' Viktor shouted. 'Certainly not from two Englishmen!'

'Do you think this could be connected to Alexei's disappearance?' she asked.

No one answered.

There was a knock on the door and a guard handed the parcel to Petrov.

'It's quite heavy,' he said as he carried it over and put it gently on Viktor's desk. 'Can I suggest that you all go out on to the terrace while I open it?'

'You don't think it could be a bomb, surely?' Sergei said.

'No but it's best to be cautious,' Petrov replied.

The family members walked out on to the terrace and stood watching through the doors from the far side of the swimming pool.

Petrov took out a knife and very carefully sliced through the tape securing the top flaps of the box. He then bent down and shone the light from the desk lamp on to the top of the box as he very slowly lifted up one of the flaps about an inch. Seeing nothing untoward he lifted the flap and then repeated the process with the others until he was peering down into the box. The box contained a large plastic bag with the top rolled up and taped down. He removed the tape and and opened the bag to see what was inside.

From outside, the family looked on as Petrov opened the box. Petrov was the most ruthless yet calmest man Viktor had ever known. But when Petrov got to the stage of opening the bag, he let out a gasp that could be heard on the other side of the terrace and staggered backwards.

Viktor rushed back closely followed by his sons but some instinct made Irina hang back.

'What is it?' Viktor demanded as he entered the study and approached his desk and the open box.

'No, Viktor, don't!' Petrov shouted. He tried to block Viktor's path but Viktor shoved him out of the way and looked inside the box.

It took Viktor a couple of seconds to comprehend what he was looking at. But when it dawned on him that he was looking into the sightless eyes of his son, Alexei, he let out a wail of anguish so loud that it reverberated around the vast villa. The bottom half of the head was badly damaged where the bullet had passed through but the top half was perfectly preserved.

Sergei and Georgy looked into the box and like Petrov staggered back in horror. Irina stayed outside. Her instinct had been right.

Viktor sat down and took a deep breath.

'Who could have done this?' he demanded.

No one replied.

'You told me we had no opposition down here!' he shouted accusingly at Petrov.

The usually unflappable Petrov was for once on the defensive.

'But we don't,' he stammered. 'No one, not here or back home would do this.'

'Well they have, haven't they?' roared Viktor. 'What the fuck do you think *that* is?'

'There must be some new outfit we don't know about,' Georgy said. 'Using our method is a deliberate challenge. They have started a war.'

'Too fucking right!' Viktor shouted. 'They'll wish they'd never been born! I will kill them all! Slowly. And all their families too!'

'I don't get it,' Petrov said. 'If there was any outfit capable of taking us on, I would have heard about it.'

'If you're so fucking clever, how do you explain this?' Viktor continued.

At that moment, Viktor's mobile rang. It was sitting on the desk and started ringing, buzzing and flashing. Everyone stared at it. Only Viktor's inner circle had the number. Yet the display showed an unknown number.

Viktor picked it up.

'Who is this?'

'Viktor Durchenko?'

'How did you get this number?'

'Your cowardly son gave it to me in a desperate attempt to save his life.'

'When I find out who you are...'

'I will tell you exactly who I am. Three weeks ago, your son beheaded my son. Now you know how it feels. Only at least your son was dead when I removed his head.'

'So you think that makes us even? I'm going to bring hell down on to you and your family!'

'I have no family now. Whereas you...I'm going to kill every one of them and then you, and bring an end to your reign of terror.'

The caller disconnected and Viktor stared at the phone in disbelief. He relayed the contents of the conversation to the others.

Petrov was secretly relieved. At least he couldn't be blamed for not being aware of some other gang that had started a turf war.

'How can one man challenge *us*?' Sergei asked.

'We know there are at least two,' Georgy said.

'No matter,' Petrov said, once more in control. 'It will be easy to find out who this man is. He won't be able to hide down here. Within an hour, I will have hundreds of eyes and ears on the streets looking for them. I assume you'd like him taken alive if possible, Viktor?'

'You assume correctly.'

Chapter 20

After disconnecting the call, Dan got out of the car and stamped on the mobile phone before throwing it into the bushes.

When he got back in the car, Jimmy drove the ten minute journey to the brothel that he had visited a few days earlier. They had switched the plates on the hire car but had decided that this would be the last time that they would use this vehicle.

Las Chapas is an expensive residential area a few miles east of Marbella. Set on a small hill on the sea side of the N340 highway was a sprawling villa, advertised in the local press as Aphrodite's Palace where discerning gentlemen could relax in luxurious surroundings and enjoy congenial company. As Jimmy put it, it was an upmarket 'knocking shop'. When they pulled into the car park, they noticed that even at lunchtime there were quite a few cars, not all of which would have belonged to the staff. Dan and Jimmy had been hoping that it would have been less busy at that time of day.

They parked in a quiet corner of the car park and tucked their pistols into the back of their trousers and put on lightweight jackets to cover them. They then went up to the front door and rang the bell. A small grille in the heavy wooden door was opened and after they had been inspected the door opened. A woman of about fifty let them in.

'Welcome, gentlemen,' she said smiling, although Dan noted that her smile did not reach her eyes. She was an attractive but hard faced woman who spoke with an east European accent, dressed in a short red dress, red high heels and what Dan assumed were seamed black stockings as opposed to tights. She had obviously graduated from the shop floor to management level as she got older.

After she had let them in, she closed the door and retreated behind a reception desk situated to the right of the door. As Jimmy had described, Dan found himself in a large open plan hall leading through to a sitting room where the clients and hookers chatted and drank before getting down to business. He could only see part way into that room but knew that it led on to a terrace where there was a swimming pool and loungers on a large terrace. At the left hand end of the hall were the stairs leading to the upper floors.

Perhaps because they had heard new clients arriving, two scantily dressed girls came down the stairs and posed for Dan and Jimmy, smiling invitingly. They then moved into the sitting room still smiling back at Dan and Jimmy.

'They'll do for us!' Jimmy said and walked towards the sitting room.

'Wait!' the woman in the red dress shouted. 'You haven't paid your entrance fee yet! It's twenty five euros each.'

'Why should I pay an entrance fee?' Jimmy said.

'It's the house rule,' the woman replied. 'Anyway, don't I know you? Haven't you been here before?'

'We'll see if we like what's on offer,' Dan said. 'We'll have a look around and if we like it you can add the twenty five to the bill.'

'That's not the way it works!' the woman said. 'Twenty five euros each or you don't go in!'

'Or what?' Dan said aggressively.

Dan saw the woman glance down behind the desk and a slight movement of her arm. He guessed she had pressed a bell of some sort.

'Or you get thrown out,' she retorted.

At that moment, two large men came down the stairs. The first one tried to take hold of Jimmy who was nearest to the stairs. Jimmy evaded his grasp and headbutted the man who fell backwards with blood pouring from his nose. With a roar of anger, and while still lying on his back, the man pulled out a gun but before he could use it, Dan shot him twice.

The other man reached inside his jacket but before he could get his gun out, Jimmy shot him in the head. Jimmy then turned and pointed his gun at Dan who was still standing with his back to the desk. A bullet whistled past Dan's head and he turned to see the woman in the red dress falling backwards and a sawn off shotgun falling from her hands.

'Charming lady!' Jimmy grinned.

At that moment, Dan saw a glint of metal in the V shaped gap where the staircase disappeared above the ceiling.

'Down! Uzi!' he screamed, diving behind the desk.

A hail of bullets sprayed into the hall but, as the shooter had simply put his hand through the gap and fired indiscriminately, without accuracy. By now there were screams coming from the sitting room and upstairs.

Jimmy, pressed against the stairs and directly beneath where the shots had come from, reached into his pocket and tossed a stun grenade through the gap on to the landing. The noise was deafening when it exploded. Jimmy then rushed up the stairs and without hesitation shot the man with the Uzi who was staggering around in a disorientated state. He then started opening all the doors screaming at people to get out and then repeated the process on the upper floor.

A succession of girls in their underwear and men hastily pulling on their trousers hurried down the stairs and out through the open door.

'All clear!' Jimmy shouted.

Meanwhile Dan went into the sitting room and out on to the terrace and told everyone there to leave. No one needed telling twice as he waved his gun in the air.

Satisfied that the villa was empty, Dan and Jimmy worked fast. They removed two cans of petrol from the boot of their car and sprayed it all over the downstairs of the premises. Dan then lit a piece of rolled up newspaper and tossed it into the hall from outside the front door. By this time, they could hear the sirens of the approaching emergency vehicles, no doubt drawn by the sound of the unsilenced Uzi and the stun grenade.

They turned on to the N340 as the emergency vehicles turned off it and the flames started to devour Aphrodite's Palace. They then stopped to put back the original number plates on the car and drove to the airport where they returned the car and hired another from a different outlet.

Only a few minutes after the emergency services had arrived at the villa, Petrov received a phone call. He was still with Viktor, planning how they would track Dan down. He was stunned when he heard the news. In all his time with

Viktor, no one had dared to mount such an assault on one of their premises.

'What's happened?' Viktor demanded when Petrov ended the call.

'Aphrodite's Palace is burning to the ground as we speak.'

'What!' roared Viktor. 'How?'

'From what I can gather, two men gained entry posing as customers, shot dead all our staff including Iva and torched the place. That was one of my police contacts phoning.'

Viktor slammed his fist down.

'The same two men!'

'So it would seem. But now we know who they are and until now they have had the element of surprise. They cannot survive out there for long.'

'You had better be right!'

'We haven't had a challenge like this since the very early days and then we were up against large gangs. We succeeded then. We will succeed now. It's only a matter of time!'

An hour later, Petrov took another call and reported back to Viktor immediately.

'These men are clearly worthy opponents,' he said. 'The boy's father is Daniel Green, a former captain in the SAS, the British special forces. I don't know who the other man is but I think we can assume that he's a former colleague. And for all we know there could be others.'

'So that explains how they managed to take out Ivan and Dmitry, and the men at Aphodite's.'

'Exactly. But as I said, they had surprise on their side. Now we know what to expect.'

'So what do we do? Beef up security at all our premises? We don't know where they will hit next.'

'Everyone will be warned but we haven't got enough men of the right quality to adequately defend everywhere. Low grade thugs would be no match for these men. We must be proactive and concentrate our efforts on finding them. They must have a base somewhere. It shouldn't be too hard to find.'

Chapter Twenty One

The massage parlour was in the basement of a shopping centre in Calahonda, an urbanisation a few miles outside Fuengirola popular with tourists and foreign residents. Dan and Jimmy knew that because of its position, they would not be able to burn it down as any fire would destroy the neighbouring businesses as well and endanger the lives of innocent 'civilians'. They were also anxious to avoid a gun battle in such a built up area.

Unlike the villa at Las Chapas, this place was distinctly downmarket and catered mainly for the late evening crowd, stag parties and the like. The foyer was a dingy room with subdued red lighting and red flock wallpaper. A middle aged oriental woman asked for a ten euros entrance fee and handed Dan and Jimmy what could only be described as a menu setting out the various services on offer. She then told them that she would fetch the girls so that they could each choose which 'masseuse' they would prefer.

In the corner of the room, Dan noted a camera covering the entrance and the desk where the oriental woman was seated. Dan paid her twenty euros and the woman came out from behind the desk and led them to a seating area around the corner. There was another camera covering this area.

'You wait here,' she said. 'I back soon with girls.'

Jimmy sat down on a sofa but Dan remained standing. The woman then walked towards a door to the left and as soon as Dan judged that she was out of the camera's field of vision, he stepped towards her and felled her with a single blow to her neck. Working quickly while Jimmy stayed on the sofa looking as innocent as he could for the benefit of the camera, Dan tied her hands behind her with a plastic tie and placed some tape over over her mouth. Then, holding her up with one hand, he carefully opened the door she had been about to go through, ready to draw his gun from his waistband should the need arrive. The door led into a corridor with cheap looking plywood doors off to the left and the right.

Dan opened the first door to the left and shoved the semi conscious woman into the room in front of him. She fell to the floor and Dan stepped in behind her with his gun in his hand. The room was a tackily decorated bedroom only just big enough for the double bed on which lay a startled and scantily dressed oriental girl who despite the make up looked no older than her mid teens. Dan put one finger to his mouth and held the gun away from the girl. Fortunately the girl did not scream.

'You speak English?' he asked.

'A little,' the girl replied.

'Don't be frightened. I won't hurt you.'

The girl nodded.

'Where are your minders? The men?'

The girl looked confused.

'The men who work with her?' Dan said, pointing to the woman on the floor.

'In room at end,' the girl stammered.

'Left or right?'

'This side.'

'How many?'

'Two.'

'Stay here!'

The girl nodded.

Dan stepped into the corridor and beckoned Jimmy who was standing at the end of the corridor covering it with his gun.

'Two of them. Last room on the left.'

They hurried down the corridor anxious to get there before the minders reacted to the fact that both customers were now out of view of the cameras.

Dan kicked open the door. They need not have worried. Neither man was looking at the CCTV screens on a desk in one corner of the room. They were sitting at a table drinking vodka watching a porn movie on a television in the other corner.

One tried to stand up but before he got to his feet the knife thrown by Jimmy entered his chest and drove him back down again into his chair and he toppled over backwards. The other man remained seated and and tried to pull out a gun but too late as Dan had stepped behind him and snapped his neck before he could extricate it from inside his shirt.

'Piece of cake!' Jimmy said.

'It won't be from now on', Dan replied. 'They will all be expecting us when they hear about this and the other place. OK, let's clear the rooms.'

They found three other girls but there were no customers. Dan and Jimmy led the other girls to the room where Dan had dumped the 'madam'. He dragged her to her feet and led her to the room containing the two dead minders. He shoved her in and added another tie to her feet.

'Don't try to escape or you'll end up like them!' he said before returning to the first room.

The girls were all huddled together on the bed and clearly terrified. They were all about the same age and only one spoke reasonable English. Dan explained that they meant the girls no harm and were only interested in the people who had brought them to work there. The girl who spoke reasonable English interpreted for the others. One girl started crying. She blurted something out in a foreign language.

'She thinks they will kill us after what you have done,' the other girl explained.

'Who?'

'The men back at the house.'

'Which house?'

'It's a house where many girls are kept. Where we sleep. Every day we are taken to different places to work and then back to the house.'

'How many girls?'

'About twenty. Five girls in each bedroom.'

'How many men are there at the house?'

'Usually about six. They work out who goes where and take them in cars. During the day, sometimes less men as they only need to look after girls still at house.'

'Are there girls there now?'

'Yes. Daytime trade not so good so only four girls here. Other girls are supposed to sleep to be ready for night trade.'

'How did you get here?' Jimmy asked.

'By car.'

'No. I meant how did you end up working for them?'

'I was schoolgirl in Thailand. I was drugged. I not really remember journey.'

'Can you take us to the house?' Dan asked.

The girl hesitated.

'Yes, but why? What happen to us?'

'We will make sure these men never harm you again and we will release the other girls. We can take you all to the police.'

'But men boast that police work for them. Police come here!'

Dan thought for a moment.

'I know a good policeman. You can trust him. He will contact your embassies, arrange for you to go home.'

The girl interpreted for the others. They looked doubtful.

'Trust us,' Dan said. 'We will deal with the men in the house and then arrange for you to go home.'

The girls had an animated conversation amongst themselves in their own language. The girl who spoke English then turned to Dan.

'OK. What we do?'

'Get dressed and come with us. You can show us the house and wait for us as we have to act quickly before they realise what's happened here.'

The girls went off to get dressed.

'What's the plan?' Jimmy asked.

'We have to hit the house now before they beef up security which they will do when they hear about this place.'

'I agree. But what about the girls? What do we do with them? We've nowhere to take them!'

'They can wait in the car.'

'But what if there are other girls at the house in the same position?'

'I don't know. We'll have to play it by ear!'

Somehow the girls looked even younger when they reappeared in jeans, T shirts and trainers rather than their previous garb of high heels, stockings and fancy lingerie. Dan wondered about the wisdom of what they were doing as the girls all piled into the back of the hire car and they drove through the streets of Calahonda. However, it was probably just as well that the girls were there as they were all arguing about the route back to the house. After a few wrong turns they eventually arrived at a large villa at the the top of a hill set apart from the others. Dan drove past the villa and parked a couple of minutes walk away.

'You're sure that's the right house?' he asked.

'Yes,' the girl who spoke English replied.

Dan and Jimmy checked their weapons. Dan turned round and saw that the girls were terrified.

'It's very important that you stay here,' he said. 'If you run away, we can't help you and you will be in great danger from the men who employ the men in the house.'

The girl he spoke to interpreted for the others.

'How long will you be?' she asked.

'Not long. You should be safe here. But if we are not back in twenty minutes then I'm afraid you are on your own. Get a taxi to Marbella police station and ask for Inspector Valdez. Insist on seeing him and no one else.'

The girl nodded and Dan gave her enough money for the taxi fare.

Chapter Twenty Two

Dan and Jimmy walked past the villa and had a good look at the property and the next door villas. Unfortunately, the property had a high front wall with secure gates set into the wall.

'We can't go in that way,' Jimmy said. 'Our best bet is from the side. They probably look out over the back so will see us if we go from that direction.'

'Let's see if the neighbours are in,' Dan replied.

They rang the doorbell of the villa to the right and the door was answered by an elderly British man.

'Can I help you?' he asked.

'I hope so,' Dan said with a smile. 'We're looking for a property to buy in this area and we saw some estate agent's particulars with details of a property up here. It looked promising. But now I think we're lost. Maybe we're in the wrong road. You wouldn't happen to know would you if one of the properties round here is for sale?'

'Not as far as I know,' the man said.

'What about the property next door? Only we can't really see it because of the wall?'

'I don't think it's for sale. They're an odd lot. Cars with blacked out windows coming and going all times of the day and night.'

'And on the other side of them?'

'That's the Wilsons' house. They don't live there. They only use it as a holiday home. I'm sure they would have told us if they were selling.'

'Are they there now?'

'No. they aren't due out till next month.'

'We must have the wrong road then. Sorry to bother you.'

The man nodded and closed his door.

'Back to the Wilsons' then!' Jimmy said.

Fortunately it was a quiet road and while Dan kept a watch for walkers, Jimmy took only seconds to pick the lock on the up and over garage door. He and Dan went into the garage and closed the door behind them. There was a back door into the garage and that too was unlocked in seconds. They then found themselves in the back garden with a six foot wall separating them from the target property. Dan lifted himself up and had a quick look over.

'I think we're Ok,' he said. 'There's only one window facing this way and it's not level with here.'

'OK, let's do it,' Jimmy replied. 'I hope those girls have got the right house!'

They scrambled over the wall and dropped to the other side and then pressed themselves against the side wall of the villa. They waited for about a minute but all remained quiet. Dan pointed to the back of the house and they made their way along the wall. When they reached the window, they had a careful look in and saw a large kitchen diner. There was one man lounging back in a chair watching TV drinking a bottle of beer. The pump action shotgun on the table beside him confirmed that they had the right house.

They continued round to the back of the house and peered in through an open window for a different view. The man was definitely alone in the room and not looking in their direction. A little further on there was a door. Dan slowly turned the handle praying it would not squeak. It didn't but it was locked. Jimmy handed him the pick and very carefully Dan unlocked the door. Fortunately the television was on quite loud and the man did not look round.

'How do we play this?' Jimmy whispered. Suddenly Dan lurched back towards the corner of the house and the undergrowth at the bottom of the wall and came out clutching a struggling skinny looking cat, the kind of stray seen all over Spain.

'Oh, I get it. A diversion!' Jimmy said.

Dan took a peek through the window and tossed the cat into the room. It landed with a squeal. The guard looked round and saw the cat and got up swearing in Russian. He walked over and tried to grab the cat continuing to shout at it. The cat evaded his grasp and the Russian turned to chase it. He never got near it. Out of the corner of his eye he saw the door opening but before he had a chance to react Dan used one of the commando knives supplied by Ortega to slit his throat from ear to ear. The man slumped to the ground and gurgled for a few seconds before everything went quiet again.

Dan saw the cat watching from a distance.

'Thanks,' he whispered. He stood aside and the cat shot out of the door.

Jimmy went over and checked the shotgun. He gave Dan the thumbs up and pointed to the door at the end of the room. As quietly as possible, they checked all the rooms on the ground floor but they were all empty.

Dan pointed up the stairs and they slowly climbed them with Jimmy leading the way with the shotgun and Dan following with his Glock. When they reached the top, they could hear mens' voices from down a corridor, not it seemed a regular conversation but the distinctive sound of men having a good time as if they were watching a football match or something.

They crept down the corridor towards the sound coming from an open door. When they arrived at a point from where they could see through the door, they were sickened at what they saw. Three men were watching as a fourth man was raping a young oriental girl. Dan and Jimmy could see the man's buttocks rising up and down while the others were cheering him on and one of them had his trousers down and was readying himself for his turn.

The first blast from Jimmy's shotgun took off the man's hand and penis. The second and third were fired at point blank range into the stomachs of the other two men watching. Dan stepped into the room and dragged the fourth man off the girl, pushed him against the wall, shoved his gun under the man's jaw and pulled the trigger. He then silenced the first man who was writhing around on the ground screaming in agony by shooting him in the head.

'Get dressed!' Dan shouted at the girl.

He and Jimmy then tried all the other doors and found five other girls behind locked doors. They managed to get the message through that they should all get dressed and then herded them down the stairs.

'We need another car!' Dan shouted.

They found their way into the garage where there was a black Range Rover Sport. The keys were in a tray in the hall. They piled the girls into the back and opened the garage door which led on to a large parking area in front of the villa. There was a sliding electronic gate in the front wall giving access on to the road.

'Jesus! How do we get that open?' Dan shouted.

'Just get in!' Jimmy replied, starting the engine.

Jimmy revved up the engine and aimed the car at the section of wall between the sliding gate and the pedestrian gate.

'Spanish builders!' he shouted as the wall collapsed and the car shot out over the rubble.

He then drove to the other car and arrived just in time as the first four girls were just beginning to get out to run away having heard the gunfire even from that distance.

Dan jumped out of the Range Rover.

'Follow me!' he shouted at Jimmy.

He then ushered the first lot of girls back into the hire car and drove in the direction of Marbella as fast as he could without drawing attention to the car and the Range Rover behind. As he drove, he took out a mobile and punched in a number. Fortunately, Mendez was at home.

'Hola,' the now familiar gruff voice said.

'Luis! It's Dan!'

'You sound out of breath, Dan!'

'Listen, Luis, this is important. You have to ring Valdez. Tell him to send vehicles to pick up ten young oriental girls from the car park of the La Canada shopping centre. They are all kidnap victims abducted from their homes. They need repatriation. They don't trust the police but I

154

convinced them, well some of them, that they can trust Valdez.'

'What, now?'

'Yes, now! I'm dropping them there myself. We found one of the Durchenkos' prisons where they keep the girls. You could say they've been liberated! I will leave them by the entrance to the Leroy Merlin store. But tell him to hurry. Some or all of them may panic and run away!'

'I will phone him immediately. I take it you won't be hanging around to make a statement?'

'Hardly. Not with the trail of destruction we've left!'

Dan ended the connection. He and Jimmy drove straight to the shopping centre and Dan asked the girl from the first group to interpret as he explained that their only chance of escaping their captors for good was to wait to be picked up by Valdez's men. He also explained that he and Jimmy would not be able to wait with them. Somewhat hesitantly, they all agreed.

Jimmy abandoned the Range Rover by parking among the customers' cars and he and Dan watched from a distance from the hire car as the nervous group of girls stood around near the store. Fortunately, they did not have to wait for long as within five minutes a police car and van arrived. Dan was grateful to see that Valdez himself had come and was relieved when he had counted all ten girls into the van.

Chapter Twenty Three

When they arrived back at their apartment, Jimmy undid his zipped top and pulled out two huge bundles of euros. He tossed them over to Dan.

'Here you are', he said. 'This should go some way to replacing what you paid Ortega.'

'Jesus! Where the hell did you get that? There must be thousands here!' Dan replied.

'I found it in one of the rooms back at the villa. It's probably the previous day's takings awaiting collection by one of the family. I told you we'd pick up some readies at some stage!'

Later that evening, Dan pored over Mendez's file plotting their next move while Jimmy checked over their equipment which they kept in a huge canvas bag in case they had to move quickly. Dan knew that until then they had had the element of surprise in their favour and that from that time on things would become more difficult. He was also aware that the family would be using every means at their disposal to track them down. Perhaps it was time to let the opposition chase their tails while he and Jimmy took care of one or two other matters which involved them leaving Spain for a while.

The answer to that dilemma presented itself shortly after dark. On moving into the flat, Jimmy had rigged up a makeshift alarm system consisting of a red bulb which would light up if anyone approached the front door of the apartment. They had ascertained that their apartment was the only one occupied in that part of the block and anyone approaching their apartment had to walk past five empty ones.

When the bulb situated on the coffee table in full view of both men lit up, they both froze.

The front door of the apartment led straight into the living room. They had bolted it from the inside and had pushed a sideboard against it when they got back. After a few seconds they heard a faint scuffling noise from outside.

That was enough for Jimmy. He fired two bullets from his silenced Glock through the centre of the door just above the sideboard about four feet from the ground. There was a thump from the other side of the door.

'I hope that wasn't someone wanting a cup of sugar!' Dan said, as both men threw themselves to the side of the room behind the sofa.

He needn't have worried. The door splintered inwards as a hail of bullets was fired through it. Dan and Jimmy fired a few rounds back to make their assailants retreat for a few seconds, then grabbed their bag of equipment and went through the patio doors into the communal garden behind the apartment. To their relief, they found that they were not being attacked from the rear as well. Had the roles been reversed, they would certainly have mounted a two pronged attack by coming through the golf course and using wire cutters to access the garden. As it was, Jimmy's foresight in making discreet cuts in the fence when they had moved in probably saved their lives. Maybe their attackers had assumed that they would be trapped but Jimmy lifted the flap and as the attackers managed to push their way through the door and sideboard and into the apartment, he and Dan ran across the fairway and dived into a bunker just as the men chasing them reached the fence and started shooting at them.

Jimmy pulled one of the AK 47s out of their bag and returned the fire, causing the opposition to take cover.

The lights from the garden shone across the fairway but on the other side of Dan and Jimmy, the course was in complete darkness.

'Given them one more burst to keep them down,' Dan said, slinging the bag over his shoulder, 'and we can disappear. I doubt they will follow us. They won't know which way we went and will be worried we will just pick them off. My guess is that there's only about four of them and they have a man down.'

Jimmy fired a long raking burst and they then disappeared into the darkness.

About two hours later, having avoided the main road, they arrived at the now deserted car park of the La Canada shopping centre. The black Range Rover which they had abandoned there earlier was standing in splendid isolation where they had left it. After checking that there was no one around, they loaded their equipment into the back and drove off.

'Good job I kept the keys,' Jimmy said. 'I thought they might come in handy! Where are we heading?'

'Moscow,' Dan replied. 'Via Paris and London.'

Petrov was furious. Using all the resources available to him, he had made the breakthrough when a young German estate agent had told one of his men, after a five hundred euro note had been produced, about the two tough looking Englishmen who had rented an apartment overlooking a golf course. The fact that they had paid in cash added to Petrov's conviction that he had traced Green and his colleague.

Now, he was going to have to start all over again. The bungled operation had not only failed but cost him another man. When the other four had returned and nervously reported their failure, Petrov had bawled them out but in truth he blamed himself for rushing in and not planning the operation properly. As soon as he had received the information, he had assembled a team and sent them in. What he should have done was to have mounted surveillance on the apartment and either planned an assault from both sides or hit the men after they had left the apartment and were out in the open.

Viktor Durchenko had also been furious, once again banging his fists down hard on his desk.

'For fuck's sake, Vitaly! You're telling me we had them and let them escape! Are you losing your touch? Has living down here made you soft?'

Petrov remained silent, not wanting to antagonise his boss further. Viktor's face was red, his eyes were blazing and a large blue vein in his neck was throbbing.

'What do we do now?' Viktor eventually demanded after he had calmed down a little.

'It's only a matter of time,' Petrov replied. 'We have eyes and ears everywhere. They cannot check into a hotel or rent an apartment anywhere on the Costa del Sol without us knowing. We have circulated pictures of them that we got from CCTV footage to all our employees and informants. We've offered a ten thousand euro reward to anyone giving information which helps us trace them.'

'You'd better be right!'

Chapter Twenty Four

'Do you think the Durchenkos have reported this vehicle stolen?' Jimmy asked.

'I've been wondering that myself,' Dan replied, as he drove down the slip road on to the N340 back in the direction of Malaga. 'They may well have done given they have contacts in the police. Not so much to trace the car but to trace us.'

'We'd better change vehicles then.'

'That would mean stealing another as we can't hire one now. I've an idea though.'

Twenty five minutes later they drove into the short stay car park at Malaga Airport. They then walked to the long stay car park and split up. About ten minutes later, Dan phoned Jimmy on one of the mobiles.

'I've found one,' he said and gave Jimmy his location in the car park by reference to the row number.

When Jimmy arrived, he found Dan unscrewing the plates from another black Range Rover.

'The owner could come back at any time,' Jimmy said. 'We don't know how long he's been away.'

'It doesn't matter. By tomorrow morning, we'll be in France. Anyway I doubt the police will be that fussed about some stolen plates.'

Back at the short stay car park, they switched the plates and headed north. They realised that the Durchenkos probably had all the airports and railway stations covered and in any event they needed somewhere to keep their equipment.

By about noon on the following day, they were not far from the border with France. They stopped at a small town and purchased two overnight bags, a change of clothes and some toiletries. After a meal, they set off for Paris. Fortunately, they were simply waved through at the border and it was early evening when they drove into the car park of an airport hotel near Charles de Gaulle Airport. On the following morning, they parked the car in the airport's long stay car park and did their best to conceal the bag of equipment. The car had blacked out windows so they were reasonably confident that it would be safe for the next few days. Otherwise they would just have to pay Fernando Ortega another visit.

They then caught a flight to London and by lunch time, they were back in Dan's flat, planning their trip to Moscow.

At eight on the following morning, they joined the queue that forms every day in Notting Hill Gate outside the Russian Embassy for visas. Even at that time, they found about ten people in front of them but they eventually managed to get visas which enabled them to book flights in three days time.

Dan used the time to visit Richard and Carol.

'Thank God!' Richard exclaimed when he opened the door. 'We've been so worried about you!'

'Why's that?' Dan asked cagily.

'Come on, Dan, don't play the innocent! It's been all over the press!'

'What has?'

'The fact that the Costa del Sol has turned into some sort of war zone! Gun battles, buildings burnt down, holidaymakers being warned to avoid the area!'

'I haven't seen the papers recently.'

Carol then appeared.

'I bet you haven't! You haven't had time! I knew you'd do something stupid like this!' she said.

'Like what?'

'Like starting a war! At the moment the police and press are putting it down to a feud between rival gangs but sooner or later they'll realise what's going on!'

Rather than continue the conversation on the doorstep, they went inside. Dan realised that it was futile to continue to deny that he was

163

involved so he told them an abridged version of what had been going on, leaving out the more gruesome details and concentrating on the brutality of the Durchenkos and how he intended to bring them down.

'Even if it means you getting killed or spending the rest of your life in prison?' Carol asked.

'I've taken similar risks before.'

'When you were young and had the support of the British army and government!'

'They executed our son for no good reason by cutting off his head!' Dan shouted. 'Do you think I can let that go unavenged?'

There was a brief silence after Dan's outburst.

'OK, let's all calm down,' Richard said. 'Is it over now?'

'I'm afraid not', Dan said. 'I may have hurt their organisation but we're nowhere near destroying them and until we do, they will continue their reign of brutality. I can't let that happen. Some good has to come out of Tom's death and if that means ridding the world of these monsters then so be it!'

'You said *we*,' Richard said. 'Does that mean you have help?'

'A former colleague is helping me.'

'One of your old SAS chums?' Carol asked.

'Yes. I couldn't do it alone.'

Carol sighed. 'I suppose there's no point in us asking you to stop?'

'I'm afraid not.'

When Dan left a few minutes later, he was surprised that Carol hugged him. Maybe she thought that it would be the last time that she would see him. Richard walked with Dan to his car.

'Don't worry about Carol', he said. 'She just doesn't want to see you killed or in trouble. I admire what you're doing. I wish I could help but I guess a country solicitor would be more of a hindrance! But if you need any money or there is anything I can do, just let me know.'

'Thanks, Richard, I appreciate that.'

The two men embraced and Dan headed back to London.

Chapter Twenty Five

Dan had only been to Moscow once before when part of the security team for a Russian oligarch based in London, nervous about returning to his home town. Unlike St Petersburg, which is more tourist friendly, Moscow can be a very confusing city for foreign visitors.

Dan and Jimmy met up at the taxi rank at Domodedovo Airport after sitting apart from each other on their flight from London. Dan then negotiated what he considered to be an extortionate price in euros for the fare to the Kempinski Baltchug Hotel, where he had booked rooms for a week. On the journey into the city, Jimmy, who was on his first visit to Russia, was fascinated by the contrasting architecture from the baroque to Soviet concrete with a skyline dominated by the grandiose monstrosities built by Stalin.

'So why did you pick the Kempinski?' he asked. 'It must be costing a fortune!'

'It is!' Dan replied. 'But given the money you lifted from Durchenkos, we can console ourselves that they're paying! I picked it for a number of reasons. To begin with, it's the only place I know as we stayed there when I was last here. It's very central and some of the cheaper places still have 'baboushkas' spying on guests.'

'What the hell are 'baboushkas'?

'To you, ugly old women!'

'I was hoping we might get some sexy young women on parade in our hotel!'

'Unfortunately for you, the Kempinski is one of the few hotels which doesn't admit hookers!'

'Shame!'

Despite the lack of hookers though, Jimmy was suitably impressed by the Kempinski with its luxurious spacious lobby and position looking over Red Square.

'I understand the BBC have a suite in the hotel overlooking Red Square which serves as a backdrop when they do reports from Moscow,' Dan said.

'Maybe they'll report on our activities then!' Jimmy replied.

After they had checked in, they met in Dan's room to discuss what they should do. Their plan was very straightforward: to locate Arkady Durchenko, Viktor's half brother, and kill him. Dan figured that while the family were running around the Costa del Sol trying to find him and Jimmy, this was an ideal opportunity to attack the organisation on a different front. According to Luis Mendez's file, Arkady was the man who held the Durchenkos' empire together in

Moscow. Remove him and the family would come under huge pressure from rival gangs as the Durchenkos would be shown to be vulnerable and without a family presence.

However, locating Arkady was easier said than done. Not surprisingly, Luis had less information on him than the family members living in Spain. Apart from the photo provided to Luis by the Russian police, all they knew was that Arkady was a bit of a playboy but nevertheless was totally loyal to his brother and presided over the family's Moscow interests with the same ruthlessness as the rest of the family.

They had no idea where Arkady lived and had no expectation of obtaining any weaponry apart from what they could buy in the shops.

They had previously discussed that the Durchenkos were likely to own some of the best nightclubs in the city and that if Arkady was a bit of a playboy, he would hopefully frequent them. They seemed to be the best place to start, a course of action approved of by Jimmy.

When he arrived at Dan's room, he found Dan leafing through the Moscow yellow pages. Fortunately, the section for nightclubs was in English as well as Russian, no doubt to attract foreign businessmen and tourists.

When he found the right section, Dan passed the book over to Jimmy.

'What do you think?' he asked.

There were a number of ads about two or three inches square with images of scantily clad women giving the names of clubs and their addresses.

'We should try the ones with the biggest and most lurid ads,' Jimmy replied. 'If we get a map of Moscow, we can find the streets and cover different areas in an evening.'

'Or night. I bet most of these clubs don't get going till midnight and Arkady won't turn up till then. I'll go down to reception and get a map. I'll also ask the concierge what he reckons are the best clubs.'

Dan returned about ten minutes later brandishing a map and a list of names given to him by the concierge. Of the four names on the list, only two appeared in the yellow pages.

'Perhaps we should try those not in the yellow pages first', Dan said. 'Maybe they are mainly for local faces.'

'The concierge obviously thinks they are suitable for us.'

Taking the four recommended by the concierge and the ones with the biggest ads, they ended up with a list of twelve. Unfortunately, they could only find nine of the streets listed on their map.

'Those three could be in side alleys not marked on the map.' Jimmy said.

'Or some way out of town so not on the map of central Moscow. Either way, we will just have to rely on a taxi driver to get there.'

'We could give the three street names to the concierge or reception and they should be able to find them! What's a five star hotel for?'

'Good idea. Let's give them the names and ask them to mark them on a map while we go for a walk.'

Five minutes later they were walking over the bridge across the Moscow River heading for St. Basil's Cathedral and Red Square. They then walked past the cathedral and entered the square with the Kremlin to their left and the GUM shopping centre to their right. They wandered through the shopping centre with its designer shops and ornate walkways and were surprised to see that the prices were even higher than in London. When they went back into the square, they noticed a queue on the other side to steps leading down below the ground.

'What's all that about?' Jimmy asked.

'That's Lenin's tomb,' Dan replied. 'His body has supposedly been preserved and you can go down and file past it.'

'You're kidding!'

'No, really. There's been some speculation as to whether it really is him or a waxwork but anyone can go in.'

'Did you do it when you were last here?'

'No. I didn't get much free time.'

'Come on then, let's do it.'

They queued for about ten minutes and eventually descended into the dimly lit tomb past forbidding looking guards. They then filed past what appeared to a perfectly preserved Lenin in an atmosphere which could be described as reverential silence before ascending back into the Moscow sunlight.

'I can't believe that's really him,' Jimmy said.

'Maybe, maybe not,' Dan replied, 'but it's an unusual tourist attraction!'

When they arrived back at the hotel, the concierge came up to them and handed them a street map with the three missing roads marked. He pointed out to them that two of them were fairly central but as Dan and Jimmy had suspected were really no more than back alleys so the names were not on the map. The other was some way out of the centre and off the map. The concierge had marked an arrow on the edge of the map showing in which direction it was.

'Have a good time,' he said with a smirk, as he handed them the map.

'He must think we're a real couple of perverts!' Jimmy said, when they were alone in the lift.

'That's just what we want him to think!' Dan replied. 'I could hardly ask where we could find Moscow's most notorious gangster!'

Back in Dan's room, they added the locations to the map where they had marked the other nine clubs.

'There are three fairly close together and fairly central,' Dan said. 'We could walk there tonight and check them out.'

'Fine by me,' Jimmy replied. 'As there's no point in getting to them before midnight, why don't we get some sleep and then go down to dinner here?'

They agreed that Jimmy would return to collect Dan at eight o'clock.

'What gear do we wear for dodgy Moscow nightclubs?' Jimmy asked before he left.

'God knows,' Dan replied. 'I think I'll just wear a jacket and trousers with an open necked shirt. They may not let us in in jeans and T shirts!'

Chapter Twenty Six

Later on, they had a drink in the bar and then took their time over what turned out to be an unexpectedly good meal. Even so, they still had nearly two hours to kill.

'Why don't we ask our friend, the concierge, if he can recommend a bar near where we're going?' Jimmy suggested. 'Who knows, we may find Arkady in the bar and anyway, we'll learn more about the local nightlife than we would staying here.'

Somewhat to their relief, the daytime concierge was off duty but his replacement was happy to recommend a couple of bars.

In the event, they wished that they had stayed in the hotel till midnight. Both the bars were packed out, very noisy, hot and full of youngsters. No one appeared to understand English and Dan had to point to a beer bottle and raise two fingers to get a drink. There was not the remotest chance of either Arkady Durchenko turning up nor of them gleaning any information from anyone in the bar, whether staff or customers.

Unfortunately, their introduction to Moscow clubland was equally unsuccessful. Jimmy was quite looking forward to the first club, largely due to its name, The Pink Pussy. It did not live up to expectations. If the bars had been noisy, nothing had prepared them for this. The thumping dance music was so loud that conversation was quite impossible. A mass of people on the dancefloor just seemed to be jumping up and down wildly under flashing lights. In raised cages around the dancefloor, topless dancers gyrated. Not in time with the music, Dan thought, as the only thing that could be done in time was to jump up and down. They had a quick look round and soon signalled to each other that they should leave. It was almost a relief to get out on to the pavement.

'What a waste of the forty quid entrance money!' Dan complained.

'No way would Arkady go there, even if his family do own the fucking place!' Jimmy commented. 'Where to now?'

'The Paradise Club is just around the corner. Let's try there.'

The Paradise Club was not Dan's idea of paradise. It was one of the clubs down a back alley and down a long flight of steps to a basement. They had to knock on the door and be checked out through a grill before they were admitted to a small dingy foyer lit by a single red bulb.

This time the entrance fee was fifty euros each. There was a list up which showed that guests could pay in euros, pounds or dollars as well as roubles. Dan consoled himself with the thought that the euros he handed over had once belonged to the Durchenkos.

They then went through to the main bar area and about the only positive feature of the place was that there was no loud music blaring out. The only music came from an elderly pianist who even to Dan's untrained ear could hardly play a note right. The room had a depressingly seedy atmosphere, again lit dimly in red. The only women were clearly hookers who had either seen better days or were not sufficiently attractive for a better class of establishment. Since there were about twenty of them and only about ten customers spread around the room, Dan and Jimmy were immediately approached and asked in English if they wanted company.

Is it that obvious we're English? Dan thought.

'Perhaps, later,' he replied. 'We'll have a drink together first as we need to discuss something.'

The hookers reluctantly slunk away and Jimmy fetched two beers from the bar.

'At least we can hear ourselves speak,' he said. 'What do you think?'

'From one extreme to the other,' Dan replied. 'I really can't see Arkady coming to a dump like this.'

'Neither can I. Surely there must be classier places than this.'

175

'Let's drink up and move on then.'

Just as they were about to leave though they noticed that every now and again people would disappear behind a curtain. They went over to check it out to find a bouncer on the other side of the curtain barring the way to a staircase.

'Where does that lead?' Dan asked.

'To the private bar,' the man replied with a thick Russian accent. 'But if you go alone without a woman, you have to pay.'

'How much? In euros.'

'Twenty five each.'

Dan handed the man a fifty euro note and he and Jimmy climbed the stairs. As soon as they went through the door at the top of the stairs, Dan realised that they had wasted their money again. They found themselves in a room lit only by the light from the hardcore pornographic movie being shown on a large screen at the other end of the room. There were sofas scattered around the room with couples on them. On one sofa, a hooker was performing oral sex on a customer while he watched the film.

'OK, let's go,' Dan said.

They went back down the staircase. The bouncer grinned at them.

'You should have taken women with you,' he said. 'There's no refund when you come back with them.'

'We won't be coming back,' Jimmy said. 'You can keep your 'private bar.'

Unfortunately the third club proved equally disappointing. It had a small dance floor where foreign businessmen were dancing with slightly better looking hookers and there were also what appeared to a few genuine couples, probably tourists, dancing to British and American pop songs. But this was not the sort of place where Dan expected to find Arkady Durchenko. They needed to find a place where the rich and famous, or infamous, of Moscow society frequented, not some downmarket place for fleecing foreigners.

'Let's call it a night,' Dan said.

'And tomorrow?' Jimmy asked.

'We work through the list tomorrow night but during the day, I suggest we just behave like tourists.'

Chapter Twenty Seven

After two days of trudging around Moscow as tourists and another night of frustration when they visited four more nightclubs, Dan and Jimmy finally found a place which was more what they were looking for on the third night.

Velvet Dreams was the second of the two clubs recommended to them by the concierge which had not been in the yellow pages. As soon as they arrived, they realised that it was in a different league from the others that they had visited. It had a grand entrance with gold painted columns framing it. The bouncers were polite and dressed in expensive suits. When a posh chauffeur driven car arrived outside, one of them would rush to open the rear door for the arriving guests who would step on to the red carpet leading out on to the pavement.

Dan was glad that he and Jimmy were reasonably smartly dressed. Unfortunately when they tried to enter the club they were stopped by the bouncers who told them politely in perfect but accented English that it was a members only club.

'Oh, that's a shame,' Dan said pleasantly. 'We're here on business and this club was highly recommended.'

'I'm sorry, sir,' the bouncer replied. 'We have a very exclusive clientele and we cannot just let people in that we don't know.'

At that point, a smaller, older man joined them.

'Is there a problem, Andrei?' he asked.

'No, sir. I'm just explaining to these gentlemen that I cannot admit them as they are not members,' the bouncer replied.

'The club was recommended to us by a London based Russian businessman we have dealings with. He said it was the best in Moscow,' Dan said.

'He was right there,' the older man replied. 'I'm Yuri Vasin, the general manager here. Do you mind telling me his name?'

Dan was prepared for this. He had figured out that some of the clubs might be members only clubs and that was probably why this club was not advertised in the phone book. Before he left London, he had done some research on the many London based Russian businessmen and he gave the name of a fairly young Russian who was regularly seen in London nightclubs.

The manager looked at Dan closely.

'We haven't seen him for a long time,' he said. 'Do you have any ID?'

Dan and Jimmy produced their passports and the man studied them.

'Very well,' he said. 'I'm prepared to grant you temporary membership for the night. There will be a charge of one hundred euros each. Will that be satisfactory?'

'That's fine,' Dan said.

'You will pay the young lady in the foyer. But before you go in, you will understand that we need to search you.'

'That's no problem,' Dan replied.

He and Jimmy were expertly searched and the thick red cord was unhooked to allow them to enter. They paid the money to an attractive girl at a desk behind which there was a cloakroom. Dan wondered if it was the sort of place where people checked in their guns. They then walked through to the main part of the club.

'This is more like it!' Jimmy said as they entered a vast space with various different sections and levels. Unlike the previous clubs, it was not sleazy due to the opulent nature of the decor and the expensive lighting but to Dan's eye it was certainly gaudy and tasteless with gold leaf and red velvet dominating the furnishings.

There were several bars and a central dance floor. The music was not thumping dance music but seemed appropriate for an older clientele. There were certainly a lot of older men even if the women with them were generally much younger.

There were of course, hanging around the bar areas, the obligatory hookers, though Dan imagined they were known as hostesses in this establishment, and provocatively dressed dancers in cages. But in this club, they were all stunningly attractive unlike in some of the places they had been in. Of more interest to Dan was a roped off section on the other side of the club which appeared to be some sort of VIP area as there were two bouncers by its entrance.

Dan and Jimmy made their way over to the nearest bar and ordered a couple of beers. Within seconds, they were approached by two very pretty girls both wearing very short dresses and the sort of heels that are impossible to walk in. They both smiled and said something in Russian.

'Do you speak English?' Jimmy asked with a lascivious grin on his face.

'Of course,' one of the girls replied. 'You are American?'

'No, British,' Jimmy replied.

The girls giggled.

'British!' the other girl said. 'So shy and proper but I find that after a few drinks you are just like everyone else!'

'Can I get you a drink?' Jimmy asked.

'We like champagne.'

Jimmy turned towards the bar.

'*Remember why we're here*!' Dan whispered.

'We need to blend in and anyway they speak English and we need information,' Jimmy replied.

He's got a point, Dan thought.

Jimmy turned back to the girls and handed them their glasses of champagne.

'I'm Nina. My friend is Maria. Let's sit down,' the blond one of the girls said, and without waiting for a reply she led the way to a booth at the side of the club. She took Jimmy by the hand and led him to the bench seat on one side of the table, leaving Dan and the brunette to sit on the other side.

The girls had no interest in a group conversation and seemed intent on engaging Dan and Jimmy on a one to one basis, wasting no time in revealing that they were wearing stockings.

After about ten minutes, Jimmy was surprised to see Dan and his girl get up and go the dance floor until he realised that Dan really wanted to have a better look at the VIP area on the other side.

When they returned, Dan caught Jimmy's eye and nodded.

Jimmy pointed across to the VIP area.

'What goes on over there?' he asked pleasantly.

Both girls looked over to where he was indicating.

'Oh, only the owner and his friends are allowed there. We only go there if we are invited,' Nina replied.

'Who's the owner then?' Jimmy asked. 'Some oligarch I may have heard of?'

The girls looked at each other and for a split second Jimmy was sure that he saw a look of nervousness or even fear pass across their faces.

'Arkady Durchenko.'

Chapter Twenty Eight

Vitaly Petrov was a frustrated man. A week had passed and there was still no sign of Green and his colleague. He had dished out thousands of euros as sweeteners with the promise of much more if anyone spotted them. He had every employee, every contractor they had ever dealt with and even his contacts in the Police looking for them. He felt that he had virtually the whole of southern Spain covered but the men appeared to have disappeared. There had been a few alleged sightings all of which had come to nothing.

At least the attacks on their establishments had stopped for the time being but that was not enough. Viktor had lost his youngest son and suffered massive damage to his business interests not to mention all the loyal soldiers and other employees who had been killed. These men had to die and if Viktor was to have his way, die slowly, along with anyone who had helped them.

So far as the latter was concerned Petrov had made some progress. As the search continued, something had occurred to him. How had these men from England managed to get to Spain with enough arms and equipment to fight a small war?

The answer was they hadn't. They must have acquired the stuff in Spain and there was only one man apart from the family itself capable of supplying such equipment.

When the family had moved to Spain, they had soon discovered that Fernando Ortega was the biggest dealer in illegal weapons on the southern coast. Although Ortega had proved to be elusive, they had managed to trap two of his men by posing as potential clients. They had killed one and sent the other back to Ortega with a message: *if we find that you've been operating west of Malaga again, we will kill you and all your family.* Until now Ortega had stuck to that even though he had lost his most lucrative area. So far as the family were concerned the area between Malaga and Gibraltar belonged to them. They didn't care if Ortega continued to operate further east towards Murcia.

But why, Petrov thought, had Ortega ignored the threat now? Had he been led to believe the men would be operating in a different area? No, he must have been told or more likely realised who the target was for this weaponry. He had seen this as a chance to attack the family without direct involvement and for that he had to pay.

It was very late when Fernando Ortega returned to his heavily guarded villa in an upmarket suburb of Malaga. Nothing had given him greater pleasure than the gossip spreading through the Spanish underworld about the war taking place further down the coast with reports of the area being littered with dead Russians and other East Europeans. There was even speculation as to whether Alexei Durchenko had been one of the victims as he hadn't been seen at any of his usual haunts recently. There were all sorts of theories as to who might be responsible for this pleasing turn of events as most locals loathed the Russians who had muscled in and stolen their businesses.

But Ortega knew precisely who was responsible. When he had seen the Englishman's shopping list, he had known immediately that such equipment was not necessary to rob a bank, carry out a simple hit or for some drug smuggling operation. The men had the bearing and attitude of soldiers and there could only have been one target on the Costa del Sol.

He had considered refusing to do business with them for fear of reprisals should the Russians put two and two together but this had been an ideal opportunity to get his own back against them and perhaps even see them driven out of Spain back to Russia where they belonged. Still, it was a concern that the attacks appeared to have stopped although so far as he was aware the Englishmen had not been caught or killed.

All this was going through his mind as his chauffeur driven car swept into the entrance to his home and the security gate lifted to allow it to drive up to his front door.

Had he not been distracted by his thoughts he might have noticed that the guard who operated the gate did not show himself and wave from the small gatehouse. In fact, the guard was lying on the floor of the gatehouse with his throat cut and the gate had been operated by a Russian.

Ortega got out of the car and the chauffeur/bodyguard opened the electric gates of the garage to the side of the house with his remote control and drove the car into it. As Ortega was letting himself in through his front door, the chauffeur got out of the car and was immediately seized from behind. Before he could react, a sharp knife sliced through his throat. He fell to the ground and twitched for a few seconds before lying still.

The house was silent when Ortega entered it as he had expected. His wife would be in bed asleep by now but despite the lateness of the hour, Ortega was looking forward to waking her and having some fun. She was his third wife but he loved her dearly even if she was a little young for him. He skipped up the stairs and opened the bedroom door in anticipation only to be confronted by a scene of absolute horror.

His wife was lying naked on the bed, gagged, with her hands tied to the bed head behind her and her legs wide apart and tied to the frame at the bottom of the bed. She was covered in cuts and bruises and had a look of absolute terror in her eyes which met his when he opened the door.

But what was even worse was the sight of a huge cropped haired man grinning as he pulled up his trousers. Ortega's hand went instinctively towards the inside pocket of his jacket.

'I'll take that,' said a voice in English with a Russian accent from behind him.

Ortega froze as he felt cold steel against the back of his head. A hand came round and removed the gun from the holster inside his jacket.

'Been expecting us, have you?' the voice continued.

Ortega was pushed from behind further into the room. He turned round and saw a man in his early thirties with a cruel face holding a silenced pistol.

'Do you know who I am?' the man asked.

'I can guess,' Ortega replied.

'I'm Georgy Durchenko.'

Durchenko was disappointed that Ortega did not show the fear that most people did in his presence.

'Welcome to the party,' he said. 'We decided to start without you. Your wife has been enjoying a real man for a change.'

The big Russian now standing beside Ortega grinned.

'Not a man, a pig!' Ortega said and spat in the Russians face.

The Russian seized Ortega round the throat and would probably have killed him there and then if Durchenko had not intervened.

'Not yet, Petr, we need to talk to Mr Ortega.'

'I've nothing to say to you, you animal.' Ortega said.

'Oh, I think you have. Like where the two Englishmen are you sold a load of weapons to.'

'I don't know what you're talking about.'

Durckenko whipped the silencer across Ortega's face, opening a nasty wound. Ortega staggered back and sat on the edge of the bed where he tried to comfort his terrified wife. Petr dragged him off the bed on to the floor and kicked him several times.

'Where are they?' Durchenko shouted. 'If you tell me I will spare your wife!'

'You're not going to spare anyone,' Ortega said.

'You may be right,' Durchenko said with a grin. 'But you'll both die slowly if you don't tell me!'

'I have no idea where they are. Why should they tell me?'

'So you admit to knowing them?'

This time Ortega laughed.

'I admit to selling them enough guns and explosives to blow your fucking family to hell and back. But are you so stupid to think they would tell me where they are?'

Durckenko raised the gun and pointed it at Ortega's face.

'Kill the woman!' he shouted.

Petr pushed Ortega aside and jumped on the bed astride the struggling woman. While Durchenko covered Ortega with the gun, Petr proceeded to strangle the woman until she stopped moving. He then got off the bed and Durchenko handed him a pair of bolt cutters.

'I didn't really expect you to know where they are,' Durchenko said. 'But you appreciate we must make sure.'

Petr moved towards Ortega opening and closing the bolt cutters.

'Wait!' Ortega stammered. 'I know how to contact them! You could trace their mobile.'

'Give me the number!'

'It's in the bedside table. I'll just fetch it.'

'You think I'm stupid? Check the drawer for weapons, Petr.'

Petr looked through the drawer.

'No weapons,' he said.

'Let me find the piece of paper,' Ortega said.

He knelt in front of the drawer and started rummaging through it. Petr stood over him looking down. As he rummaged in the drawer with one hand, Ortega shifted his position so his right leg was further away from the watching Durchenko and slid his other hand down to his ankle and removed a stiletto blade from inside his sock.

'I think this is it,' he said.

Petr leaned further over the drawer to have a look and Ortega brought his right hand up quickly and shoved the blade into one of Petr's eyes right up to the hilt.

Durchenko saw the sudden movement and heard a kind of squelch and then to his horror Petr fell over backwards towards him with a knife embedded in his eye. The dead Russian hit the floor and Durchenko panicked. He fired several shots at Ortega killing him instantly but could not help but notice that Ortega died with a smile on his face.

Chapter Twenty Nine

'Arkady Durchenko?' Jimmy asked innocently. 'I don't think I've heard of him. What's he like?'

Nina looked uncomfortable.

'He's not the sort of man you ask questions about.'

'Really?' Jimmy continued. 'That sounds mysterious. What is he? Some sort of gangster?'

The girls exchanged nervous looks again.

'He's just our boss,' Maria said. 'We don't want to talk about him now. We just want to have some fun.' And as if to emphasise the point, she took Dan's hand, put it on the top of her thigh and snuggled up to him.

It was clear that for now the subject was over but Dan realised that the girls might well be the source of some useful information. He called over a waiter and ordered a bottle of champagne hoping that after a few more drinks, the subject could be broached again.

After a while, the girls said they were going to the Ladies but left their bags at the table and said they would soon be back.

'We need to find out all we can about Arkady. He's sitting over there now. I recognised him from Luis' photo,' Dan said.

'I agree,' Jimmy replied, 'but how do we raise the issue again when they are clearly reluctant to talk about him?'

'Yes, they seem frightened of him.'

'I think we should have a few more drinks then get the girls on their own. Let's face it, they're not sitting with us for fun. They're expecting us to pay them to shag them. They couldn't be making it more obvious!'

Dan smiled. 'And you think we should go along with that in the interests of information gathering?'

'Too bloody right!'

'OK. We'll see what the deal is.' Dan handed Jimmy a wad of the Durchenkos' euros. 'My impression is that Nina seems the more likely to open up. Maybe you should take her back to the hotel if she'll go.'

'You're the boss!' Jimmy said, grinning as the girls returned.

After another bottle of champagne which Dan ensured was mainly drunk by the girls, Jimmy put his arm around Nina and whispered in her ear.

'Why don't we find somewhere more private?'

Nina giggled. 'I thought you'd never ask!'

'What would it take for you to come back to my hotel with me?'

'For the whole night?' she asked.

'Well, there's only a few hours of it left! But I'm sure we can find a way to amuse ourselves!'

'750 euros,' Nina said, without hesitation. 'Payable up front.'

'No problem.'

'Really?' Nina seemed genuinely pleased. 'What are we waiting for then?'

She stood up and pulled down her tight fitting dress. Jimmy stood up too.

'We're off,' he said. 'We'll see you guys later. Are you OK to settle the bill here, Dan?'

'Fine,' Dan replied. 'Enjoy yourselves.'

Dan watched as Jimmy and Nina walked hand in hand towards the foyer.

'So, that just leaves us,' Maria said seductively, rubbing her exposed thigh against Dan's.

'What do you have in mind?' Dan asked.

'You could take me back to your hotel too or we could go to one of the upstairs rooms here.'

Dan hesitated.

'I'm not sure,' he said, moving away from Maria.

Maria sensed his reluctance.

'But I've spent over an hour with you!' she said. 'I'll get into trouble if we don't...do business.' She glanced around the club.

'How do you mean?' Dan asked.

'We are watched the whole time,' she said in a low voice. 'The time I have spent with you will have been noted. I'm expected to do more than drink with the customers.'

Dan realised that Maria was not going to give him any more information about Arkady where they were, particularly as she was now worried about getting into trouble. He thought about giving her whatever she wanted to charge for sex for information instead but knew that would look very suspicious and might even freak her out. OK, what the hell, he thought.

'All right,' he said, 'how much to go upstairs?'

'300 euros. But you can pay in pounds if you prefer.'

'Euros are fine,' he said, standing up.

As if on cue, a waiter appeared and handed him a bill. Dan gave the waiter 400 euros and told him to keep the change.

Dan then followed Maria to a door at the side of side of the club which led to a staircase. On the first floor, Maria led him down a corridor and into a room off to the right.

Dan was surprised at how lavishly the bedroom had been decorated. He had been expecting a rather grubby, functional room with little more than a cheap double bed. But the room followed the style of the club downstairs with ornate furniture covered in red velvet and gilt. The bed was a king size bed draped with a dark red bedspread and matching cushions. There were gold embroidered red matching curtains and Dan could see a fully fitted en suite bathroom through a door to one side of the bed. Over the bed, there was a large mirror on the ceiling and a state of the art flat screen television on the wall opposite the bed.

Maria followed his gaze as she unzipped her dress and let it fall to the ground, leaving her in just her bra, thong, stockings and high heels. She stepped over and put her arms round Dan underneath his jacket.

'You want to watch a film?' she asked.

'Not really,' Dan replied, feeling himself react to the scantily clad body pressing against him.

'Are you sure? I could show you a good one of me with three men. Some men like to watch me being fucked before they do it themselves,' Maria breathed seductively.

Dan shook his head. Maria shrugged and removed his jacket. She threw it on to a chair and then started undoing the buttons of his shirt. She sank to her knees dragging her hands down Dan's chest so he felt the combination of their coolness and the light scratching of her long painted nails. She then removed her bra before unbuckling his trousers and releasing him. In contrast to her hands, her breasts felt warm as she pressed them against him. She then moved away slightly and he once again felt the coolness of her hand followed by the wetness of her mouth.

After about a minute, she stood up and removed her thong. Dan stepped out of his trousers and boxer shorts and threw off his shirt. Maria then took hold of him and he realised that she was slipping on a condom.

Why Dan chose that moment to ask his question, he didn't know.

'So, have you been up here with Arkady?' he said in a low voice.

Maria's eyes widened in a mixture of surprise and horror. She put her index finger to her mouth and made a faint shushing noise. She then looked around the room and pointed to the walls.

Dan realised immediately that she was signalling that the room was bugged for sound and that there was no hope of him gaining any information at all from this escapade. Angry and frustrated, he pushed Maria down on the bed. If she was surprised in the change in attitude by this previously fairly passive client, she did not show it. She simply opened her legs and beckoned him down on her.

Dan accepted the invitation and rammed himself into her. He didn't care if Maria's screams of pleasure were genuine or not as they bounced up and down on the bed with his furious pumping. When he had finally released all his frustration he rolled over and lay on his back.

After a short pause, Maria broke the silence.

'Wow!' she said. 'Where did that come from?'

Dan didn't reply.

'So much for the English being shy and reserved!' Maria continued. 'Anyone would think you hadn't had sex for ages!'

It occurred to Dan that she was right. But he'd come here for information, not sex and he hoped that Jimmy was having better luck. He got up and tore off the condom, tossing it into the toilet in the ensuite. He then went over to his jacket.

'300 euros, you said?'

'Yes, but you don't have to be in such a hurry!'

Dan walked over and put the money down on the bedside table beside the girl. He looked down at her and saw that she was blinking away tears.

'What's the matter?' he asked.

'Nothing,' she said sulkily.

'Come on, what is it?'

'I really enjoyed this evening, which is rare in my job. But you've turned out just like all the others. As soon as you'd had your fun, you can't even be bothered to talk to me.'

Dan sat down on the bed beside her and took her hand.

'I'm sorry. I didn't mean to seem callous. But I've got a lot on my mind. Which obviously I can't talk about,' he pointed to the walls as Maria had done earlier. 'It's not you. I had fun too.'

Maria nodded and squeezed his hand. She watched as he got dressed and noticed for the first time the scars from bullet and other wounds. She got up and gave him a hug before he left.

'You take care, Englishman,' she said.

'Yeah, you too,' Dan replied. He kissed her forehead and left.

Chapter Thirty

Jimmy noticed that as he and Nina walked through the foyer, the cloakroom girl picked up a phone when she saw them and within seconds a taxi appeared at the entrance for them. Nina seemed impressed when Jimmy gave the driver the name of the hotel.

'Nice hotel,' she said. 'I'm looking forward to this!'

Jimmy put his arm round her and she was quite happy to engage in a bit of foreplay in the back of the cab.

'I'm supposed to take the money before I allow you to to handle the goods,' she joked. 'But I guess I can trust an English gentleman!'

'Gentleman! I don't know where you got that from! I can't imagine what sort of Englishman you've met before if you think I'm a gentleman.' Jimmy said, laughing.

Unlike Dan, Jimmy had no intention of raising the subject of Arkady Durchenko until after he had made his sacrifice in the interests of gathering information. He lay on his back with Nina lying facing him and her arm across his chest.

'Don't get too relaxed,' he said. 'That was just the starter. The main course is still to come!'

Nina giggled.

'I can't wait!' she said.

'Well, you'll have to wait a few minutes. I'm not getting any younger!'

'How long have you worked at the club?' Jimmy asked after a pause.

'About two years.'

'Do you like it?'

'Things could be worse, I guess.'

'How did you end up there?'

Nina sighed.

'The usual story. I had a dead end job in a dead end town and someone offered me the chance to come and work in Moscow. To be honest, I had a rough idea what it would entail but I thought it would be glamorous and I might meet a nice rich young man.'

'And it hasn't turned out that way?'

'Hardly! To begin with, I was treated well, given nice clothes, English lessons. Then I was asked to be 'nice' to certain important people and before long I was put to work in the club and then forced to appear in films on some days.'

'And this Arkady is your boss?'

'Yes. Though I have as little to do with him as possible. My immediate boss is the club manager.'

'What's he like?'

'Providing you do what you are told, he's ok, I suppose. But step out of line and you're in big trouble!'

'Couldn't you just leave and get another job?'

Nina laughed.

'You have no idea what it's like here. They consider that they own us. The last girl who tried to run away was found dead, naked and mutilated in a skip.'

'You said you have as little to do with Arkady as possible. Why is that?'

'He's the worst of the lot. He's a pig!'

'How do you mean?'

'He comes to the club nearly every night and some nights he chooses one of the girls to take home with him. We all try to avoid that.'

'Why?'

'He's cruel and a pervert.'

'Really? Surely you get a lot of that sort of thing?'

'Not like him. Sometimes he makes us perform with a couple of his bodyguards while he watches. Other times he gets violent. He put one girl in hospital. Yuri, the club manager was furious. Not of course out of concern for the girl but because she couldn't work for a month.'

'How often do you have to go back to his place?'

'It depends. If you please him, you go back more often. But if you don't, you risk a beating!

202

But fortunately there are a lot of girls so not that often.'

'Does he always go to that club?'

'Yes. His family own other clubs but they are not so good and the best and most expensive girls work in my club. He likes to entertain his friends and business associates there and show off. Often he will call over a girl to go upstairs with one of them. You then have to perform for nothing, so you earn nothing.'

'Does he stay till the club closes?'

'No. He usually leaves at about two or three o'clock.'

'No doubt with a large group of bodyguards!'

'Not really, no. Just his driver. There's plenty of security in the club and no one would dare attack him anyway. I think he has a bullet proof car though.'

There was silence for a while while Jimmy thought about what he'd learned.

Nina then reached between Jimmy's legs. 'Do we have to talk about that bastard? I think you said something about a main course...'

'So I did!' said Jimmy and rolled on top of her.

Petrov was furious again and if Georgy had not been Viktor's son, he would have felt the back of Petrov's hand. Petrov had wanted to deal with Ortega himself but Georgy had insisted that he be allowed to go and Viktor had agreed.

'So let me see if I've understood this correctly,' Petrov said coldly. Viktor was watching the exchange from behind his desk. 'Despite the fact that you were covering him with a gun, this small middle aged man managed to kill Petr, one of our most loyal soldiers. You then killed Ortega but left without Petr's body.'

'Yes.'

'Why didn't you take Petr's body? You had two men outside who could have carried the body.'

'I..I don't know. It didn't occur to me.'

'It didn't occur to you that by leaving his body, you have left a direct link between the incident and us?'

'I didn't think there was time.'

'I thought you just said it didn't occur to you. Which is it?'

Georgy did not answer.

'I'll tell you what happened.' Petrov continued. 'You panicked. The operation went wrong when Petr was killed, and you shot Ortega and ran.'

'That's not what happened.'

'Really? My police sources tell me that Ortega was hit four times and two more shots hit the wall behind him. So that doesn't indicate panic?'

Once again, Georgy did not reply.

'What did our police sources say about Petr?' Viktor asked.

'Petr had no ID on him, of course,' Petrov replied, 'but that police officer, Valdez, the one who arrested Alexei, is showing an interest in the case.'

'The politicians we own are getting very nervous,' Viktor said. 'They were happy that things seemed to be quietening down but now there are lurid headlines about rape and murder and an unidentified man dead at the scene believed to one of the assailants and of east European origin.'

'The whole thing should have been handled more discreetly,' Petrov said, looking at Georgy.

When Georgy had gone, Viktor sighed.

'We can never retire, Vitaly. How can we leave things to the younger generation?'

'They haven't had to fight their way to the top like we did. It's been too easy for them.' Petrov replied. 'They haven't learned from their mistakes as we did. They have always had us to clean up the mess.'

Chapter Thirty One

It did not take Dan and Jimmy long to formulate their plan. Attacking Arkady in the club was out of the question. They would never get near him and even if they did, they would never leave the club alive. Without weapons, they had no chance of mounting either an assault on his car while en route or his home which was no doubt heavily protected.

That left the small window of opportunity when Arkady left the club and walked to his car. Even that seemed an impossible task as they could not wait right outside the club and the time when Arkady walked through the door and along the red carpet to his car would only be a matter of seconds. They therefore needed to gain some more time and realised that they would need some sort of diversion.

They visited the location during the day and worked out that they could not wait opposite the club as there was no cover and they would be seen by the bouncers and others. They would also have to cross the road and even at that time of night they could not rule out the possibility of passing traffic holding them up when every second counted.

However, the club was on a corner and they decided that the only option was to wait around the corner out of sight of the bouncers and take it in turns to keep a watch on the red carpet. They would not have a view of the entrance so would not see Arkady until he was already on the carpet but they were a lot closer than being across the road.

Dressed in black jeans, dark hooded tops and baseball caps, Dan and Jimmy began their vigil at 1.30 am. Fortunately the streets were fairly quiet and the corner where they were standing was not directly under a streetlight. Occasionally when a car went by they huddled together pretending to be a couple of lowlifes in conversation. Tucked inside his top, Dan was holding a bottle full of petrol which they had siphoned off from a parked car earlier in the day. The bottle had been specially selected from a shop on the basis that it looked fairly fragile and liable to break easily. Stuffed in its neck was a petrol soaked rag. In the pocket of his fleece, Dan fingered a cheap lighter which nevertheless lit very easily. Strapped to his calf, Jimmy had a sturdy, razor sharp kitchen knife, also purchased earlier.

After about an hour, Jimmy, whose turn it was to peer around the corner, saw a big black limousine pull up outside the club and a large brutish looking man got out of the driver's door and walked towards the club.

'We could be on!' he said to Dan beside him. 'That could be the driver going to fetch his boss!'

Dan took the bottle out. The plan was simple. Wait till Arkady got in the car, then Jimmy would create the sort of diversion that they had used when they had killed Alexei's bodyguards. Dan would then hurl the Molotov Cocktail into the car and Arkady would be incinerated. Jimmy would deal with the driver and they would then run away and disappear down side streets before anyone else could react.

The only problem that they foresaw was the possibility that that Arkady might have one of the girls with him. In that event, Dan would try to get her out of the car but if he couldn't, he would have to proceed anyway as they would not get a second shot.

Unfortunately, he did have a girl with him. Jimmy saw the bouncer first, preceding his boss to open the rear door. He had a side view of Arkady and could see that there was a girl on the other side.

'Shit! There's a girl,' Jimmy said but as the timing was so tight, he could not wait for Dan's reply.

He staggered out and lurched towards the car, looking like a drunk or someone on drugs. He saw Arkady get into the back of the car followed by the girl. The driver turned and looked at him and closed the car door. Jimmy appeared to stumble and fell against the car. The driver roared with anger and pushed Jimmy to the ground and started kicking him.

Meanwhile, Dan nipped past the two of them and yanked the rear door open. Fortunately, Arkady's lack of manners in getting into the car first meant that the girl was nearest to him.

'Get out!' he screamed at the girl in Russian. Then he recognised her. It was Maria. He lifted his head up saw that she recognised him. But she was frozen with fear as he stood there holding a Molotov Cocktail in one hand and a lighter in the other. Everything then seemed to happen in slow motion. He transferred the lighter to the hand holding the bottle and reached in with his right hand. Maria hesitated and then took his hand. He pulled her violently from the car as Arkady's hand reached into his jacket. As Dan transferred the lighter back to his other hand, he could see Arkady withdrawing the gun from his jacket. Dan lit the rag as the gun moved towards him and hurled the bottle into the car while at the same time slamming the door with his other hand.

The bottle exploded but the armoured nature of car prevented the windows from blowing out and Arkady's screams being heard on the outside.

At the same time, Dan heard a scream of 'no' from behind him. He span round in time to see

Maria jump to her feet and fling herself in front him as one of the bouncers opened fired with a pistol. The bullet struck Maria in the chest and she slumped back against the car. Before the bouncer could fire again, Dan grabbed the gun with one hand and bent the bouncer's elbow back with his other. The gun went off and took off most of the bouncer's face and Dan wrenched it out of his hand.

Meanwhile, Jimmy jumped to his feet while the driver was distracted by what was going on behind him. He seized the bouncer around the neck and rammed the kitchen knife up into his heart. As he fell, Jimmy relieved him of the gun in him shoulder holster.

By this time, more security staff were appearing and Dan and Jimmy took cover behind the car as shots were fired.

Dan and Jimmy fired back and the security staff retreated to the club and behind the pillars.

There was now no chance of a quick exit. After more shots were exchanged, a car turned the corner.

'Cover me!' Dan shouted. He then ran in front of the car and pointed his gun at the driver.

'Out!' he screamed in Russian. A young man jumped out of the car and ran away, leaving his girlfriend screaming in the passenger seat. Dan ignored her and jumped into the driver's seat. He pulled up beside the limousine which was shielding them from the club, Jimmy jumped into the back of the car and Dan accelerated down the street.

However, after only a couple of hundred yards, Dan saw in his mirror another car bearing down on them. Shots were fired and the rear window was blown out. Dan pushed the ancient VW as hard as he could but it was no match for the chasing vehicle. He swung the car from side to side to avoid being hit and careered around corners.

'I'm out of ammo!' Jimmy shouted.

'Take this! There's a few rounds left.' Dan tossed the bouncer's weapon over to Jimmy. The girl beside him was still screaming and he pushed her down as far as he could. Fortunately, she realised that she was well advised to keep her head down.

'I'll try and take the driver out,' Jimmy shouted. 'When I say, let the other car catch us right up and stop weaving about!'

After a few seconds, they came to a straight stretch of road.

'Now!' Jimmy shouted.

Dan straightened up and slowed down. The other car came close up behind them and almost rammed them. Jimmy leant out of the back window and emptied the remaining rounds of the gun into the following car's windscreen where he estimated the driver was. A few seconds later the road bent to the left. Dan swung the car into the corner but to Jimmy's satisfaction, the other car went straight on and ploughed into a wall.

'Result!' he exclaimed, grinning.

Dan found his way back to the centre of the city and stopped to let the terrified girl out. Before doing so, he made a show of looking through her bag and removed a document which appeared to have her address on it. He pointed to it and signalled to her that if she didn't keep quiet, they would come after her. He pointed two of his fingers at her head as if they were a gun. He then put the document in his pocket. The girl seemed to get the message and nodded vigorously. They then abandoned the vehicle in a car park and walked back to the hotel. They tidied themselves up a bit before going in, trying to look as if they had had a good night out.

An hour and a half later, they checked out and settled into the back of a chauffeur driven Mercedes provided by the hotel for their trip to the airport for the early morning flight to London.

'Let's hope there's no reception committee for us at the airport!' Jimmy said.

'I doubt it. I don't think anyone at the club knows their attackers were English. They'll assume we're rival gangsters, Russian, Chechen, whatever. They may make the connection when they report what's happened to Spain. No doubt the Durchenkos can fax over pictures and the

212

CCTV can be checked. But they don't know what night we went to the club even if we went at all. We'll be long gone by then.'

'Nina certainly won't say anything.'

'Sadly, neither will Maria. Fancy her taking a bullet for me like that!'

'What about the police?'

'Yes. I did wonder whether we should lock that girl in the boot of the car with some air holes. But I thought we'd put her through enough. She will have realised we're British or American. If she reported it to the police, and we have to assume she did despite my attempt at a threat, they might check out the airport but I doubt she would recognise us and how many people carry out a hit at 3.00 am and are booked on a 7.00 am flight?'

At the airport, they split up and checked in separately. Apart from the usual security, no one appeared to pay them much attention and they were relieved when the flight took off on time.

Chapter Thirty Two

Yuri Vasin was a worried man. The club manager and his security chief, Stepan Leskov, were in his office wondering when they should report what had happened to Petrov in Spain and what the reaction would be.

Vasin had spent over two hours dealing with the police and they were still at the club interviewing staff and taking photos of the scene. Vasin knew that several senior police officers were on the family payroll and were regularly entertained at the club, but seemingly not the officer in charge of the investigation. When Vasin had referred to the 'good relationship' between the club and certain of his colleagues, the officer had seemed unimpressed. He had pointed out that whatever friends the club might have at headquarters, they would not be able to help in this situation. One of Moscow's most prominent celebrities had been assassinated in a particularly gruesome way, a man and a woman had been shot dead and another stabbed to death outside the club and after a car chase, another man had been shot dead, the car had crashed and three other men had been badly injured. A full investigation was called for not least because questions were likely to be asked as far up as the Kremlin about what had happened.

It was nearly 5.30 am in Moscow and Vasin calculated that it would be 3.30 am in Spain. But he knew that he had to make the call. He had feared and despised Arkady Durchenko but he feared Petrov and Viktor Durchenko even more. To delay further in reporting such an incident could prove, quite literally, fatal.

Vasin was also worried about his future, regardless of the reaction from Spain. Arkady Durchenko may have been an arrogant prick but at least no one had dared to start any turf war against the Durchenkos. Well, not until now. Who on earth could have mounted such an operation? Leskov had already complained that with two men dead and three others out of action for weeks or months, his resources would be fairly thin if another attack was launched. They could bring in men from the other clubs but they were nothing like the same calibre.

The two men glanced at each other and Vasin picked up the phone and dialled the number in Spain. He had never had to phone Spain before as Arkady had always handled that side of things.

At that time of the morning the call went through to the gatehouse of the villa in Spain. Vasin identified himself and asked to be put through to Petrov.

'Are you mad?' the guard had asked. 'At this time in the morning?'

Vasin had replied that it was an emergency and explained briefly what had happened. The guard had sworn. 'Rather you than me!' he had said and connected the call to Petrov's room.

Petrov answered on the second ring.

'Yes?' he barked. 'Who is this?'

'Mr Petrov, this is Yuri Vasin from the Velvet Dreams Club in Moscow...'

'This had better be good, Vasin!' Petrov shouted.

'Er, there's been an incident I thought you should be told about immediately...'

Vasin described what had happened. Petrov, who had still been lying down, sat up immediately.

'An *incident*?' he shouted down the phone. 'That's not an incident. It's a fucking *disaster*!'

The Columbian hooker lying next to him sat up too.

'What's going on?' she asked blearily.

Petrov shoved her forcibly out of the bed.

'Get dressed and get out!' he shouted.

'I beg your pardon?' Vasin said.

'Not *you*, you idiot!' Petrov roared. He took a deep breath and continued in a calmer voice. 'OK, now tell me again in more detail exactly what happened.'

Fifteen minutes later, after Petrov had got as much detail as he could from Vasin and given instructions as to how security should be increased at all their establishments, he explained to the shocked family who had assembled in Viktor's study what had happened. He was met with a stunned silence.

'Who would dare kill Arkady?' Viktor eventually asked.

'Green and his colleague?' Sergei suggested.

'Surely not,' Georgy said. 'They can't be in Moscow!'

'What do you think, Vitaly?' Viktor asked.

'I think Sergei is right,' Petrov replied after a pause. 'It all fits. No one has dared to attack us for years in Moscow. Is it just coincidence that we are attacked now when the two men attacking us down here appear to have disappeared? The attack was carried out by two men. From what I gather, the guns they used after they had killed Arkady were taken from our own men in close quarter combat. If we had been attacked by say Chechens, I would have expected a whole team of men armed with automatic weapons.'

Petrov headed for the door.

'Where are you going?' Viktor asked.

'To phone Vasin back and get him to send men to the airports and stations. It's worth a try. I doubt they will hang around in Moscow now.'

But by the time the call was made, Dan and Jimmy had passed through security at the airport and the search came to nothing.

Chapter Thirty Three

After landing at Heathrow, Dan and Jimmy went straight back to Dan's flat and slept for a couple of hours. Dan then phoned the colleague at work, who had traced Alan Campbell and Jimmy for him. He had previously phoned him before leaving for Moscow and asked him for another favour.

'There are no Natalya Durchenkos that I could trace in London,' the colleague said, 'so I tried to trace the Natalyas. You wouldn't believe how many Natalyas there are in London. So I gave up on that and had a brainwave. I checked out her mother and found out that Irina's family name was Dragunov. And guess what? I found a Natalya Dragunov! She runs some youth stage and arts outfit.'

'That's brilliant, Gary! Are you sure it's her?'

'Yes, I sent someone down to check her out with the photo you sent over. She's a real looker. I've seen the surveillance photos he took.'

'Did you get a home address as well?'

'Yes, he followed her back to a ritzy apartment block in Chelsea.' He gave Dan the address of the business premises and the apartment block. 'My operative slipped into the foyer behind her and saw that the lift went to the top floor. There's only one penthouse flat there.'

'That's fantastic, Gary! I owe you.'

'You can buy me lunch when this is all over!'

'All what?'

'Come on, Dan. We do read the news here! We know what you're up to and we're all behind you.'

Inspector Valdez was not a happy man. He was under considerable pressure to solve the string of violent crimes which had taken place along the most exclusive part of the Costa del Sol. The press were making unfavourable comparisons with Mexico and the drug wars going on there. Tourism was suffering. His problem was that he knew very well who had committed most of the crimes. He had had a good idea right from the start but after he had picked up the hookers from the shopping centre car park following the call from Luis Mendez, he had gone to see his old friend and mentor and asked him what he knew.

'Are you asking as a police officer or a friend?' Luis had asked.

'Would it make any difference?'

'Probably not.'

'I can't receive information as a friend and ignore it as a police officer.'

'I know. It was a silly question.'

'So, what's going on, Luis? How did you get the tip off about the girls in the car park?'

Mendez had shrugged.

'It was Green, wasn't it?' Valdez had persisted.

'What if it was? What would you do about it?'

'Shortly before your call, a Calahonda resident had reported gunfire from a villa and then a car smashing through a wall. We found five dead east Europeans at the house, one with his throat cut and the others with bullet and shotgun wounds. There was clear evidence that the girls had been held there. The girls just said that two men helped them escape. I showed them Green's picture and they refused to identify him but I could tell from the reaction of one or two of them that they recognised him.'

'And am I supposed to feel sorry that these men are dead?'

'Come on, Luis. We can't have people running around the Costa del Sol carrying out executions, whatever their motive and however evil their victims are.'

'I understand your position, Jose. But remember how every time we tried to investigate the Durchenkos, we were blocked by our superiors who in turn had been leant on by politicians. Remember how you were ordered to close down the investigation against Alexei. Where the Durchenkos are concerned there is no justice in Spain. And I bet those same superiors and politicians are clamouring for the arrest of those who have dared to stand up to them!'

'So what should I do?'

'Do you have any direct evidence linking Senor Green to these matters?'

'No.'

'Then you continue to investigate but until you have any evidence against any individuals, there is surely no one to arrest. Even if you could find them.'

However, Dan Green had clearly not been responsible for the most recent incident which had occurred in Malaga. The notorious arms dealer, Fernando Ortega, his wife and two of his men had been brutally murdered at his home. But the fifth dead body pointed directly to the Durchenkos. DNA evidence had revealed that this man had raped Ortega's wife and then strangled her. The evidence all pointed to the conclusion that Ortega had somehow managed to kill this man before he himself was killed. The man's colleagues had clearly panicked and then fled the scene.

Although the man had carried no ID, Valdez had been fairly sure that he was Russian. After Valdez had faxed a picture of him to the Russian police, they had identified him as one Petr Bortsov, a man with a long criminal record for violence and a known associate of Vitaly Petrov, the former KGB officer, who was now Viktor Durckenko's right hand man and the most feared man after Viktor himself on the Costa del Sol.

Valdez had been delighted. The Durchenkos were always very careful not to leave any link with themselves but this time they had made a mistake. He had obtained an arrest warrant for Vitaly Petrov to take him in for questioning. Although he had known that Petrov would refuse to answer any questions and would walk free after hiring a hotshot lawyer, just to arrest him would be a minor triumph and might rattle the family a bit more. He had heard that they were frantically searching for the men who had been attacking them and the rumours of Alexei's demise had also reached him.

However, on arrival at the gates to the villa, he had been refused admission and when he had demanded access to Petrov and shown the arrest warrant to one of Petrov's deputies, the man had laughed and told him to check with HQ.

'I think you will find that the warrant was issued in error and has been cancelled,' the man had said with a smirk on his face.

Valdez had phoned his office and found to his fury that the warrant had indeed been cancelled. He had driven straight back and had a huge row with his immediate superior, who claimed that he had been ordered by the chief himself to cancel the warrant.

'Senor Petrov is an important businessman and you cannot arrest him just because someone he once knew has a criminal record and has been found dead.'

Valdez had stormed out of his superior's office, slamming the door, and returned to his own. 'Maybe Luis is right,' he thought. 'If I can't investigate some crimes properly, then maybe there are others which will prove equally difficult to solve.'

Chapter Thirty Four

'I thought Luis said Natalya had nothing to do with the family business,' Jimmy said, after Dan had told him about the result of his enquiries about her.

'He wasn't sure,' Dan replied. 'So we may as well check it out for ourselves. Anyway, it's probably best if we don't go back to Spain for a few days. They will have realised by now it was us who killed Arkady and they will be expecting us back to resume our campaign against them. They'll be on full alert, checking transport hubs, hotels and everything. Let them chase their tails for a while. There's no hurry. In the meantime, we can see what Miss Dragunov has been up to!'

'Ok. But the fact that she uses her mother's maiden name rather than the family name and lives here rather than in Spain or Moscow suggests she wants to put distance between herself and the family.'

'Maybe. But let's find out.'

'What do you propose then?'

'We could start by having a look at her business premises.'

A couple of hours later, they took up a position in a coffee bar looking out across Brewer Street in Soho towards the premises of the grandly named International Youth Stage School. The shop window had a black background with pictures of children aged from about twelve to sixteen singing, dancing and acting on a small stage. To the left of the shop window was a black door. After an hour of drinking coffee and in Jimmy's case eating pastries, they learnt very little. A couple of teenage girls had gone in and then an older man carrying some sort of heavy equipment.

'Maybe we should just go over there and see what's going on?' Jimmy suggested.

Ok. You go,' Dan replied. 'There's no point in both of us showing our faces at this stage. You could pretend to be someone checking out the school for his daughter.'

Dan watched as Jimmy walked across the road and tried the door. It was locked so Jimmy rang the bell.

The door was opened by an attractive girl in her twenties dressed in jeans and a tight top.

'Can I help you?' she asked in a South London accent.

'I was just passing and wondered whether this might be the sort of school which would suit my daughter,' Jimmy said with a smile. 'She's mad about the stage.'

The girl stood aside.

'Come in,' she said pleasantly, 'and I'll tell you what we do here.'

The girl led Jimmy down a short corridor into an office and sat down behind a desk.

'Please. Sit down.' She pointed to a chair in front of the desk. 'How old is your daughter?'

'Thirteen.'

'And what is she interested in?'

'Er...how do you mean?'

'Well, basically we do dancing, singing and acting here.'

'Oh, yes, I see. She likes dancing.'

'OK. We do various dance classes here. They take place either in the school holidays, weekends or after school hours. And if you sign up to a course, you can come in and practice any time.'

'That sounds great. Have you got a brochure?'

'Yes, of course.' The girl reached into a drawer and handed Jimmy a glossy brochure. 'The courses are described in here. I'll put this separate sheet in which has the prices. Unfortunately, we are booked up for the summer but new courses will be beginning in September on Saturdays and from 5.00pm weekdays.'

'That's a shame. How do I book a course for September?'

'Just give me a call on this number.' The girl pointed to a number on the back of the brochure. 'Tell me what you're interested in and I'll see what's available. I'm Janet by the way.'

'Is this your school then?'

'Oh, no! I just man the office and take the bookings.'

'Would it be possible to have a look round while I'm here?'

'Oh, I'm sorry. I can't show you round today as we've got some girls doing their final rehearsal for a show they are putting on at a wedding. So I can't let you into the stage area.'

'No problem. Another time maybe.'

'Yes, certainly. Just give me a call when you want to come and we'll arrange a convenient time.'

Jimmy stood up.

'Thank you, Janet. You've been most helpful.'

The girl smiled and accompanied Jimmy to the door.

Jimmy went back to the coffee bar and told Dan what had happened. Dan had a quick look through the brochure.

'What do you think then?'

Jimmy shrugged.

'It seemed OK to me. The girl was very friendly. It's a shame I never got a good look round but I assume the stage area is shown in the pictures in the window.'

'These courses are very expensive!' Dan said, as he looked at the separate sheet that the girl had inserted in the brochure.

'Well, you're not planning to book one are you? Anyway, I imagine people are prepared to pay through the nose to give their kids a chance of pursuing their dreams!'

'I guess so.'

'And penthouse flats in Chelsea don't come cheap!'

At that moment, the door to the school opened and a stunningly attractive woman came out. She had long blond hair and high cheekbones. She was dressed in black leather trousers and high heeled ankle boots and a white T shirt with some sort of metallic decorative design on it.

'The lovely Miss Dragunov, I presume!' Jimmy said.

They watched as she hailed a taxi and was driven away.

'What now?' Jimmy asked.

'I think I'd better get to know her,' Dan replied.

Chapter Thirty Five

Natalya Dragunov was bored stiff. She declined the offer of coffee and was relieved when her dinner companion asked for the bill. She had only agreed to have dinner with him because she had thought that he might be able to put some business her way. However, during the course of the meal, it had become abundantly clear that his only interest was in getting her into bed. She wouldn't have minded if he had been remotely attractive but he was everything she loathed in a man. No class and no taste despite his apparent wealth. In fact, he reminded her why she had left Russia in the first place. He would have gone down well in Moscow society with his shiny expensive suit and chunky gold jewellery. She bitterly regretted wearing such a short skirt and had lost count of the number of times that she had had to remove his hand from her thigh.

Fortunately, she had not had to make much conversation as her companion had spent virtually the whole meal talking about himself. In fact the only thing he hadn't boasted about was the size of his penis, leading Natalya to the conclusion that he was fairly inadequate in that department. That thought was the only thing that had amused her all evening.

From their window seat in a pub just across the road from the restaurant in Sloane Square, Dan and Jimmy could just about see the table where Natalya and her companion were sitting and could see the bored expression on her face.

'I don't think she'll be going home with him tonight!' Jimmy said.

'Let's hope not,' Dan replied.

Outside the restaurant, the man predictably put an arm around Natalya and invited her back to his place for coffee. She politely declined, wondering how obtuse the man must be not to pick up on the negative vibes from her. She also declined his offer to share a taxi with him as she lived nearby and preferred to walk. Her disappointed suitor hailed a taxi for himself and to Natalya's relief she was finally free of him.

Since it was a pleasant evening and she did only live ten minutes walk away, she decided to walk rather than hail a taxi of her own. She was thinking about what a rotten evening she had had when it took a severe turn for the worse. A tough looking man appeared at her side as she walked.

'Fancy a drink, darling?' he said.

She had been approached in the street many times by men wanting to chat her up or take her out, but she was well capable of brushing them off with a putdown and in the light of her experience in the restaurant was in no mood for taking any prisoners.

'Piss off, loser!' she snarled and walked on quickly.

But the man kept up with her.

'Who the hell do you think you are, slag?' he replied aggressively.

'How dare you talk to me like that! Just go away, you pathetic little man!' Natalya responded.

'I'm not being told what to do by some East European tart!'

The man grabbed her by the arm. Natalya swung her other arm at him to try to get away but he parried her blow easily and dragged her into an alleyway between two shops. Natalya could not believe that this was happening in Chelsea. She tried to scream but the man put one of his hands over her mouth and pushed her against the wall. He put his other hand up her skirt and tried to pull her knickers down as she struggled and tried to kick out at him. Just as she was beginning to realise that she had no chance of fighting the man off, there was a shout from the street.

'Hey! What's going on there?'

The man stopped pulling at her knickers and looked back towards the street. The man who had shouted ran to them and Natalya's assailant released her and turned towards the man rushing towards him.

Dan punched Jimmy in the stomach and as he doubled over headbutted him, careful to ensure he made contact with Jimmy's forehead rather than his nose or mouth so as not to do too much damage. It made an impressive cracking sound and Jimmy went down and stayed down.

Dan turned to Natalya, who by now was hysterical.

'Are you OK?' Dan asked, putting one of his hands on her shoulder to steady her.

'I...I think so,' Natalya replied.

'Let's get out of here before he wakes up,' Dan said and gently led her back towards the street.

'We should call the police,' he said.

'No it's OK. I'll be all right. I don't want to involve the police,' Natalya said. 'I just want to forget about it.'

'If you're sure? But I'm not leaving you in this state. You've been badly shaken up.'

'I only live a few minutes away. I should have taken a taxi.'

'I will walk you home. But why don't we stop at that bar over there first. You could do with a brandy.'

Natalya hesitated.

'I understand your reluctance,' Dan said. 'You've just been attacked by one stranger and now you're with another.'

'No, no, you're very kind,' Natalya said. 'I suppose I could do with a drink.'

Dan found a quiet table for Natalya and went to the bar to get the drinks. She asked for a Vodka and he ordered a double for her and a lager for himself. She finished the drink in two gulps and he replenished her glass immediately.

After a few minutes when the alcohol began to take effect, Natalya began to feel better. For the first time, she began to assess her rescuer. She noted his handsome, strong face. He had a military bearing and as he had demonstrated, clearly knew how to look after himself. Unlike her ghastly dinner companion, he seemed more interested in her than himself and the conversation flowed easily. Soon, she found herself laughing and enjoying herself, relaxed in his company.

Dan saw that Natalya had started to relax. To begin with, she had been understandably wary of him and selfconsciously pulling her skirt down every few seconds as if trying to protect herself. Now, she had stopped doing that and Dan noticed the glances from a number of men in the bar.

After about half an hour, Natalya said that she felt tired and asked Dan if he would mind walking her home. She took his arm as they walked the short distance to her apartment block.

'I'm really grateful for what you've done,' she said. 'I don't know what would have happened if you hadn't showed up.'

'I'm just glad that I did,' Dan replied.

'I would ask you up but after what's happened...'

'No problem. I quite understand. But you could show your gratitude by agreeing to have dinner with me?'

Natalya smiled, pleased that he had asked to see her again.

'I'd be delighted.'

'Tomorrow?'

'Why not?'

'Give me your number and I'll give you a call to make the arrangements.'

Dan programmed Natalya's number into his phone and after giving her a brief kiss on the cheek, watched as she entered the block and then the lift, turning to give him a little wave before she got into it.

Back at Dan's flat, Jimmy was sitting watching television with a pack of frozen peas pressed to his forehead.

'How did it go?' he asked.

'Like a dream. I'm taking her out tomorrow night,' Dan replied. 'But I'm pretty sure she's not involved with the family business.'

'Don't be fooled by her looks!'

'I'll try not to be. How's the head?'

'You didn't have to hit me that hard!'

'It had to be realistic! Were you really out?'

'No. I heard your sympathetic rescue act. It's the only way you'd pull a bird like that! Next time I'll do the rescuing!'

Chapter Thirty Six

Their establishments were all on full alert but there had been no further attacks. Despite the threats issued and the inducements offered, there had been no sightings or reports of the two Englishmen. On several occasions there had been false alarms when reports of two Englishmen of the right sort of age had been made only for them to turn out to be tourists on a golfing holiday.

'Do you think they've stopped after killing Arkady?' Viktor Durchenko asked.

'No I don't,' Petrov replied. 'They can't stop. Green knows that we will keep hunting him and eventually will find him. So it's them or us. This will be played out until either we find them and kill them or they kill all of us.'

'How can two men destroy an organisation of our size?'

'I agree. But they've shown they can do a lot of damage. We must find them as soon as possible.'

'They must be lying low, hoping we will drop our guard.'

'Perhaps. But I don't believe they are in Spain, or surely we would have heard something.'

'Maybe they have friends out here who are hiding them. They could be in a villa somewhere and we'd never hear of it.'

'So why did they rent an apartment when they first came here?'

'Because we did not know about them then. They may have called in a favour now we are looking for them. Some ex army colleague who has retired down here perhaps.'

Petrov nodded. It was certainly a possibility and he had already considered it. But he was not prepared to simply wait for the next attack.

'They may have returned to England to wait there till we drop our guard.'

'What do you suggest?'

'I've found out that Green lives in a modern apartment block in an area of London known as Docklands. I suggest we send a team of four men over there to check it out. We have contacts in London who found out his address for me. They can also arm our team.'

Durchenko considered this for a moment.

'OK, do it.'

Dan phoned Natalya the following morning and she seemed pleased to hear from him. He suggested that they had dinner in an Italian restaurant that he knew in Kensington Church Street. She said that she would meet him there but he insisted on picking her up and said that he would park outside her block at about eight and ring her bell for her to come down. She told him that it was the top bell and that she would be ready.

Jimmy was sceptical about Dan's chances of finding out whether she was involved in the family business by taking her out to dinner.

'You just want to shag her, don't you?' he said, grinning.

'That's not what this about,' Dan replied. 'Have you got a better idea?'

'Well, we could break into her studio after hours and have a look round. Or maybe I could break into her flat while you're having dinner?'

'Too risky. The studio is almost certainly alarmed and I expect her penthouse is like a fortress! And any break in would put her on notice if she's up to something. This way with a bit of luck I will get an invite back to her flat and will get an opportunity to look round.'

'What do you want me to do?'

'Nothing. I think I can handle this on my own!'

''Handle' being the operative word!'

Chapter Thirty Seven

Dan realised that he would never have been able to achieve what he had so far had Jimmy not agreed to help. But sometimes he found Jimmy's attitude a little hard to take. Jimmy seemed to be enjoying the whole thing despite the dangers not just from the Durchenkos but also the authorities in the countries whose laws they were breaking. To him, this was just another adventure with the opportunity along the way to kill a few bad guys, pick up a few euros and maybe bed a few women as well. Dan had to keep reminding himself that Jimmy had not lost his only son.

Thus, he had resented Jimmy's insinuation that he was more interested in having sex with Natalya rather than ascertain where she stood, if at all, in the family hierarchy.

These thoughts were running through his mind as Dan stood outside the entrance to Natalya's block and watched through the glass doors as the lift descended from the top floor to the bottom. However, they were soon dispelled when the lift door opened and Natalya appeared. She looked absolutely stunning. Her blond hair was beautifully coiffeured and her lipstick matched the nail varnish on her long finger nails. She was wearing a simple but elegant short black dress which accentuated every aspect of her figure, showing off her her ample cleavage and bronzed legs perched on black suede shoes with heels which must have been six inches high. Her legs had a glossy look to them and Dan wondered if women rubbed some sort of cream into them to make them look like that.

Natalya came through the door and kissed Dan on the cheek, giving him a whiff of an expensive perfume. They walked to his car which was right outside and Dan opened the passenger door for her. As she slid into the passenger seat, Dan didn't know whether to look at the expanse of thigh she revealed as she got in or down her cleavage. As he tore his eyes away, he felt embarrassed as he saw the seductive look on her face which told him that she knew exactly where he had been looking.

As he walked round to the driver's side, he reminded himself again what this was all about. It was just part of the mission. Nothing else.

The journey to the restaurant took about ten to fifteen minutes and the conversation consisted of small talk about London, the traffic and other inconsequential subjects. Dan decided to wait until they were in the restaurant before he began questioning her about what he was really interested in.

Unfortunately, Natalya seemed determined to spend the whole meal flirting and showed no inclination to get involved in any detailed conversation about herself. She deflected any questions about her background and family by simply saying that she had moved to London a few years ago and that her family all lived abroad. She told Dan about her stage school but he realised that she was telling him nothing more than he had already found out from Jimmy's visit to the school. The only thing that she volunteered was that she loved working with young people and helping them start their careers.

Dan kept trying to find out more but knew that he could not press her too hard or she might become suspicious.

'Why all the questions, Dan?' Natalya said over coffee. 'You don't have to pretend interest in my life.' She smiled seductively.

'I'm not pretending,' Dan replied. 'I really am interested in you.'

'Come on,' Natalya said smiling. 'We both know what this is about.'

'Do we?'

'Of course. You Englishmen can be so upright and proper.'

'Tell me then.'

Natalya smiled across the table at him. She then pushed her knees against his and gently rubbed them against him. She leant across the table and took one of his hands and while staring into his eyes, put half his index finger in her mouth and gently sucked it for a few seconds before removing it.

'I can tell you fancy me. I could tell that as soon as we met.'

'Was I that obvious?'

'Yes, but you did try to hide it!'

'Sorry!'

'Don't be! I fancy you too so why don't you get the bill and we will have our brandies back at my place.'

Dan needed no second invitation. He called over the waiter. Even if the meal had not been productive so far as information was concerned, he had at least got his invitation back to her apartment.

Chapter Thirty Eight

Natalya took Dan's hand as they walked to his car. Once in the car, Dan found it difficult to concentrate on driving. Natalya leaned towards him and spent the whole journey stroking the inside of his left thigh. She seemed to delight in his discomfort. Once, when he stopped at traffic lights, she took his left hand and put it between her own thighs and gently rubbed them against his hand.

When they arrived at her apartment block, she directed him around the corner and down into the underground car park. As soon as he had parked she leant across and kissed him, at the same time moving her hand up his thigh. She giggled when she found what she was looking for.

'It must have been an uncomfortable journey for you, trapped in there.'

She undid his belt and zip and reached inside his boxer shorts.

'That's better. Now he can breathe!'

She bent down and closed over him with his mouth. As her head bobbed up and down, Dan realised that she was not going to stop. He gently tried to move her head away but she resisted and carried on more vigorously. Eventually, he pulled her head away just as he was about to reach the point of no return. Natalya laughed.

'What's the matter? Don't you want to come?'

'Yes, but not here! Why don't we wait till we get upstairs?'

Natalya continued to tease him.

'Oh my god, you're not one of those men who comes once and then that's it for the whole night?'

'Well, I er....'

'Believe me,' Natalya continued, 'No one is like that with me! I could get you going again in the time it takes for the lift to go up!'

'I'm sure you could. Maybe it's my age, but my days of having sex in a car ended twenty years ago!'

'OK, no problem. But you're very easy to tease!'

After a steamy ride up in the lift, they practically fell through Natalya's front door and over to the huge white leather sofa facing floor to ceiling windows looking out over the Thames.

'Don't worry,' Natalya said, 'no one will see us this high up. Unless of course a helicopter passes by. In which case, good luck to them!'

She extracted herself from Dan's arms and quickly removed her dress and underwear. Dan stared appreciatively at her completely hairless body. She smiled at him and then set to work undoing his trousers for the second time. She

245

pulled down his trousers and boxer shorts and he kicked them off his feet. She couldn't be bothered with his shirt and immediately climbed on top of him and guided him into her. Dan doubted whether it was ten seconds before they both exploded.

'Oh god,' Natalya sighed. 'I've been waiting for that all evening.'

'OK,' she continued, 'let's get to know each other better in the bedroom.'

She stood up and led Dan by the hand into her bedroom, a lavishly furnished room down the corridor from the living room. She pulled back the bedcover and helped Dan take his shirt off.

'You wait for me in bed while I go and get some champagne. I have changed my mind about the brandy. I'm in a champagne mood now!'

Dan did as he was told and got into the bed. As soon as Natalya had disappeared, he jumped out again and quickly looked in all the cupboards and drawers. As expected, there was nothing apart from clothes and accessories. He got back into the bed and wondered how he would manage to get an opportunity to look around the rest of the apartment. He calculated that she had already had a vodka and tonic and the best part of a bottle of wine. He had only had half a glass as he had been driving. Maybe if he ensured that she drank most of the champagne and did his best to tire her out, he might get a chance later but the way things were going it was likely to be him who ended up tired out!

Natalya seemed to have been gone a long time and Dan assumed she had gone to the bathroom but she eventually reappeared with an open bottle of champagne and two glasses.

She poured some champagne into the glasses and handed one to Dan. She then got into bed beside him and snuggled up to him as she drank her champagne. Dan stroked her hair and sipped his champagne, hoping that Natalya would quaff hers back fairly quickly so that he could refill her glass.

However, after a few minutes she put down her glass and felt between his legs again. Perhaps it wasn't quite as short as the time that it would take for the lift to go up but Natalya had not been exaggerating. Dan felt himself reacting and had no alternative but to put his own glass down.

This time they were not as frantic as before. They both took their time and after a few minutes, Dan rolled on top of Natalya and entered her again. After a while, Natalya pushed him over on to his back and climbed on top of him. Dan was already beginning to understand that this was her preferred position. She sat upright on him facing the wall behind him and gently rocked up and down until she gradually increased the pace. Dan could tell from her breathing that she was building up to a climax. He reached up and fondled her nipples. She looked down at him.

'Yes, yes, yes,' she said breathlessly as she once again increased the pace.

Dan too could hold back no longer. He thrust upwards as he reached his climax. Natalya screamed loudly as she bounced up and down but just as she screamed there was a loud crack which came from behind her. Dan looked up at her and her head seemed to explode and blood and brains spattered the wall behind Dan and dripped down on him.

Dan's confusion lasted a millisecond before his instincts took over. He thrust the now lifeless Natalya off him to one side and rolled off the other side of the bed, knowing that his efforts were hopeless as the shooter would have plenty of time to readjust his target before Dan could get anywhere near him. He jumped to his feet expecting at any moment to feel the searing pain and hear another crack from the silenced pistol but to his astonishment he saw Jimmy leaning against the doorframe holding a Sig Sauer pistol in his hand.

'What the fuck are you doing?' Dan screamed at the top of his voice.

'Saving your arse, that's what,' Jimmy replied. 'Think yourself lucky I waited till you'd come! Christ, she makes a racket doesn't she?'

'What the hell are you talking about? And where the bloody hell did you get that pistol?' Dan raged.

Jimmy did not reply but used the long silenced pistol to beckon Dan over to the door. Dan walked over and stood in the doorway naked looking to where Jimmy was pointing the pistol. Dan walked down the corridor and looked into the living room. In the middle of the floor lay a man dressed in black from head to toe. He was lying face down and was obviously dead. A huge pool of blood leading from a gash in his neck had soaked into the white carpet and blood had sprayed across the room on to the white leather sofa Dan had been on less than an hour earlier.

Chapter Thirty Nine

Previously

Although Dan had said that he could handle things on his own, Jimmy thought that there was no harm in watching his back. Besides, he had nothing else to do that evening except watch the telly. He had realised that he would not be able to tail Dan to Natalya's apartment block by public transport or taxi so he had gone straight to the restaurant.

He arrived before them and was relieved when they turned up that nothing untoward had happened when he hadn't been around. He couldn't see their table from outside the restaurant but when they came out, it seemed clear that they were going back to her flat for some action. He hailed a taxi and gave the driver the address of Natalya's apartment block. He asked to be dropped off on the corner about a hundred yards from the block so that no one would see him. He then found a doorway in the block opposite from where he could keep a discreet eye on the entrance.

Jimmy reckoned that he was wasting his time. They had seemed to be well into each other. Here he was stuck outside while Dan was shagging one of the tastiest bits of skirt he'd seen for years! He decided to give it an hour and then leave.

After nearly an hour, he spotted something that woke him up and put him on full alert. A swarthy looking man dressed in black was walking down the street towards the block. There seemed to be something odd about him. He was looking around as if unsure where he was or, and this troubled Jimmy more, as if checking no one was around.

Jimmy had a dilemma. If the man went into the block, how could Jimmy get in? He could try ringing Dan but what if he didn't answer? The man stopped at the entrance and looked around again. Why? Jimmy thought. Then the man walked over to the entrance with a key. Jimmy had to do something. He did not look like the sort to own a flat in that block. In fact, to Jimmy's experienced eye, he looked like a pro.

Jimmy ran over to the man just as he was entering the block.

'Hold on,' he said. 'This saves me getting my key out!'

The man glowered at him but said nothing. How could he? Jimmy thought. He could hardly keep me out or he would really draw attention to himself trying to exclude a resident.

They both walked over to the lift. Jimmy held back and ensured the other man went in first, and sure enough, he pushed the button for the top floor. Jimmy pushed the button for two floors below.

'Nice weather for the time of year,' Jimmy commented as the lift went up.

The other man grunted and deliberately looked away from Jimmy. When the lift stopped, Jimmy stepped out and immediately located the stairs and rushed up the next two flights. He peered round the corner and saw the man approaching the only door on the top floor.

Jimmy had already removed one of Dan's kitchen knives from his jacket pocket. The other man paused at the door and put his ear to the door. Then he produced a key. But it was what he produced in his other hand that spurred Jimmy into immediate action. The man drew a silenced Sig Sauer from his pocket and put the key in the door. By the time he had turned it, Jimmy was already halfway across the gap between them. The man glanced towards Jimmy, a look of shock on his face, but before he could bring the pistol round, Jimmy was on him pushing him into the apartment and putting an arm around his throat. With his other hand he shoved the knife into the man's neck right up to the hilt and then pulled down on the handle. Blood spurted everywhere but Jimmy kept hold of the man until he stopped struggling, then walked him further into the apartment and gently lowered him to the floor.

'But how do you know Natalya was responsible for this?' Dan asked, still shocked by the turn of events.

'Who else knew you were here? But anyway there's cast iron proof. This guy was a professional hitman. All he had on him was some cash and this phone. Probably East European, not Russian, as you will see from the text. Judging by his looks I'd say Bulgarian.'

Jimmy tossed the phone over to Dan. It was open at the message inbox. There was one text in English sent about forty five minutes previously.

'Green here in apartment. Unarmed. Will be in bedroom.'

'Oh, and just in case you're still not convinced, here's her phone which I found on the sideboard.' Jimmy tossed a second phone over to Dan who saw the same message in the sent folder. Now he knew why it had taken her so long to fetch two glasses and a bottle of champagne.

'Sorry, Dan, but she stitched you up good and proper. She planned to have her evil way with you, then off you. Good job Uncle Jimmy was watching your back!'

'God, I've been a right prick, haven't I? She had almost convinced me she had nothing to do with her family. She said she just wanted to help young people.'

'That's what she called it, is it?'

'What do you mean?'

253

'Well, after I'd dealt with matey here, I heard you two at it in the bedroom and decided to have a look round. I found a locked cupboard by the telly and guess what I found inside?'

Jimmy walked over to the sideboard and removed a handful of DVDs.

'Have a look at these!'

Dan walked over and looked at the glossy covers. Once again he was stunned. The DVDs were produced by 'Natalya Productions' and the covers depicted hardcore pornographic images of young teenage girls, almost certainly under sixteen, having sex with much older men.

'I'm afraid that's what she meant by working with the young,' Jimmy said, putting another DVD into the player by the television. 'And let's have a look at this one.'

'There's no need. I don't want to look at kiddie porn!'

'Bear with me. You need to see this.'

Jimmy switched on the television and after fiddling around for a while eventually got a picture. Shielding Dan from the picture, he fast forwarded it until he came to a suitable passage. He then stood back.

'Check this out.'

Dan was shocked yet again. Two mature women were lying side by side on a double bed with their legs in the air being 'serviced' by young boys who looked as if they about fourteen.

Other young boys were standing around, seemingly waiting for their turns. But what really shocked Dan was that one of the women was Natalya, apparently enjoying herself considerably.

'The other woman is the so called office girl I spoke to when I made my visit to the school,' Jimmy said.

'Jesus,' Dan said. 'Evil must run through this family.'

'What now?'

'We go home. But tomorrow, we shut this school down once and for all!'

'What about the mess here?'

'There's not a lot we can do. We could put the gun in his hand, making it look as if he shot Natalya but where does that get us? That doesn't explain who killed him.'

'Your DNA is all over the girl.'

'There's nothing we can do about that. If they ever trace me I can just say I left before this happened. So I'll leave my fingerprints but I suggest you wipe down everything you've touched. Anyway unless Natalya has a cleaner coming soon with a key, it could be ages before this is discovered.'

'OK. Then I'll take the gun with us. Given that they are on to us here, it may come in handy.'

Little did Jimmy know how soon it would come in handy.

Chapter Forty

On the journey back to Docklands, Dan felt a little guilty about his earlier annoyance with Jimmy. But for Jimmy's thoroughness and vigilance, Dan would almost certainly have been dead by now. He was angry with himself for letting his guard down and letting himself be beguiled by Natalya. Jimmy may have a carefree and gung ho attitude on the exterior but he was a true pro and whereas Dan had been living a safe, comfortable existence since leaving the army, Jimmy had maintained his skills in some of the world's most dangerous trouble spots. He resolved to place more reliance on Jimmy's instincts in future.

As it happened, Dan had an earlier opportunity than he would have imagined to repay Jimmy with a piece of potentially life saving vigilance. As he drove down the road leading to his apartment block, he spotted the glow of a cigarette in a car parked on the right about fifty yards from the entrance to his block and the underground car park. The light was just sufficient for him to see the silhouettes of four men in the car.

Marat Banin had been pleased when Petrov had selected him to lead a team to go to London to see if Green was holed up there. Until recently, he had enjoyed his time in Spain. It had proved to be a relatively cushy life after the locals had been subdued. With no opposition, Banin's most onerous task had been to ensure the smooth running of some of the family's establishments. Good pay and as many women as he could handle was all he required. But now things were different. The whole organisation was on full alert. It felt like they were under siege not knowing when the enemy would strike next. Everyone was running around like mad trying to trace the two Englishmen who had dared to attack them and kill so many including Alexei and Arkady. Viktor and Petrov were in permanent bad moods, shouting at everyone and demanding progress in the search.

So the opportunity to get away for a few days was a welcome break. The chances were that they would not find Green but if they did, he knew that failure would not be tolerated. Nevertheless, if they could find and kill either Green or his companion or preferably both, it would be a huge feather in his cap and likely to lead to advancement in the organisation.

They arrived in London at five o'clock travelling in pairs so as not to draw attention to themselves. After hiring a car, they went straight to the address in Southall on the outskirts of London where Petrov had said they could pick up weapons. A surly looking man, who appeared to Banin to be of Armenian extraction or from somewhere in that part of the world, simply handed them a bag containing four handguns and ammunition and then slammed the door. Petrov had already arranged for the payment to be made.

They then checked into a relatively cheap and anonymous hotel in Lancaster Gate, a cosmopolitan area with as many foreigners as locals, before driving east to check out Green's apartment block.

The area seemed deserted when they arrived at about nine o'clock but a number of the apartments had lights on. Banin guessed that most of the flats were occupied by people who commuted into central London during the day. The area by the waterfront did not look like an area where families lived.

Banin sent one of his men to ring Green's bell. He was not surprised that there was no answer.

'He could still be up there,' one of his men said.

'Maybe,' Banin replied. 'But even though we could probably get someone to let us into the block through the front doors, what then? Smash down his door? We don't know the layout of his apartment. One burst from an Uzi and we're all dead. Anyway, this isn't Moscow. The slightest disturbance and another resident will call the police.'

'And if he isn't there, he'd go to ground and we'll never find him,' another man added.

'So what do we do?' the first man asked.

'We wait to see if he comes out or returns and if he does, we take him in the street and drive off before the police are even called.'

'What if he drives out of the underground car park?'

Banin handed the man a pair of binoculars.

'It's your job then to check any car that comes out then. If it's him, we follow and wait for a time to draw level so we can take him out.'

'How long are we going to wait?'

Banin thought about it for a moment.

'Till midnight. Then we'll go back to the hotel and be back here by seven.'

There were predictable groans.

'We're not here to enjoy ourselves,' Banin said. 'These men are extremely dangerous and if we don't kill them, they may well kill us, if not here then in Spain.'

Dan drove straight past the entrance to the block and the car park.

'Where are you going?' Jimmy asked.

'There are four men sitting in a car just before the entrance.'

'Christ, I missed that!'

'I only saw them because one of them is smoking.'

'What do you reckon?'

'I reckon they're waiting for us. Who sits in a car in an area like this unless they're waiting for something or someone? And why four of them?'

He pulled up at the side of the road after turning left twice.

'What do you suggest? We could drive to a hotel.'

'We've got to go back to the flat at some stage.'

'We could drive into the car park. They might not realise it's us.'

'If they do, they could call for reinforcements and simply wait. It wouldn't deal with the problem.'

'We could call the police anonymously and say there are four heavily armed men in a car.'

'We could. But again it doesn't solve the problem. They or others would be back.'

'So what do you suggest?'

'I think we should deal with them now.'

'With one gun with fourteen rounds left?'

'Assuming they didn't clock us as we drove past, we have the element of surprise. But we can't just walk up to the car and blast them while they're sitting there. We have to be sure. They could conceivably be late night workers waiting for their shift!'

Dan outlined his plan.

'You're taking a hell of a risk!' Jimmy said. 'What if they've got a rifle with sights? They wouldn't even have to leave the car.'

'Unlikely. But if you get close enough and see that's what they're doing, you can start shooting and I'll run for it!'

Dan doubled back and parked in a side street some two hundred yards from the car with the men. Jimmy crossed to the right side of the road and ducked down behind another parked car. There were not that many cars parked in the road and he counted five between himself and the car with the four men in it. Fortunately, the lighting in the area was poor. Then, remaining in a crouched position, he moved from one car to the next until he was behind the last one with a gap of some twenty yards to the car with the men.

Meanwhile, Dan walked down the left side of the road as if he was coming from the local Docklands Light Railway station. Though looking ahead, he was able to keep the car to his right in the corner of his vision.

After nearly three hours cooped up in the car, Banin was ready to call it a night when he looked in the nearside mirror and saw a man walking down the other side of the road from behind them towards the block.

'There's someone coming,' he said calmly. 'It could be him. Stay still.'

All four of them checked their weapons. The tension in the car rose. No one spoke till Dan was only about ten yards from the car.

'It's him!' Banin hissed. 'Wait for my signal.'

Banin waited until Dan had passed their car and was about to turn towards the entrance.

'Now!' he said, and all four car doors opened.

Jimmy could see Dan walking down the road but his attention was fixed on the car. He knew exactly where Dan would be when the attack started if he had been in the car and as if on cue the car doors opened at that point. These were clearly not shift workers. He saw at least one gun as the men got out of the car.

He waited until the men were fully out of the car before making his move. Then he stood up and walked forward, dropping the two men who had got out of the rear doors with two shots into the centre of their backs.

Banin heard the muffled cracks from the Sig Sauer and knew exactly what had happened. They had fallen into a trap. But Banin did not make the fatal mistake that his colleague who had got out of driver's door did. This man turned round at the sound of the cracks and, disorientated as to precisely where the shots had come from, had no chance of locating his target before two more precise shots from Jimmy hit him in the chest and forehead. This gave Banin the chance to get out of the line of fire and by the time his dead colleague hit the ground Banin was already across the road and diving over the low wall into the forecourt of the apartment block.

Before the third man hit the ground, Jimmy swung his gun round towards the fourth just in time to see him diving over the wall. He let off two more shots but to no avail.

As soon as the car doors opened, Dan started to run. He heard the cracks from Jimmy's gun and was relieved to hear no other shots. He ran into the forecourt and ducked right behind the low wall and a large plant pot. He turned round to see what was happening in time to see Banin diving over the wall on the other side of the entrance. Banin saw him immediately and realised he was a sitting duck for Dan. He tried to make himself as small as possible behind the corresponding plant pot on his side but when no shot came, it dawned on him that Dan was unarmed.

Now it was Dan trying to make himself as small as possible behind a pot. Banin raised his gun towards Dan but did not dare to raise himself above the wall.

'Tell your friend to back off,' he said in a thick Russian accent.

When Dan did not reply, Banin fired an unsilenced shot which broke off part of the pot reducing Dan's protection as well as reverberating around the forecourt. Lights started to come on in the block.

'Tell him to back off now or the next shot is for you! I have a clear shot now,' the Russian shouted.

Jimmy was in the middle of the road covering the wall but not knowing precisely where the Russian was.

'What's your situation, Dan?' he called out.

'He's got a clear shot,' Dan replied.

'Throw your weapon over the wall!' Banin shouted.

'Why? So you can kill both of us?' Jimmy shouted back.

'If you throw the weapon over the wall, I will back away and we all live to fight another day,' Banin replied.

There was a long pause.

'OK,' Jimmy said. 'I guess I'll just have to trust you.'

He threw the silenced Sig Sauer over the wall and Banin watched it clatter across the forecourt. He stood up with his gun still trained on Dan. He glanced over at Jimmy, who stood there with his right arm by his side. Banin then smirked.

'Maybe you shouldn't have trusted me after all, Englishman.'

He then turned back towards Dan but before he could fire, Jimmy brought up his left hand which had been concealed from the Russian and fired three shots into him with a gun belonging to one of the dead Russians. Jimmy had picked it up off the road while Banin was still crouching behind the wall as soon as he had heard what Banin was proposing.

Dan stood up.

'What if he had stuck to the deal?' he asked.

Jimmy grinned. 'He'd have found me equally untrustworthy!'

At that point they could hear sirens.

'Come on, let's go!' Dan said. He picked up the Sig Sauer and they ran towards the river pausing only to throw the gun into the water as they did not want the police to make any connection between what had happened here and what had happened in Chelsea. They ran around the block and picked up Dan's car. By the time the police arrived, they were driving out of the area looking for a hotel.

'The area will be a crime scene for days,' Dan said, 'but as a resident I'll be able to return to the flat and pack our gear.'

'Back to Spain then?'

'Yes. Back to Spain. But only after we've closed down Natalya's school.'

'I can't wait!'

Chapter Forty One

After a night spent in a hotel near Canary Wharf, Dan and Jimmy decided to leave Dan's car in the hotel car park and take public transport into central London. They arrived at the International Youth Stage School at about eleven. The door as expected was locked so they rang the bell. There was no answer so Dan pressed the bell again and kept his finger on it.

Eventually, they heard the sounds of bolts sliding back and the door opened a crack.

'We're closed today,' a female voice said. 'Oh, it's you. You were here a couple of days ago, weren't you?'

'That's right,' Jimmy said. 'It's Janet isn't it? I've brought a friend who is also interested in the school.'

'Well, I'm sorry, I can't let you in today. We're very busy. You should have rung for an appointment. Perhaps another time?'

'I didn't need an appointment last time. We just need a few minutes of your time.'

'You'll have to come back another time. I'm sorry. I have to go now.'

The girl went to close the door but Dan put his foot in it preventing her from closing it. He could have simply kicked it open and forced his way in but he did not want to do that in a busy street in the middle of Soho.

'We're supposed to meet Natalya here. She said that it would be all right to call round today,' he said.

The girl was taken aback by the reference to Natalya.

'You know Natalya?' she asked.

'Yes, we do and we also know all about Natalya Productions,' Dan replied.

The girl glanced up and down the street at the mention of Natalya Productions.

'I don't know what you're talking about,' she said and tried again to shut the door.

'Look, Janet,' Jimmy said, 'I wasn't being entirely straight with you when I visited you last time. We work for Natalya's family and her father asked us to test your security. That's why I called pretending to be the father of a prospective pupil.'

'You know Natalya's father?' Janet asked, shocked at what Jimmy had said.

'Yes, we've come over from Spain to check on the family's security arrangements at their establishments in London. I don't know if you've heard but there have been some significant security problems in Spain.'

'I don't know anything about that.'

'We've arranged to meet Natalya here to discuss things further. Isn't she here yet?'

'No, she should be but she hasn't turned up yet.'

'Well can you let us in? Her family won't be very happy if you don't co-operate with us. You've nothing to worry about. I was quite impressed with the way you dealt with me last time.'

'Well, I suppose...OK. You had better come in.'

Janet stepped back and allowed Dan and Jimmy in. She shut and bolted the door and led them to the same office that Jimmy had been in previously. As she went round her desk, Jimmy noted how tight her jeans were over her pert bottom but his feelings towards her had completely changed after what he had seen on the DVD. As Dan had with Natalya, he felt foolish that he had been taken in by her on the previous visit and considered her to be a 'nice girl'.

Dan was meeting her for the first time and as far as he was concerned, she was just a slag and a child molester.

After Janet had sat behind her desk, Dan and Jimmy sat in the only other two chairs in the room.

'Right,' Dan said, 'You're going to tell us exactly what goes on here before we go and take a look for ourselves.'

'I thought you already knew.' Janet thought for a moment. 'If you were meeting Natalya here, why didn't you say so to begin with?'

'Ah, the penny drops!' Dan said. 'Natalya won't be coming here today. Or indeed, ever again.'

'Who the hell are you? I want you to go. Now!' Janet said, unable to hide the anxiety in her voice.

'Or what? You'll call the police? I don't think so.'

'I'll call security!'

'Go ahead then.'

Janet picked up the phone and dialled two digits.

'Wayne, can you come to my office immediately?'

The three of them waited. About half a minute later, a huge man entered the room, probably about thirty, close cropped hair and tattoos down his arms. He would have looked tough to normal people but Dan and Jimmy were not normal people. They looked at each other and smiled.

'These men are leaving,' Janet said. 'See them out, Wayne.'

'We're not leaving', Dan said.

The man was stupid as well because he actually smiled at the prospect of throwing Dan and Jimmy out, wholly failing to recognise that either of them could have dealt with him with one hand tied behind their backs.

Jimmy produced coin.

'Heads or tails?' he said to Dan.

'Tails,' Dan called.

Jimmy flipped the coin.

'Over to you, then.'

Janet and Wayne were bemused by this. Dan stood up and faced Wayne who looked down at Dan with an expression on his face which suggested he was going to enjoy what followed.

'Go on, then, fat boy. Make your move,' Dan said pleasantly.

Wayne's expression turned to one of anger. He swung a large fist towards Dan who swayed out of the way and used Wayne's own momentum to snap his arm like a twig. At the same time he kicked back and down with all his weight into Wayne's right knee. There was a sickening crack but before the scream was out of Wayne's mouth, Dan swung round with his elbow wrenching Wayne's jaw out of its socket and rendering him unconscious before he crashed to the ground.

While this was going on, Janet leapt to her feet but before she could scream, Jimmy was behind her desk, seizing her by her hair and smashing her face down on the desk before pressing the barrel of the gun he had used to kill Banin against the side of her head.

'OK,' Dan said, 'My friend is going to release you and you're going to sit back down in your chair and answer our questions. If you don't, you'll end up like that.' He pointed to the unconscious Wayne whose right arm and leg were both bending the opposite way to that which they should have been.

Janet nodded and Jimmy pushed her back into her chair.

'Now, Janet, or should I say 'Candy Love', tell us about this so called school.'

Dan had noted from the DVD that 'Candy Love' was Janet's stage name for her role in the film.

'There is a school here with real pupils,' she said. 'Only it doesn't make any money. In fact it makes a loss.'

'So it's a front for Natalya Productions?'

Janet shrugged and Dan assumed that she agreed.

'So how does it work?'

'The school is closed when we're filming. The genuine students are informed by email when the school will be closed.'

'Like today?'

Janet hesitated. 'Yes, like today.'

'How long have you worked here?'

'Two years.'

'How did you get involved?'

'I've been in the industry for years. I met Natalya and she offered me a regular job at much higher pay than I could get elsewhere.'

'What industry? The child porn industry.'

'No. The adult movie industry.'

'So, straight porn rather than child porn?'

'It's hardly child porn! There's no one under about fourteen and they know what they're doing.'

'So you think it's OK to film children having under age sex?'

'The boys love it. What teenage boy wouldn't want to shag me or Natalya?'

'And the girls?'

She shrugged again.

'My uncle and his friends started shagging me when I was twelve. That's life.'

'So just because you were abused, it's OK to abuse others?'

Janet didn't reply.

'How do you recruit the kids?'

'From the Stage School. It's easy. The boys don't need much persuading and some girls would rather be stars in our movies than have no showbiz career at all. No one gets hurt.'

'You call this show business? How many are involved?'

'For obvious reasons it's a small team.'

'And they're all here today?'

Again a pause. 'Yes.'

'Shall we go and say hello then?'

Dan stood up and Jimmy led Janet over to the door. Pushing her ahead, they went down a dark corridor to another door with a combination lock on it.

'Open it!' Dan ordered.

Janet punched in the numbers and Jimmy opened the door and pushed her through it. The scene that met Dan and Jimmy sickened them. They found themselves in a large room painted black with a stage at one end. On the stage under harsh lights was a mattress with a man of about fifty taking a young teenage girl, aged no more than about thirteen or fourteen, from behind. A cameraman was filming and taking close up shots and a soundman was holding a padded boom over the action. Two other men of similar age and another young girl were waiting in the background in dressing gowns, no doubt for their turn to be filmed.

As Janet followed by Dan and Jimmy burst into the room, everyone turned to look in their direction.

'What the fuck?' shouted the cameraman, a revolting looking individual in his fifties, with a long straggly grey ponytail and tattoos which would have been more appropriate on someone over thirty years younger. 'You can't come barging in here! Janet, who the hell are these people?'

'Oh, no,' squealed the man being filmed. 'I've lost my erection now!'

Jimmy didn't hesitate. He jumped on the stage and kicked the man's legs from under him so he fell on his back.

'It's the last erection you're ever going to have!' he shouted, and proceeded to stamp as hard as he could on the man's genitals. After a while, Jimmy was fed up with man's screaming and kicked him in the head rendering him unconscious. He then grabbed the camera and smashed it on the floor before seizing the cameraman and shoving the barrel of the gun into his mouth and so far down his throat that the cameraman began to gag and struggle.

'Just say the word, Dan, and I'll blow this fucker's head off!'

Dan knew that he didn't mean it. They had agreed that unless they were faced with guns, there would be no shooting.

Dan noticed that there was a baseball bat among the many props at the side of the stage. He walked up on to the stage and looked at the scene.

'Is there somewhere to put the children for a few minutes?' he asked looking at Janet.

'There...there's a storeroom behind the stage,' she stammered.

'Take them there,' Dan ordered.

Janet ushered the two girls behind the stage, more than happy to leave the area.

'Natalya Productions is finished,' Dan said to the others, who were standing there quaking. 'Natalya herself is dead. And you all will be too if you carry on in this vile business. We will come back and find you. We should call the police but we don't want any involvement with them either. But you have to pay the price for your crimes.'

Dan seized the cameraman who Jimmy had now released and threw him unceremoniously off the stage. He then went and picked up the baseball bat. He and Jimmy jumped down from the stage and Jimmy grabbed the cameraman's right hand and held it down by the forearm on the stage. Dan then wielded the baseball bat and smashed the cameraman's hand against the wooden stage. The cameraman let out a howl of agony which Dan cut off by knocking him unconscious.

'He won't be operating a camera again,' Dan said dispassionately.

By now, the soundman and the other two performers were moaning and weeping with terror.

Dan walked up on to the stage with the bat.

'Please, please, no,' one of them men wailed.

The soundman was only about nineteen or twenty. Dan looked at him as he moaned with fear.

'Don't ever get involved with this sort of thing again,' Dan said. The boy nodded vigorously.

'Go behind the stage to the storeroom with the others.'

The boy ran off as quickly as he could. Dan turned to the other two.

'You make me sick,' he said. 'Take off your dressing gowns.'

The men hesitated but when Dan lifted the bat, they obeyed instantly. Dan looked at their puny bodies with contempt then he went round and smashed every piece of equipment he could find as he vented his anger.

'Watch them, Jimmy, for a moment.'

He then went behind the stage and found Janet, the soundman and the two young girls. He ignored the first two and addressed the girls.

'I'm not a social worker, as you may have gathered, and if you want to ruin your lives that's up to you. But do you really think this is a glamorous way to get on stage, making seedy films produced by society's scum? So other seedy men can watch you being abused and masturbate.'

He didn't know whether it did any good. The chances were it didn't. They probably came from broken homes and would end up dead, murdered or through drugs or Aids by the time they were twenty five. But it made him feel better.

He walked back on to the stage and he and Jimmy ushered the naked child abusers back down the corridor to the front door.

'I'm going to open this door and throw you out now,' Dan said. 'Don't even think about coming back for your clothes. Just run. When I leave about a minute later, if you are still in sight, you will know what to expect.' Dan held up the bat and the men cowered away.

'Understood?'

The men looked at each other and nodded.

Dan slid back the bolt and opened the door and Jimmy shoved them out into the street. They looked back briefly but seeing Dan and Jimmy in the doorway they ran down the street as fast as they could.

'I reckon you let them off lightly,' Jimmy said. 'You should have used the bat on their balls!'

'I was going to. But they're such pathetic creatures. After smashing the cameraman's hand, I just couldn't face doing it to all of them. Maybe I'm going soft.'

Chapter Forty Two

On their way to the underground station, Dan and Jimmy saw the first editions of the London Evening Standard being stacked up at a newsvendor's stall. The headline read '*Gun battle in Docklands leaves four dead*'. They both picked up a copy to read on their journey back to Canary Wharf.

The article described how a gun battle between rival gangs had taken place outside a luxury block of flats. Four men, white and believed to be of East European origin were found dead at the scene. Three weapons were recovered. The men had carried no identity and police were appealing for witnesses. The paper had managed to speak to a couple of residents in Dan's block who spoke of hearing some loud cracks followed by the sound of four or five loud gunshots. The reporter had correctly surmised that the initial cracks had come from one or more silenced weapons. He also pointed out that this had not been the more common form of gun battle in London between feuding gangs on South London housing estates but appeared to be evidence of London's infiltration by violent East

European gangs. He asked what the police and the mayor intended to do about such an outrage.

After picking up Dan's car from the hotel car park in Canary Wharf, Dan and Jimmy were not surprised to find the area outside his block still crawling with police, press and onlookers. The car was stopped by the police and Dan identified himself as a resident in the block. After explaining that he and his colleague had been away for the night on business and therefore had not heard or seen anything, he was waved through down a section of the road which had not been cordoned off and which had been left open for residents to enter their car park. Dan noticed that save for a narrow path to enable residents to have access, the whole of the forecourt had also been cordoned off.

Back in Spain, Petrov had been furious when Banin had failed to telephone him with a report on his progress the previous evening. When he failed to ring in the morning, Petrov rang Banin's mobile. It rang for a long time and Petrov was about to disconnect, when it was finally answered. Petrov waited for Banin's voice but no one spoke. Petrov was immediately suspicious and continued to wait. Eventually, a voice spoke in English.

'Who is this?'

Petrov said nothing.

'This is Detective Superintendent Robinson...' the voice continued, but Petrov disconnected at once.

He rushed into Viktor Durchenko's study and told his boss what had happened.

'Let's put Sky News on,' Viktor said. 'It looks like Banin is either dead or has been arrested.'

It did not take them long to find out what had happened as it was the lead news item and was being covered in depth.

'I think we can safely assume that the four dead men are all ours,' Petrov said.

'For God's sake!' Viktor raged, 'Do we employ idiots? Has living down here made them all soft? How can four men, including two former Spetnaz operatives, all get themselves killed?'

Petrov did not reply. This was the second time that they had located the two Englishmen and the second time that his men had come off worst. This time with all four dead. He was still confident that sooner or later the Englishmen's luck would run out but at what cost? They had had to send Georgy to Moscow to try to stem the growing rumours there that the Durchenkos were losing their grip on things. Apart from Arkady's death, news of what had been happening in Spain had reached Moscow and some of the rival gangs, particularly the Chechens, had begun to take liberties that previously would have been unthinkable. He would rather have gone himself to reinforce the family's control over things but Viktor had insisted that Petrov remain in Spain until Green and his companion had been dealt with.

Viktor picked up the phone on his desk and dialled a number. When there was no reply, he slammed the phone down again.

'I can't get hold of Natalya,' he said. 'She's not answering her mobile.'

'We've no reason to believe that just because Green has returned to London he has gone after Natalya,' Petrov said. 'Natalya lives under a different name and no one outside the family has any idea that Natalya Productions is one of our interests. But if we haven't got hold of her by this evening, we could tell Georgy to come back tomorrow via London to check on her.'

'Is that wise, sending Georgy to London with just one bodyguard accompanying him, while Green is there?'

'Green won't be there tomorrow.'

'How do you know that?'

'He will be on his way back here. He now knows we know where he lives and are prepared to go after him there. Whatever he had intended before, he knows that his only hope is to finish what he started. He can't afford to wait until we send another team to find him.'

'So what do you suggest?'

'We have no choice but to wait until either one of our contacts down here locates him or he shows his hand. We have the airports and stations covered but I'm sure he will drive as we cannot cover every road in Spain. He will need a base and we have every hotel in the area covered and will hear if anyone matching their description tries to rent an apartment or villa. Sooner or later, he will be found and dealt with.'

'You'd stake your life on that?'

'I may have to!'

Dan and Jimmy took the early morning Eurostar to Paris and Dan was relieved when they arrived at the long stay car park at Charles de Gaulle Airport and found the black Range Rover where they had left it, together with their mini arsenal of weapons. After the incident with the Durchenkos' men, Dan and Jimmy had felt naked when they had had to dump the Russian's gun in a waste bin near St Pancras International Station and the magazine in a different bin just in case it fell into the wrong hands. However, they had seen nothing suspicious at the station and nothing at the Gare du Nord at the other end.

They were in no hurry and decided to take a leisurely trip back down to Spain as first, they did not want to get stopped for speeding in a stolen car full of weapons by either the French or Spanish police and secondly, they knew that the

Durchenkos would be expecting them and would be at their most alert on the next couple of days after the shoot out outside Dan's apartment block. Besides, they had not yet worked out where they were going to stay when they reached the Costa del Sol, although Dan said that he might know somewhere.

Chapter Forty Three

Georgy and his bodyguard arrived at London Heathrow at about noon, by which time Dan and Jimmy were already in Paris. As soon as he had cleared customs, he rang his father to be told that not only had there still been no contact with Natalya, but also there was no reply at the stage school. Had there been any contact with Natalya, he would have stayed at the airport and taken the next flight to Malaga. He had no particular wish to go and see his sister. The two of them had never really got on and Natalya had always thought herself to be superior to Georgy. While she had been getting the best education that money could buy in Moscow, he had left school as soon as he could, preferring to get involved with the more seedy and violent side of the business. He had taken great pleasure at the age of sixteen in hanging an old tyre around the neck of one of his father's rivals and then setting light to it and watch the man die in agony.

For all her airs and graces, Natalya was now the one involved in the most seedy side of the business of all, in Georgy's view, though he had to admit that her brand of pornography was extremely profitable. He also had to admit that

Natalya was as ruthless as any other member of the family. When one of her young 'starlets' had had second thoughts about what he had been doing and threatened to tell his parents, Natalya had sent her tame Bulgarian minder to burn down the family house with them all in it.

Since it was the middle of the day, he decided to visit the school first as he was sure that somebody would be there and probably Natalya herself, particularly if they were filming. He too thought it unlikely that Green would have found out about the school let alone what really went on there. He was therefore surprised when found police tape across the door. He walked on wondering what to do when he saw a pub a little further down the street.

Georgy may have been cruel and sadistic but he was good looking and could be charming when he wanted. He also spoke fluent English without much trace of an accent. He told his thuggish looking companion to wait outside and went into the pub. The pub was not very busy as by this time, local workers were making their way back to work. He sat at the bar and ordered a pint of bitter from the pretty barmaid, whose accent suggested she came from Poland or the Czech Republic or somewhere like that.

He caught her eye and smiled and before long they were making small talk. He could see that she fancied him but sadly, he didn't have the time to take it any further.

'What's happened up at the stage school?' he asked, after a while. 'I see there's police tape over the door and it appears to be locked up?'

'Oh God, there was a real bust up there yesterday,' the girl said. 'There must have been a big fight because three people were taken out on stretchers with very serious injuries. And guess what, I didn't see it because I was behind the bar here, but customers told me that two men were thrown out of the place stark naked and ran down the road past the pub! Anyway, the police were called and the place has been locked up since then.'

'Any idea what it was about?' Georgy asked.

'Maybe it was some sort of extortion racket. You know, the school refused to pay and some gang decided to make an example of them.'

'Do you pay extortion money here?' Georgy asked.

'Well, no, not as far as I know.'

It was inconceivable that Natalya would not have reported it to the family if some idiots were trying to extort money from her, Georgy thought. This was not looking good. He did not believe in co-incidences. He left the pub and telephoned his father. Viktor told him to go straight to Natalya's apartment in Chelsea. He had a key so could let himself in. But Viktor told him not to approach the block until Igor had thoroughly checked out the neighbourhood.

Forty minutes later, Igor entered the pub on the corner of Natalya's road. Georgy was waiting for him at a window table.

'It all seems clear,' Igor said. 'No sign of the police or anyone watching the premises. I let myself into the foyer and waited in the stairwell but nobody followed me in.'

'Ok, let's go,' Georgy said.

The two of them walked down to Natalya's block and took the lift to the top floor. Georgy stood back while Igor unlocked the door of the apartment. They immediately saw the blood on the floor leading from the hall into the living room. The man in black was still lying face down on the living room floor with a huge patch of dried blood on the carpet beneath him. Georgy used his foot to tilt the man's face towards him. He recognised him as Natalya's Bulgarian minder.

Igor went back into the hall to check the rest of the apartment.

'Oh shit!' Georgy heard him say. 'Georgy! You'd better come here!'

Georgy walked into the bedroom. Natalya was lying naked on her stomach diagonally across the bed, her right arm dangling over the side of the bed. He knew it was her from the tattoo in the small of her back despite the fact that half her head was missing and seemingly spattered all over the wall behind the bed.

For the first time in his life, Georgy experienced an emotion which until then had been completely alien to him. Not sorrow or anguish or even horror at finding his sister's body like that but fear, despite the fact that he was in no immediate danger. First his brother, then his uncle and now his sister, not to mention all the other men who had died in Spain, Moscow and now London. Who the hell were these two men who seemed to be destroying everyone and everything in their path? What monsters had Alexei unleashed on them?

Chapter Forty Four

By the time Georgy was making his gruesome discovery, Dan and Jimmy were halfway through France and at the end of the day checked into a hotel in Perpignan near the Spanish border. While they were having a drink on the terrace, Dan used one of their mobile phones to ring Luis Mendes.

'I take it you are not in Spain?' Luis asked.

'What makes you say that?' Dan asked.

'Because it's been so quiet! Apart of course from the Ortega incident.'

Luis told Dan about the murder of Fernando Ortega, his wife and two of his men and how excited Jose Valdez had been to find a known associate of the Durchenkos dead at the scene.

'It came to nothing of course,' Luis continued, 'Jose was humiliated by his superiors and prevented from carrying on any meaningful investigation into the link. But that may help you.'

'Why?'

'Because the more his superiors frustrate his attempts to bring down the Durchenkos, the less likely he is to pursue someone with the same aims notwithstanding the flagrant breaches of the law!'

'Anything else I should know?'

'Only that the Durchenkos are doing everything they can to find you. Be very careful when you return as there are eyes and ears everywhere! I take it you are going to return...?'

'Oh, yes, we'll be back very soon!'

'By the way, news has reached us down here about Arkady's unfortunate demise in Moscow. I suppose it's just a coincidence that that should happen while you're out of Spain...'

'Of course.'

Dan ended the conversation and relayed what Luis had said to Jimmy.

'They raped and tortured Ortega's wife before killing them,' Dan said, 'But apparently Ortega managed to kill one of their top enforcers before he died.'

'I assume they realised where we had got our weapons and were either seeking retribution or seeing if he knew where we were.'

'Probably both.'

There was silence for a moment.

'Best not to dwell on it,' Jimmy said. 'Ortega was no saint. He supplied arms to criminals for a living. He was happy to do business with us.'

'And he knew exactly what we were going to do with the weapons.'

'Any more thoughts as to where we might stay when we get down there?'

'There is one person who might be able to suggest somewhere.'

'Mendez?'

'No. I don't want to involve him. He's done enough for us. He is after all a former police officer and one of his best friends is investigating what we've been doing!'

'Who then?'

Dan looked through his wallet and took out a business card. He then picked up the phone.

'Who are you phoning now?' Jimmy asked.

'I'm going to try to arrange a date,' Dan replied, and dialled a number.

'Goth Heaven,' a female voice said, when the call was answered.

'Is that Dana?' Dan asked.

'Yeah,' the voice said, 'who is this?'

'You may not remember me but I called into your shop some time ago now looking for a former employee of yours, Sandra Wilson.'

'Oh, I remember you all right. What can I do for you, Mr Private Investigator?'

'Well, er, you said that if I was returning to the area, I should give you a call.'

'I did indeed. But I didn't really expect to 'ear from you.'

'Well, I'm coming back to the area in a couple of days with a colleague to continue my investigation and I just wondered if you'd like to meet up?'

'Your investigation into the whereabouts of Sandra Wilson?' There was a hint of sarcasm in the girl's voice.

'Well, I couldn't really tell you everything. The investigation is a little more complicated than that.'

'You don't say!'

'Look, I'm sorry. Maybe I shouldn't have phoned.'

The girl laughed.

'Don't worry, I'm only teasing you again. I don't care about your poxy investigation. It wasn't that I was interested in!'

'Ok. So you'd like to meet up?'

'When are you arriving?'

'The day after tomorrow. Thursday.'

'OK. I close the boutique at nine. Why don't you come then?'

'That's fine. Er, there's one other thing you may be able to help with.'

'Go on.'

'My colleague and I need somewhere to stay and I wondered if you knew anywhere discreet? Maybe someone who could put us up. We'd pay well as it's all on expenses.'

There was a pause.

'Look, mister, you ring me up out of the blue with some cock and bull story about an investigation. That's fine if you just want a date. But now you're asking me if I know somewhere discreet you can stay. I don't even know your name! What's wrong with a quiet hotel?'

'You're right, of course. I shouldn't have asked. My name's Dan by the way.'

'For all I know you're drug dealers or something.'

'I promise you we are not drug dealers or criminals.' Dan wondered whether Jose Valdez would have agreed with the latter. 'The truth is that we are investigating a criminal gang and that's why we need somewhere discreet.'

'Supposing I could find somewhere. How much are you prepared to pay?'

'Say 250 euros a night for the two of us? Cash.'

There was another pause.

'OK. To be honest, I could do with the money. I've got a spare room in my apartment. Would that suit you?'

'That would be perfect! So we'll see you at your boutique on Thursday then.'

'Hold on. Let's just get one thing straight. You keep going on about 'we'. I do most things but I don't do threesomes!'

'Of course. You will find my colleague is very straight laced!'

Chapter Forty Five

The whole family, or what was left of them, and Petrov had assembled in Viktor's study to listen to Georgy's report as soon as he had arrived back. He had of course telephoned as soon as he had discovered Natalya's body but he now filled in the details.

Most mothers would weep on hearing that their daughter had been killed but Irina was not most mothers. She had not wept when she had first heard of Natalya's death and she did not weep now. She sat there stony faced and waited patiently while Georgy gave a detailed description of what he had found out about the goings on at Natalya Productions and what he had found at Natalya's apartment. When he had finished, she was the first to speak. She normally would not dream of interfering in her husband's affairs for fear of feeling the back of his hand. But nothing was going to hold her back now. She stood up and looked at the four men in turn, Viktor, Sergei, Georgy and of course, Petrov.

'I cannot believe that you have allowed this family and our businesses to be decimated, our children slaughtered, our loyal soldiers slaughtered. We're becoming a laughing stock! Two men and you can't stop them!' she raged.

Viktor slammed his fist down on his desk.

'Shut up, woman!' he shouted. 'How dare you talk to me like that!'

Irina walked over to his desk and leant towards him.

'I have never defied you before, Viktor Durchenko,' she said, 'but you know I'm right! You need to stop this now. If you don't, our rivals will sense our weakness and we will be finished!'

He stared at her. The other three men sat motionless. He wanted to smash his fist into her ugly face. But he knew she was right.

'We're doing everything we can,' he eventually said.

The tension in the room eased but Irina would not let them off the hook.

'Well it's not enough is it?' she said. She then rounded on Petrov. 'And what about you, Vitaly? Our master tactician. The man who strikes fear into our enemies. They don't seem very frightened of you, do they?'

'We will catch them, Irina,' he replied. 'It's only a matter of time.'

'You've been saying that for ages. They are not supermen. They bleed like everyone else. I expect you to take them alive because I personally want to cut their hearts out!'

With that, she stormed out of the room.

Dan and Jimmy spent the following night at a small hotel on the outskirts of Madrid and timed their journey so that they arrived in Puerto Banus at just after eight thirty in the evening. Dan felt tense as he drove into the town not so much because they were entering a danger area but because this was where it had all begun with Tom's brutal murder. He drove into the underground car park under the main square behind the waterfront and parked. Jimmy opened the glove department and took out the two Glocks. He offered one to Dan. Dan shook his head.

'We have to look like tourists,' he said. 'It's far too hot for jackets. Where are we going to conceal them?'

Dan was wearing a polo shirt and lightweight trousers. Jimmy had a loose fitting short sleeved shirt on.

'If you switched to a shirt like mine, you could stick it down your waistband.'

'This girl thinks she's going on a date. What if she puts her arm around me?'

'Well, we're not going out there unarmed.'

Jimmy reached into the back of the car and retrieved a shoulder bag of the type tourists often use to carry their cameras and valuables.

'I'll put them both in here and leave you two free to put your arms round each other!'

They agreed that Dan would go to the shop alone and say that Jimmy was parking their car. Jimmy would watch from a discreet distance.

Dan put on a pair of sunglasses and a baseball cap and took the exit which he judged to be nearest to the boutique. Jimmy followed about fifty yards behind. When he approached the shop, Dan took off the hat and sunglasses. He rolled up the hat and stuffed it in his trousers pocket and hooked the sunglasses in the neck of his polo shirt. Jimmy sat on a bench in the square and watched as Dan entered the shop.

Dana and a young girl, who Dan assumed was her new assistant, appeared to be tidying up ready to close. Dana looked over and smiled when she saw Dan.

'Perfect timing,' she said. 'Penny, you can go now. I'll finish up here.'

Penny picked up her bag from behind the counter and gave Dan a shy smile as she left.

'See you tomorrow, Dana,' she called out happily.

'Yeah, if we're still in business,' Dana said after she'd gone.

'Things not going too well?' Dan asked.

'Haven't you 'eard? There's a recession on. Particularly in Spain!'

'There still seem to be loads of tourists about.'

'There are, but they're not spending the money like they used to. Particularly on leather fetish goods! I'm not sure how long I'll be able to keep Penny on. She was so glad to get the job. Anyway, you've haven't come to hear about my problems. I hope you've come to take my mind off them.'

She walked over and stood on her toes to kiss Dan. Despite her high heels, he towered over her. She was much as Dan recalled. About thirty; bleached blond swept back hair, cut short and held in place by lashings of hairspray; heavy purple eye make up which extended in a line about half an inch beyond her eyes, ornate silver earrings and purple lipstick. She was wearing a tight black vest over her ample bust, a short black leather skirt and black ankle boots. Just the sort of person to be seen with, Dan thought, when you're trying not to attract attention!

'So where's this friend?' she said. 'I was only kidding, you know.'

'About what?'

'About not doing threesomes!'

She then burst out laughing.

'Your face! You may be a big tough guy but you're so easy to wind up!'

Dan laughed too.

'He's just parking the car. I said we'd meet him out in the square.'

'OK, then, let's go. I'll just lock up.'

After she had locked the door, Dana wasted no time in taking Dan's arm.

'Dan and Dana,' she said, smiling, 'It's got a nice ring about it!'

Jimmy was surprised on two counts as he saw them walking across towards the square. Dan had given him some idea as to what to expect but he hadn't expected Dana to be such a sexy piece of work. But what surprised him more was to see Dan laughing and joking with her, clearly enjoying her company. Understandably, Dan had been a bit uptight about things since he had first approached Jimmy. Jimmy would have been too if his son had been murdered. But Dan looked genuinely relaxed with Dana and did not appear to be acting.

'Crikey!' Dana said, after Dan had introduced her to Jimmy. 'Another muscleman! I'll certainly feel safe with you two about!'

'Shall we find somewhere to eat?' Dan said.

'Do you guys want to dump your stuff in my flat first?' Dana asked.

'How far away is it?' Dan asked.

'It's that one up there. Fifth floor,' she replied, pointing up at a flat in the large block which overlooked the square.

Dan and Jimmy were impressed. The flats had large balconies with trailing plants hanging down. Dan had noticed the block when he had last been there and admired the flats and how well kept they appeared to be.

'Where's your car?' Dana asked.

'In the car park under here,' Dan replied.

'Well, you can put it in the block's underground car park. I have a space down there but don't have a car myself.'

They drove around to the block's car park and Dana used a small fob on her keyring to open the gate. After they had parked, Dana gave Dan the fob.

'Here, you'd better have this,' she said. 'I hardly ever use it. But don't forget to give it back when you leave.'

They took the lift up to the fifth floor and Dana led the way to her flat. It proved to be as impressive as it had looked from the outside. It had spacious well proportioned rooms and a large terrace looking out over the waterfront shops and bars towards the sea.

'Wow, do you own this place?' Jimmy asked.

'That's a good question,' Dana replied. 'It was owned by a middle eastern guy I used to live with for about five years. He was very rich and set me up in the boutique. But he eventually left me for a teenager and returned to Dubai. I think he felt guilty because he said I could keep the flat. I 'aven't seen or heard from him for over three years. But there's no paperwork to prove it's mine even though all the bills are now in my name. So I guess I'd have trouble selling it. But at least I can live here rent free!'

She showed Dan and Jimmy the spare room. She noticed them look at each other when they saw that there was only a double bed in the room.

'I can sleep on the sofa,' Jimmy said.

Dana looked at Dan and smiled cheekily.

'That may not be necessary,' she said. 'We can work out the sleeping arrangements later.'

She offered them a drink.

'Aren't we going out to eat?' Dan asked.

'That's already sorted. I've booked a table at a restaurant on the waterfront for ten. No one eats here much before then.'

This worried Dan. He had been hoping to go to a discreet restaurant away from the crowds. But then again, he thought, sometimes the best place to hide is in a crowd. They would be looking for two men, not two men and a woman. And as far as he was aware, they only knew what he looked like, not Jimmy. Then Dana said something which put Dan further at ease.

'The table's booked for four.'

'Four?' Dan replied.

'I told you I didn't do threesomes! We don't want Jimmy sitting there like a gooseberry. When you said you were with a colleague, I asked one of my friends to join us. I can always cancel her if you prefer....'

'No, no, no,' Jimmy said quickly. 'That's absolutely fine!'

'You don't mind a blind date then?'

301

'Hopefully it's your twin sister!'

Dana giggled.

'You are a cheeky boy aren't you? She's nothing like me but I'm sure you won't be disappointed.'

Chapter Forty Six

And Jimmy wasn't disappointed. The three of them arrived at the restaurant first and Dan chose a seat facing the wall, leaving Jimmy with the task of looking out for trouble. What Jimmy did see after about ten minutes was an extremely attractive woman making her way over to their table. She was probably in her late thirties, possibly early forties, but she had a fine figure shown off by a long slinky brown dress matching her hair with a long slit in it and high heeled sandal type shoes.

Dana had been right. She was nothing like her. She was introduced as Elaine and she too had a fashion boutique, though as she was quick to point out, her clothes were rather more conventional than Dana's.

It occurred to Jimmy that maybe he should have been paired up with the girl who came from Canvey Island and Dan should have been with the posh totty but he certainly wasn't going to complain. Elaine proved to be good company and by the end of the meal, he had her to himself as Dana seemed determined to monopolise Dan.

Elaine also proved to be very observant. Jimmy was professional enough despite the company and the drink to keep a close watch on the comings and goings at the restaurant and anyone who seemed to be paying them undue attention. Fortunately, the only attention appeared to be from men looking at Dana and Elaine rather than Dan and Jimmy.

'I'm not boring you, am I, Jimmy?' Elaine asked, with a flirtatious smile. 'Only you seem to spend a lot of the time looking around the restaurant.'

Oh, no, not at all!' Jimmy replied. 'I'm just not used to this sort of place. I'm just fascinated by the people here. I'm sorry if I appeared rude.'

'Well, I'll have to see what I can do to make you pay more attention to me.'

Until then, Elaine had been careful to keep the slit in her dress closed with the material held between her thighs but she opened them slightly and the slit opened as the material slid down the outside of each leg. Jimmy could not help staring as Elaine's legs were revealed right up to the top of the slit which only ended about three inches from her crutch.

'Well, that got your attention!' she said. 'That's the trouble with dresses like this. You have to hold them together when you're sitting down or you can end up looking indecent!'

She pulled the left side of the dress which was visible to other diners back over her knee but made no attempt to cover her right leg.

'You can be indecent with me anytime!' Jimmy replied.

Elaine raised an eyebrow and held eye contact with him.

'What shall we do now?' she asked, addressing the others as well.

'Let's get the bill and have coffee at my place,' Dana suggested.

Everyone agreed and Dan settled the bill.

On the way back to Dana's flat, she and Dan led the way with Dana again holding on to Dan's arm. Jimmy put his arm around Elaine and confirmed what he had already worked out that she was not wearing a bra.

Back at the flat, Dana asked if everyone wanted coffee.

Elaine looked at her as if she was mad.

'Stuff coffee,' she said, and led Jimmy into the spare bedroom.

Dana walked up to Dan and put her arms around him.

'I told you we could work out the sleeping arrangements later. It looks like you're in with me. Unless of course, you'd prefer the sofa...'

Dana took Dan by the hand and led him to her bedroom. He was stunned when he entered the room. Whereas the other rooms he had seen were tastefully decorated and furnished, this room had been kitted out in the style of Dana's boutique. The walls and floor were black. The ceiling

305

consisted of vast mirrors. The room was dominated by a huge bed with an iron frame with a shiny purple bedspread and purple satin pillows. There was a purple velvet chaise longue and a couple of other similarly upholstered chairs. Purple and gold brocade curtains were drawn. There was a large ornate dressing table on which were tall gold coloured candelabras with purple candles as well as perfume bottles and a collection of sex toys. At least, Dan assumed that they were sex toys as he had never seen most of them before.

Dana walked over and lit the candles. She turned off the subdued lighting that she had switched on when they had entered the room. The candles flickered and produced a ghostly effect reflected in the overhead mirrors. She then walked over to Dan, who appeared to have been rendered speechless.

'Well, what did you expect?' she said softly. 'You must have realised that I don't do vanilla!'

She pulled her vest over head and threw it to one side. She then unzipped and pushed down the leather skirt, revealing that she wasn't wearing any underwear. She left the stilettoed ankle boots on and then started to undress Dan. She helped him off with his polo shirt, pausing to look at and gently finger the numerous scars from bullets and other weapons inflicted all those years ago.

'I knew you were a dangerous man from the first time you walked into my shop. But something told me you're a good guy. I hope I'm right.'

She then led him over to the bed and made him sit on the edge while she removed his socks and shoes. She then pulled him up again and undid his trousers, pushing them and his boxer shorts down to the ground. He stepped out of them. She looked down at him and smiled.

'My, my,' she said. 'You're going to have to be patient though.'

Dan thought back to when he had been in a similar situation with Natalya and the contrast between then and now. Why didn't he just grab Dana and push her down on the bed? But Dana had taken complete control and he felt powerless to resist. She gently pushed him back on the bed on his back and arranged him so his head was on the pillows. She then knelt between his legs and slowly moved each of her hands up his legs, gently touching him there but continuing her journey with her hands up his body. She lifted his arms above his head. Now she's going to get on me, Dan thought. But she didn't. She moved up his body until she was sitting astride his chest. She then reached out to the side and moved her hands slowly up his right arm until it was fully stretched out. He then heard a click and suddenly realised that she had handcuffed his hand to the iron bedhead. His first reaction was to resist. He pulled at the restraint but Dana lay down on top of him and whispered in his ear.

'Just relax. Trust me. You won't regret it.'

She caressed his chest with one hand and moved her other hand down and gently stroked him it. He stopped struggling and amazed himself by allowing her to handcuff his other hand to the bedframe as well. She then got off the bed and came back with two long pieces of chiffon like material. She pushed his legs apart and tied each of his ankles to the bottom of the bedframe. She then put a blindfold on him.

'Now', she whispered in his ear seductively, 'enjoy!'

They woke up at about ten. Dana had eventually released him and the rest of the night had been spent more conventionally. She made some coffee and told Dan that she had to open up the shop at eleven. She left a key on the dressing table so he could come and go as he pleased.

'I must give you some money,' Dan said.

'What, for services rendered?'

'No, no, I didn't mean that. For the rent.' Dan was embarrassed.

Dana laughed. 'I know what you meant,' she said. 'I'm only teasing you again!'

Dan counted out 1750 euros and handed them to Dana.

'Here's a week's worth,' he said. 'I don't know how long we'll be staying. We may have to leave quickly.'

Dana took the money.

'After a night like that, it's quite a turn on to be handed a wad of cash. Make sure you don't leave without saying goodbye. Mr Private Investigator!'

After, Dana had left, Dan went out into the living room to plan the day. Jimmy walked in looking a little groggy.

'All right?' Jimmy said. 'Good night?'

'Yes, fine,' Dan replied a little defensively, having no intention of going into detail with Jimmy as to what he'd been up to. 'You?'

'Yeah, great.'

'I assume Elaine's gone?'

'Oh, yeah, she didn't stay the night. She left after a couple of hours to relieve her babysitter and feed her cats! So what's the plan then?'

'How do you fancy robbing a casino?'

'Now you're talking!'

Chapter Forty Seven

Dan and Jimmy looked like typical tourists as they walked along the beach dressed in swimming trunks, T shirts, dark glasses and in Dan's case a baseball hat. Jimmy carried a beach bag ostensibly containing a beach towel but what was well concealed was the fact that it was wrapped around their handguns. They had taken a bus to El Rosario, an upmarket residential area about five miles east of Marbella and walked down to the beach from the dual carriageway where the bus had dropped them.

It was a hot day and there were a lot of people out sunbathing, swimming and walking up and down the beach by the water's edge. After a few minutes, they saw a modern, white rectangular building with a flat roof and a terrace and swimming pool separating it from the beach.

'I think that's it,' Dan said.

According to Luis Mendez's file, the casino had opened about ten years previously. It had been owned by a Spanish family but had changed hands three years ago. It was now registered to an offshore company. It had come to Luis's attention that a large proportion of the clientele was Russian as were some of the members of staff.

Luis had decided to make some enquiries and eventually traced a member of the Spanish family who had been prepared to speak to him on a confidential basis. He had confirmed what Luis had suspected. The sale had been a forced one for a knockdown price. The family had been approached and offered what they considered to be half its actual value. They were told that it was in their own interests to accept the offer or the consequences would be severe. Initially, the family was outraged and threatened to go to the police but they had soon changed their tune when one of the younger female members had been badly beaten and raped in her own home and told by a man who fitted Petrov's description that if the offer was not accepted in twenty four hours, the price would go down by ten per cent every day thereafter and members of the family would start dying.

'It doesn't look like a casino from here,' Jimmy said.

'Apparently it's very discreet and for high rollers only.'

'So there will be plenty of cash around?'

'I would imagine so. Let's take a closer look.'

Just to one side of the building was an attractive looking 'chingurito', a beachside bar and restaurant of the type seen along the whole of the coast in that area of Spain. Access to it was from the beach or the road leading down to the beach. Dan and Jimmy walked across the terrace to the road behind from where they could walk around the casino. There was a discreet sign referring to the Sunshine Casino and Beach Club, an entrance which fronted the road and a car park which was half full. Dan assumed that at busy times, the customers would park in the road leading down to the premises or the small road running parallel to the beach to the east of the casino leading to the beachside villas.

'Why don't you go and check it out, opening hours and such like?' Dan suggested. 'I'll order you a beer at the beach bar.'

A few minutes later, Jimmy joined Dan at the beach bar. He had a leaflet with him and handed it to Dan.

'The casino is open from midday till 4.00 am,' he said. 'The beach club is open from ten but only to members. You don't have to be a member to go to the casino. Entry for non members is fifty euros and the dress code is jacket and trousers. The girl I spoke to said some people dress a bit more formally at night but as long as you look reasonably smart they will let you in. You do however have to show ID.'

'Security?'

'Difficult to tell from the foyer but there are two guys manning a metal detector and then there is a staircase leading up to where I assume the casino is, with the beach club on the ground floor.'

'What do you reckon then?'

Jimmy shrugged. 'Well, they're going to be on the lookout for you, aren't they? So far as we know, they don't know who I am yet. Why don't I go there this evening as a punter and take a look inside. There are bound to be cameras everywhere. We need to work out how to get you in undetected and of course, these little babies.' He tapped the side of the beach bag with his foot. 'You can then have a nice romantic evening with the lovely Dana.'

'No way! We don't know for certain they haven't identified you. I will be outside with the car. In fact I can have dinner here from where I can just about see what cars come down the road leading to the beach. I will give you one and a half hours exactly from the time you step inside the door. If you're not back by then, I'm coming in with enough metal to blow the detector's fuse!'

Jimmy laughed. 'Of course, I'll have to look like a genuine punter.'

'I'll give you a couple of thousand euros to play with. Try not to blow it all at once and make sure you don't win!'

'What? You've got to be kidding!'

'No, I'm serious. The one thing casinos don't like is people who win. If you start getting lucky you will draw attention to yourself and the guys monitoring the cameras will be having a very close look at you.'

'Yeah, I guess you're right. I'll console myself with the thought of what we're going to take from them next time.'

'If we can find a way to do it.'

'Trust me, Dan. I will find a way. I'm not missing this opportunity!'

Later that evening, Jimmy was back well within the hour and a half. He joined Dan at his table on the terrace and ordered a beer and a plate of Spaghetti Bolognese when the waiter came over.

'I only lost five hundred euros!' he said.

'I take it you had no problems then?'

'No. No one seemed to pay me much attention. It wasn't particularly crowded but there were quite a few people there. I spoke to one guy at one of the tables who said the busiest time was about midnight when people came in after dining out. But Luis was right when he referred to high rollers. My two grand was like chicken feed to most of the punters there! People were changing wads of five hundred euro notes for chips and betting thousands on every roll of the wheel!'

'So plenty of cash about?'

'Oh yes. Some of it Middle Eastern as well as Russian.'

'And the security?'

'Discreet but fairly heavy. There are cameras everywhere and there's a balcony which looks down on the casino floor. Every so often a couple of tough looking guys walk round it and have a good look down on what is going on.'

'Can we do it?'

'It won't be easy. But yes, we can.'

Jimmy then proceeded to tell Dan what he had in mind.

Dan could have done without another night of kinky sex with Dana and would happily have substituted himself for the more than willing Jimmy. But he did not want to offend his temporary landlady and consoled himself with the thought that it was just another of those things he would have to put up with for the sake of the mission.

Chapter Forty Eight

On the following day, he and Jimmy finalised their plans. They debated at length the best time to hit the casino. During the day there would be less customers about but that would make them, and in particular Dan, more conspicuous. Further, if the proceeds from the night before had been banked, there could be far less cash about. The best time for cash would be after midnight but the casino would be at its most crowded then and that could hinder them and also pose a risk to customers if anything went wrong. In the event, they decided to go in that evening at the roughly same time Jimmy had gone in the previous evening, at about nine.

Dan dropped Jimmy off and parked the Range Rover around the corner from the casino in the road running parallel with the beach facing away from the casino.

Jimmy entered the casino after paying the entrance fee and passing through the metal detectors. He purchased a thousand euros worth of chips and sat down at a roulette table and started playing. At about nine twenty, he pocketed his remaining chips and made his way to the gents toilets off a small corridor at the

north western corner of the building. He ignored
the urinals and went to the last cubicle and locked
himself in. Behind the toilet was a window which
only opened about three inches before being held
by a metal stay. Jimmy opened it as far as it
would go and then unlocked the door to check
that no one else had come into the toilets.
Satisfied he was alone, he locked himself in
again, wrapped his jacket around his left hand and
wrist and then immediately smashed the flat of
his hand against the window frame. It was the
sort of blow he would have used to drive a man's
nasal bone into his brain and, as he had
anticipated, the metal stay gave way with a loud
crack and the window opened fully. Fortunately
the glass did not break so he did not need the
protection provided by his jacket. He put his
jacket back on and took out a mobile phone on to
which he had earlier download a flashlight app.
At precisely nine thirty he held up the phone and
flashed the light once.

Dan was hiding in the bushes on the other side
of the car park looking up at the window. When
he saw the flash of light, he checked that the car
park was clear and hurried across it. He was
dressed in a lightweight white jump suit with a
white rucksack on his back. In his hand, he held a
rope with one end secured to a metal hook. He
stood back from the sheer white wall and threw

the hook up and towards the open window. Fortunately his aim was true.

Jimmy was standing to one side of the window pressed against the side wall of the cubicle so as not to be hit by the heavy metal hook but, anticipating its arrival, he managed to half catch it and prevent it clattering into the ceramic bowl of the toilet and making too much of a noise. He immediately secured it, waved out of the window to signal to Dan and within seconds Dan appeared at the window. Jimmy helped to pull him up, pulled up the rope behind him and closed the window.

'We must stop meeting in toilets!' he whispered to Dan. 'People will get the wrong idea!'

Dan shrugged off the rucksack and removed his jumpsuit. Under it, he was dressed in a smart jacket and trousers. He also took off his white trainers and put on a pair of black loafers which he removed from the rucksack. He then removed the Glocks from the rucksack, handed one to Jimmy with a spare magazine and tucked the other into his waistband.

At that moment, they heard someone enter the toilets. They kept silent and listened while they heard a tap running, a drier operating for about twenty seconds and then the door opening again. Jimmy opened the door gently and checked that the coast was clear.

Dan went over to the mirror, put on a pair of spectacles with clear glass in them and studied his appearance.

'I don't fancy you with a beard,' Jimmy said. Earlier that day, they had visited a theatrical costumiers and bought the glasses and a short false beard for Dan.

'I'm relieved to hear it,' Dan replied. 'I think I look rather cool.' He bundled up the jumpsuit, rucksack, trainers, rope and hook and stuffed them in the basket for used hand towels. He then scrunched up some hand towels and threw them into the basket to cover things up.

'OK, let's do it!' he said and left the toilets.

Jimmy followed a couple of minutes later. He watched Dan buy some chips and sit down at a Blackjack table. No one paid much attention to him. Jimmy went back to the Roulette table that he had been on previously. From there he had a clear view of both Dan and the cashier's area situated to the left of the entrance but to Jimmy's right from where he was looking. The area consisted of a cash desk behind which sat the two cashiers, a young woman and a middle aged man. Between them and the customers was a high grill consisting of metal bars.

At about ten, Jimmy caught Dan's eye and nodded. Dan got up from his table and went and stood to the right of the cash desk. Jimmy got up and walked over to the cash desk. There were no other customers there. He stood close to the grill concealing so far as was possible his front from the balcony above.

'Yes, sir? What can I do for you?' the girl asked in an East European accent. At that moment, Dan went and stood at the grill in front of the male cashier as close as he could to Jimmy so as to shield him from view as much as possible.

Jimmy opened his jacket and produced the gun. With other hand he took out a very large folded up plastic bag. Dan showed the male cashier the gun in his waistband.

'If either of you move your hands before I tell you to, you're dead. Understand?' Jimmy said.

The girl and the man beside her nodded immediately.

'You,' he said to the girl, 'hand me stacks of five hundred euro notes until I tell you to stop.'

The girl started handing them over immediately. Jimmy stuffed them into the bag as quickly as they came. Dan and Jimmy had anticipated that the chances of them getting away without any problem were minimal. At best the alarm would be sounded as soon as they left the cash desk but then any shooting would be confined to the staircase and entrance as they made their getaway with little risk to the other customers. More likely someone would want to buy or change some chips and see what was going on in which case they would leave immediately and the same scenario would apply. But the luck which they had enjoyed so far was about to run out. Their worst case scenario came about. The girl saw that Jimmy was both watching her and her colleague while loading the money into the bag and Dan was looking back most of the time at the casino and up to the balcony. While continuing to pass over the money, she used her knee to activate a silent alarm. Her bravery was to cost her her life.

Out of the corner of his eye, Dan saw a man rush to the balcony and raise a machine pistol.

'Uzi!' Dan screamed, just as he had in the first brothel that they had raided. Dan flung himself to his right and Jimmy to his left as a hail of bullets rained down on where they had been standing. The bullets smashed into and through the metal grill, killing the two cashiers immediately. One of the bullets ricocheted off one of the metal bars and Jimmy felt a searing pain in his side. Dan was already bringing his gun up as he hit the ground. He fired three times before the shooter could let off another burst. The man dropped his gun and collapsed, his weight causing him to crash through the wooden balustrade and fall face down on a Roulette table scattering chips as he landed.

The casino was in chaos. People were screaming and trying to hide under the tables. Dan and Jimmy got to their feet. Jimmy had dropped his gun when he had been hit but picked it and the bag up and they headed for the staircase. More shots were fired. Dan turned at the top of the stairs and fired some shots into the air so as not to hit any customers but to ensure the other shooters kept their heads down. They hurtled down the stairs as the two guards manning the metal detector appeared at the bottom, guns in their hands. Dan and Jimmy took them down before they could even get a shot off.

They then ran out across the car park and towards their car. Before they got around the corner, more shots were fired at them.

'Start the car,' Jimmy shouted. 'I'll hold them off.'

He ducked down behind the corner and fired a few shots towards the casino. The men shooting at them ducked down behind cars. There was another black Range Rover parked near the entrance. Jimmy had noticed it when he had entered the casino and wondered then if it belonged to the Russians. This was confirmed when one of the men shooting got into it from the side that was shielded from Jimmy.

Jimmy aimed his gun and fired several shots. None of them went anywhere near their attackers but he managed to shoot out both the tyres on the side of the Range Rover which was facing him. He then jumped into the passenger side of their car and Dan roared off down the road.

'I don't think they'll be following,' Jimmy said. 'I shot their tyres out.'

He held his side as he now became conscious of a severe burning pain. He could feel that blood had soaked his shirt and run down inside the waistband of his trousers.

Dan looked across.

'How bad is it?'

'There's a lot of blood but I don't think it hit anything major.'

Dan spotted something and screamed to a halt.

'Take your jacket off,' he said as he left the car. 'I'll be back in a mo.'

At the end of the road was another beach restaurant. Dan had seen an elderly women loading lace tablecloths into the boot of her car, parked just up from the restaurant. He had seen these vendors before selling the cloths to diners at the restaurants. This one was probably going home for the night. He rushed up to her.

'How much are the tablecloths?' he asked the surprised woman.

'They are very nice,' she said. 'Beautifully made. Two hundred and fifty euros.'

'I'll take one,' Dan said to the surprised woman, who would have accepted seventy five euros. He counted out the money.

'But which one?' she said.

'That one,' Dan said, snatching the tablecloth in the woman's hands.

The woman watched bemused as he ran back to the car.

'Here,' Dan said, thrusting the tablecloth at Jimmy. 'That's the most expensive bandage you'll ever have! Use it to staunch the wound. But hold on, let's just have a look.'

Dan switched on the interior light and lifted Jimmy's soaked shirt away from the wound.

'The bullet's cut right across your side, probably down to the bone, causing a six inch gash. It will need stitches.'

'Well we can hardly go to a hospital. You can stitch it back at Dana's.'

'With what? A normal needle and thread?'

'Why not? You'd do it in the field.'

'And scar you for life!'

Jimmy laughed. 'You think I care about that. It will just be one more war wound to impress the ladies with!'

'Anyway we don't want Dana getting suspicious. I've got a better idea.'

Chapter Forty Nine

After the gunfire had ceased, the screaming finally stopped and a few of the customers tentatively made their way towards the exit. When news filtered back that it was safe to leave, a mass exodus began as the remaining customers hurried down the stairs to their vehicles.

The casino manager, Yuri Strelkov, surveyed the wreckage of his premises. He was beside himself with worry and anger and teetering on the brink of panic. His anger was not so much directed at the men who had robbed him but at the man who lay spread-eagled across one of the Roulette tables. If he had not already been dead, Strelkov would have been tempted to kill him himself.

When the alarm had gone off simultaneously in his office and the guards' room, Strelkov had checked the monitors and realised exactly what was going on. The premises were already on a state of high alert on Petrov's orders and Strelkov had been in no doubt that the two men huddled together at the cashiers desk were the two men being desperately sought by the organisation along the whole coast. Here was an opportunity for him to show Petrov and the family that he was one of their most able employees. The men would not have known that an alarm had been set off and Strelkov had already been planning as he left his office how a trap could be set at the bottom of the stairs and the men killed or better still apprehended alive without any undue disruption to the casino.

Now, thanks to the buffoon lying across the Roulette table, he was in big trouble. As Strelkov had left his office, he had seen the man rush out of the guards' room on the other side of the balcony and, before Strelkov could stop him, lean over the balcony and open fire. As far as Strelkov was concerned the trigger happy idiot had got what he deserved. Now Strelkov was going to have to explain to both the police and Petrov what had happened.

His immediate concern was the police. He was well aware of the organisation's connections in the police and indeed high ranking police officers often attended the casino. But explaining how one of his own men had managed to gun down two cashiers and cause a gunfight leading to a mass panic was a different matter.

He wondered whether he could blame the death of the cashiers on the robbers. But why would the robbers have shot the cashiers? Because they had seen the alarm being activated! But wouldn't any half decent police inquiry reveal that the shots had come from the balcony above? And what was he going to do about the man on the Roulette table? It suddenly occurred to him that the whole incident would have been recorded on the casino's CCTV system. He rushed up to his office. He could devise a story for the police later. His first priority was to delete the digital film.

He was sitting at the bank of monitors frantically deleting the film when the rest of his men returned.

'I'm afraid they got away, Yuri,' one of them said.

'You don't say,' Yuri responded.

'We'll have to phone the police,' the man said.

'I know that, but we've got to work out what to tell them. That's why I'm deleting the film. I'll phone the police in a few minutes. In the meantime, you had better get rid of your guns.'

But he was too late. One of the customers had already called the police as was clear from the sound of approaching sirens.

Ten minutes after the first police cars had reached the casino, Inspector Valdez arrived. He had already given orders that none of the staff be allowed to leave and that they should all be kept together until he arrived. After surveying the scene, the rough sequence of events had seemed fairly clear to him. It was obvious from the position of the man on the Roulette table, the broken balcony, the dead cashiers and the bullet holes in the wall on the balcony behind the broken area that there had been an exchange of fire leading to the death of the cashiers and the man on the table.

He then proceeded to interview each member of staff. The bar staff and waitresses, who were locals, largely confirmed what he had suspected. After taking their statements, he allowed them to leave. None of the Russians said anything save that they had not seen anything. When Valdez asked Strelkov why the CCTV images had been deleted, why a member of his staff had seemingly been in possession of an Uzi and why a search by his men had revealed several handguns in excellent condition which appeared to have been thrown into the surf on the beach, he had merely shrugged. Valdez shrugged too and promptly arrested all the Russians for the illegal possession of firearms.

An hour later, Petrov stood in front of Viktor Durchenko's desk and relayed to his boss what had happened. Strelkov had eventually been allowed to make a phone call and with some trepidation had called Petrov and told him the sequence of events.

Viktor sat behind his desk motionless. He stared at Petrov and said nothing. Petrov felt distinctly uneasy. He would have been happier if

Viktor had slammed his fist down and ranted and raved.

'There is however some good news...' Petrov continued.

'We've been robbed of nearly half a million euros,' Viktor interrupted, 'three more of our men are dead, Strelkov and the rest of his men have been arrested and it will be weeks before we restore confidence in the casino, if we ever do. Do tell me what the good news is, Vitaly!'

'One of them was wounded in the gunfight. Possibly quite badly. Strelkov's men found a trail of blood leading down the stairs and all the way across to where their car was parked. We don't know if it was Green or the other man.'

'Well I suppose that is something.'

'It sounds like he will need medical treatment. I have all the hospitals covered.'

'And I assume we now have images of the other man.'

'Er, no, I'm afraid not. Strelkov deleted all the CCTV film before the police arrived as he didn't want the police to see one of our own men gunning down the cashiers.'

'That man is lucky he had a swift death!'

'That was Strelkov's view too.'

'And what about Strelkov and his men?'

'You won't be surprised to hear it was Valdez who arrested them. But I can get them out. Eventually. The casino won't be reopening any time soon so it won't do them any harm to reflect on their mistakes for a couple of days.'

'This Valdez is becoming a nuisance. Do you think we should be thinking about a more permanent solution to his interference?'

'Not at the moment. Our friends in high places are becoming very nervous. Killing a senior police officer would not go down well. Besides, I rather enjoy humiliating him!'

Chapter Fifty

Dan drove as fast as he dared to Malaga. He could not afford to be stopped by the police with Jimmy slumped beside him with a blood stained tablecloth tied tightly around his middle, not to mention the weaponry and equipment in the back.

He parked the car just around the corner from the bar where they had made contact with Fernando Ortega. Leaving Jimmy in the car, Dan went into the bar alone. Once again, the hubbub of noise died down as people turned to stare at him, some of them with hostile expressions on their faces. Dan felt somewhat comforted by the Glock in his waistband. He went straight up to the bar where the same barman as before looked at him with contempt.

'I want to see Ortega's man. As soon as possible please.'

The barman said nothing. He removed the top from a bottle of beer and pushed it over to Dan. Dan pushed some money across and sat at a table near the door.

On this occasion, Dan did not have to wait before the big man who had approached them before came in. He did not sit down.

'You know Senor Ortega is dead?' he asked.

'Yes,' Dan replied. 'That's why I asked to see *you*.'

'I'll say this for you, Englishman. You've got nerve in coming here. Fernando Ortega was a popular man around here and many people blame you for his death.'

'Look, I'm sorry about Ortega's death but you all knew exactly what I wanted those weapons for and were more than happy for me to take on the Durchenkos. Please, sit down.'

The man hesitated and looked around as if he did not want to be seen associating with Dan. Eventually, he sat down.

'Well, what do you want?'

'I need your help.'

'I can't get you any more equipment. Only Senor Ortega had the contacts...'

'I don't need equipment. I need a doctor.'

The man looked at Dan.

'No, not for me. For my colleague.'

Dan told the man about the raid on the casino and that Jimmy had been hit.

'So I need a doctor who can check him out and stitch him up with no questions asked,' Dan continued.

The man thought for a moment.

'Where is he now?'

'In the car around the corner.'

'Wait here,' the man said. He got up and left the bar.

Dan had a feeling of déjà vu. Five minutes later, the man returned.

'Ok,' he said, 'We go in your car. I will direct you. But this will cost you.'

'Don't worry about that,' Dan said, getting up. He led the way to the car. Jimmy grunted when they got in. The man seemed to relax a bit once they had set off and gave his name as Raoul. He directed them to a poor residential suburb of Malaga and they parked outside a rundown house on a corner.

'So who is this doctor?' Jimmy asked.

'He was struck off because of his drinking,' Raoul replied.

'Bloody hell,' Jimmy said. 'Are you sure you don't want to stitch me up, Dan?'

Raoul went and knocked on the door while Dan helped Jimmy out of the car. Luckily, there was no one else about apart from a mangy looking dog who looked at them hopefully in case they threw him something to eat.

The door was unbolted from the inside and a wizened old man looked out at Raoul and beckoned them in. The place stank of alcohol. He led them through into an old fashioned kitchen where a large wooden table had been cleared. The old man gestured to Jimmy that he should get on the table. There was a brief conversation between the two Spaniards in Spanish. Dan caught enough to hear that the doctor, or rather ex doctor, wanted a thousand euros.

'Tell him if he does a good job, I'll pay him two thousand,' Dan said.

The old man clearly understood that and grinned. He removed the tablecloth from around Jimmy and after inspecting the wound, he gabbled something in Spanish to Raoul. This time Dan did not understand what he said.

'He said the bullet may have grazed a rib but there's nothing broken. He's going to stitch you up.'

The man produced a needle and injected Jimmy in the area around the wound. Jimmy was pleased to see that the man's hand was not shaking too badly. While they were waiting for the anaesthetic to take effect, the man produced a bottle of liquor and four grubby looking glasses. Dan declined but the other three had a large slug each.

'What the hell!' Jimmy said. 'He probably can't function without it.'

The old man then set about stitching Jimmy up and Dan had to admit from what he could see that the man made a pretty good job of it.

When he had finished, Dan gave him the money and the man said something in Spanish.

'He said that the stitches should stay in for at least a week. But he should take it easy for another week or two,' Raoul said. 'Do you want to come back for them to be removed?'

'No,' Jimmy said. 'We can manage that. And I certainly won't be taking it easy for long!'

'So, will you be continuing your campaign?' Raoul asked, when they were in the car taking him back to the bar.

'What do you think?' Dan replied. 'It's them or us now.'

'Closing down brothels and casinos and killing their soldiers and even their relatives will hurt them but you will never defeat them until you have killed Viktor Durchenko and Petrov. And you will never do that unless you find some way to entice them out of their fortified villa or somehow manage to get inside the villa.'

'We're well aware of that,' Dan said as he parked the car near the bar.

'You will never get into the villa with just the two of you,' Raoul continued.

'So do you have any suggestions?' Dan asked.

'Fernando Ortega was my friend as well as my boss. As were the other men who died. From what I hear, Viktor and Petrov will not be leaving the villa until you have been caught and dealt with. So if you decide to attack the villa, I may be able to arrange some help.'

'What sort of help?'

'Myself and maybe three or four other men.'

Dan looked over his shoulder at Raoul.

'I know what you're thinking, Senor,' Raoul continued. 'We may not be up to the standard of special forces but we know how to handle ourselves and we wouldn't let you down.'

Dan and Jimmy exchanged glances.

'Maybe,' Dan said, 'when the time is right.'

'Then when the time is right, call this number,' Raoul said. He wrote a number down on a scrap of paper and handed it to Dan. 'We will be ready.'

Dan took the number and put it in his pocket.

'Thanks. You must let me pay you something for your help tonight.'

Raoul shook his head. 'I don't want your money. I just want you to rid this coastline of those Russian bastards. Every single one of them.'

'We'll see what we can do,' Jimmy said.

With that, Raoul got out of the car and melted away into the darkness.

'What do you think?' Jimmy asked. 'Can we use them? Can we trust them?'

'I certainly think we can trust them. They seem to hate the Russians as much as we do. And he wouldn't take any money. He knows we're awash with it after robbing the casino and could have asked for virtually any fee he wanted.'

'But a bunch of middle aged Spaniards who the Russians had no difficulty driving out of town?'

'I don't like to remind you, Jimmy, but we're practically middle aged now. If they're well motivated, know how to shoot and have us to lead them, why not? As long as they don't shoot us by accident, what harm can they do?'

'Ok, so what now?'

'Well, whether you like it or not, you're going to have to take it easy for the next week. We'll tell Dana you've got food poisoning or something. We can plan our next move while you're resting. Providing Dana's happy to put us up and we keep our heads down, we can keep them guessing as to what we're going to do next.'

'And I can spend the time counting all that money we lifted!'

Chapter Fifty One

When they arrived back at Dana's apartment in the early hours of the morning, she was still up and the sight of Dan helping Jimmy into the apartment and then into his room did not improve her humour. She assumed that they had been out drinking and that was why Jimmy needed assistance. Dan decided to leave it at that as food poisoning did not seem to be a viable excuse for Jimmy's indisposition at that time of night.

'I've no illusions that this is going to be a long term relationship, Dan,' Dana said, 'but having let you into my home and my bed, I'd have thought that I could expect better than you and your friend comin' back after two in the morning blind drunk.'

'I'm sorry. I know it looks bad,' Dan replied, 'but for what it's worth, I'm completely sober. I was driving. We had to meet someone and well, as you can see, Jimmy had a bit of a skinful. It won't happen again.'

He moved closer to Dana.

'Well, I suppose you don't smell of booze.'

'I haven't had a drink all night!'

'OK, I'll give you the benefit of the doubt! Do you fancy a drink now?'

'Actually, I wouldn't mind a brandy.'

'How about if I bring it through to the bedroom?'

'Sounds good to me!'

The following week was frustrating for both Dan and Jimmy. For the first few days, Jimmy remained in the apartment either watching television or lying on a sun lounger on the balcony. At least Dan could go out but he knew that there was no point in him taking any further action against the Durchenkos until Jimmy was fit again.

He spent a lot of time studying their villa from the vantage point that they had used previously watching the comings and goings. As far as he could tell, neither Viktor nor Petrov left the villa. Apart from tradesmen, the only other visitors appeared to be the hookers bussed in to entertain the troops.

Dan also had lunch with Luis Mendez who was very interested to hear about the events that had taken place in Moscow and London. Dan was also interested to hear about the arrests that had taken place at the casino when Valdez had arrived but was not surprised to hear that after a couple of days, the Russians were released from custody.

'Don't let Jose catch up with you,' Luis said, 'Nothing would please him more than to see the Russians destroyed but he's still a policeman and you and your colleague are prime suspects in a number of crimes that have taken place recently!'

'Being hunted by the Russians and the police doesn't make things easy!'

'I wouldn't say you are being hunted by the police. So far as I'm aware, Jose hasn't issued an arrest warrant for you but he would certainly like the opportunity to question you.'

'Can you help keep him off our backs?'

Luis shrugged. 'Maybe. I'll do what I can but he's coming under tremendous pressure to stop the war which appears to have broken out down here. You should really think about bringing things to a conclusion as soon as possible.'

For the first few evenings, Jimmy made his excuses and stayed in the apartment, cooking himself a meal. Dana seemed quite happy with that arrangement as it enabled her to go out with Dan. Although Dana turned a few heads, Dan was reasonably confident that a couple would not attract the attention of the family's informants and in any event, they would drive out to a beachside restaurant of the type only frequented by tourists and expats. Dan began to become quite attached to Dana, who despite her unusual style of dress and her kinky habits in the bedroom proved to be engaging company. She even succeeded in getting Dan to relax in what was proving to be a long and for the most part tedious week. Dan knew that Luis Mendez had been right. It was time to bring things to a conclusion or sooner or later their luck would run out.

A week after the stitches had been put in, Jimmy insisted that Dan remove them. Dan had favoured leaving it for another couple of days but Jimmy would not hear of it.

'We've got to get moving,' Jimmy said, echoing Dan's own thoughts. 'We can't hang around much longer without making a decisive move.'

Dan used a pair of Dana's tweezers and some nail scissors that he had found on her dressing table to take the stitches out. The wound still looked fairly red and raw and Jimmy commented that it felt a bit tight as he moved his arm around.

'But I'm fine,' he said. 'I can't wait to get out of this place and get going again!'

Chapter Fifty Two

Rudi Morales lived his life in a constant state of fear. Before the Russians had come to the Costa del Sol, life had been one big party. He had made a good living supplying cannabis and cocaine to tourists in Puerto Banus. He had a flash sports car, a speed boat and dressed in designer clothes. He was well known around the bars and clubs and there was always a plentiful supply of girls. He had even had his own minder, an amiable gentle giant of a man, whose main function was as a status symbol but who very occasionally had to give a slap to a slow paying punter.

All that had changed one night when he and Pedro had left a club in the early hours of the morning. As they had been about to get into their car, hoods had been placed over their heads and they had been bundled into the back of a van. Demands to know what was going on had been met with a kicking by men who spoke in a strange foreign language.

After a journey of about twenty minutes, they were dragged out of the van with the hoods still over their heads and then frogmarched into a building and shoved down on to hard seats. They were then bound tightly to the seats before the hoods were removed. Rudi saw that they were in some sort of derelict barn. Four tough looking men dressed in black suits stood watching them and smoking until a car drew up outside. Their kidnappers immediately stubbed out their cigarettes and Rudi noticed that a couple of them smoothed down their suits and almost stood to attention.

Rudi could feel his heart pounding as two men walked into the barn. The first man was obviously the leader as the other walked a couple of paces behind. The man strode over with barely a glance at the other four. He was older than the others and had a completely shaven head and a face which struck even more fear into the already terrified Rudi. Curiously he was wearing a black overcoat despite the fact that even at that time of night, it was still reasonably warm.

The man stopped in front of them and without saying a word, he undid his coat and produced a silenced pistol. Without hesitation he shot Pedro in the head. Pedro's body and the chair to which it was bound clattered to the floor and the man then levelled the pistol at Rudi's head. Rudi lost control of his bladder and closed his eyes hoping that he would feel no pain. But nothing happened. There was no crack from the pistol, not that Rudi would have heard it before the bullet smashed through his skull, and no pain. After a few seconds, he opened his eyes. The man had lowered the pistol and was grinning. He looked down at the pool of urine which had dripped down Rudi's legs on to the floor.

'You Spanish really are disgusting,' the man said in English with a thick accent. 'Don't you agree?'

Rudi said nothing. The only sound he could make was a whimper. The man responded by hitting Rudi across the face with the long barrel of the pistol, not hard enough to knock him out but hard enough to split open the skin over his cheekbone.

'I asked you a question. You will answer it. I know you speak English.'

Rudi nodded vigorously, tears running down his face.

'I can't hear you,' the man continued and raised the pistol again.

'Yes, yes, yes,' Rudi squawked. 'Please don't hit me again. I'll do whatever you want!'

'That's better,' the man continued and lowered the pistol again. 'I will tell you what I want. You work for me from now on. Do you understand?'

Rudi nodded but the man raised the pistol again.

'Yes, yes, I understand,' Rudi stammered. 'I work for you now.'

'Good. We finally understand each other.' The man gestured at Pedro's body. 'You will have our protection now. You won't need him. But let what happened to him be a lesson to you. Cross me in any way and you will end up like that.'

And so Rudi had ended up working for the Russians and his indolent, hedonistic lifestyle came to an end. His regular supplier disappeared (probably dead as Rudi imagined) and the Russians supplied him with all his drugs, not just cannabis and coke but serious stuff like crack cocaine and heroin. They expected him to keep scrupulous records and they set him targets, demanding an explanation if he should fall short of a target. He found himself working three times as hard as previously for half the money. He had contemplated running away and making a fresh start somewhere else but he had soon realised that that was not an option. He had not seen the shaven headed man again but the man to whom he had to report, Pavel, was almost as scary. He had told him that if he tried to run away, his elderly mother would be killed and then his sister and her children. Then eventually they would track him down and make him beg for an end as swift as Pedro's.

The only things that had amused Rudi recently were the rumours that the Russians themselves were under attack. The newspapers had been full of the incidents at the casino and various other locations and although the papers did not say so, it seemed pretty clear to Rudi that those establishments had been controlled by the Russians. Further, Pavel seemed desperate to trace two Englishmen and had told Rudi to keep his eyes and ears open for two fit looking men of about forty. He had been shown a photo of one of them and been told that they might be driving a black Range Rover.

If these were the men who had been attacking the Russians then Rudi would have been more likely to wish them luck rather than turn them in. Save though for one thing. Pavel had promised a ten thousand euro reward for anyone who gave information leading to them being traced.

As Rudi was discreetly passing a wrap of heroin to a hooker in the main square, he glanced up and saw a black Range Rover driving out of the underground car park of the apartment block on the other side of the square. To begin with, as the woman passed him a fifty euro note, he did not make the connection but when the car was facing him, he looked through the windscreen and saw two men both wearing sunglasses and baseball hats. Rudi only caught a fleeting glance of them but somehow they did not strike him as tourists nor as locals.

As the woman moved away, he was in two minds. He did not want to phone Pavel and risk his wrath if these were not the men being sought but on the other hand, ten thousand euros was a lot of money. Maybe with that, he could get his whole family away from the area, perhaps to somewhere like London.

He took out his mobile and dialled the number.

'Da? What do you want, Rudi? This had better be good!' Pavel grunted.

Rudi winced. 'Those two men you are looking for...'

Suddenly, Pavel's attitude changed.

'You've seen them?' he said eagerly.

'I don't know. I might have done. You said to look out for...'

'What have you seen?'

Rudi described what he had seen and identified the block from which the car had emerged. Pavel seemed pleased with his information.

'Er, you said there would be a ten thousand euro reward if I managed to find them?'

'Yes, yes. If it's them you'll get your money. We keep our promises. Good or bad. You just remember that.'

With that, Pavel ended the connection. Now it was he who was in two minds. There was of course nothing conclusive about the information that he had received. After all, they were not sure that the Englishmen were still using the stolen black Range Rover and anyway there were loads of black Range Rovers in and around Puerto

Banus. And two men wearing sunglasses and baseball caps in what to Pavel was infernal heat?

Nevertheless, he felt obliged to relay the information to Petrov. The consequences of having received information which may have led to the two men and not reporting it were unthinkable. He knew that Petrov was fed up with investigating what till now had proved to be false leads but at least the decision would be his.

In fact, fed up though he might be with pursuing false leads, Petrov was becoming increasingly frustrated at the lack of progress being made in tracing the men and was coming under considerable pressure from Viktor.

'Go to the apartment block yourself,' he said to Pavel. 'Ask around. See if any of the other occupants know who these men are. If you don't get anywhere, get someone to watch the building to see when they return and get the number of the car. I can get one of our contacts in the police to see who the car is registered to.'

Chapter Fifty Three

Petrov would no doubt have been interested to know that while he was talking to Pavel, he was in fact under observation, or rather to be more accurate the villa was under observation. Dan and Jimmy were in their usual position, hidden in the undergrowth, watching the villa through binoculars.

'Any suggestions?' Jimmy asked.

'Well, we know there is a gatehouse with at least two guards in it at all times; we can assume that the wall and grounds are alarmed; there are guard dogs and probably at least a dozen more men in addition to the family up at the house.'

'So a piece of cake then?'

'Hardly! What I'd like to know is whether there are any alarms on the outside of the wall.'

'I doubt it. Why would they need alarms on the outside when they've got them on the top if someone tries to climb over?'

'You're probably right. And if so, when it's dark we could get to the wall and work our way back towards the gate without being seen.'

'How will that help us?'

Dan explained to Jimmy what he had in mind.

'Bloody hell!' Jimmy said. 'That sounds like fun! You think Raoul and his boys will be up for that?'

'I don't see why not. I can't think of another way.'

'OK. We'd better stay here till it gets dark and then see how easy it is to get to the wall. If there are alarms we can run for it.'

They waited patiently till darkness fell then separated and approached the wall from different sides of the gate. Careful not to make too much noise, they crawled through the scrub until they reached the dirt track road which ran along the wall and past the gate. Jimmy reached a position about fifty yards past the gate to the left from where they had been watching the property and Dan reached a position about fifty yards to the right.

Although the scrub through which they had approached was in darkness, light was shining out through the wrought iron gates from the lights in the gatehouse and along the drive leading to the house. There were no lights in the road so the light got progressively lighter towards the gate.

It occurred to Dan that if he had been asked to advise on security for the villa, he would have suggested lighting on the outside of the wall and CCTV cameras at various positions along the wall so that the men in the gatehouse could observe the road along the whole length of the wall.

They had synchronised their watches and at the agreed time, they hurried across the road and pressed themselves against the wall. They then made their way slowly towards the gate from opposite directions, keeping close to the wall. They reached the gateposts together and then stopped as if they had gone further they would have been visible from the gatehouse.

After the agreed five minutes, nothing had changed. There was no movement from the gatehouse and therefore clearly no alarm had been triggered. Dan gave Jimmy the thumbs up sign and they both retraced their steps and met back at their vantage point.

'So do you think it will work?' Dan asked.

'They won't know what's hit them,' Jimmy replied. 'When do you want to do it?'

'I'll phone Raoul and see how quickly he can get his team together.'

'Are you going to tell him the plan?'

'No way. All he needs to know is when it's on and I want to check his team out before we set off.'

'And if you're not happy?'

'Then I guess it's down to you and me.'

'It won't be the first time!'

Chapter Fifty Four

Dan had reached the main square in Puerto Banus and was only about fifty yards from the entrance to the car park under Dana's apartment block when Pavel made his move. Having reported back to Petrov after making the inquiries at the apartment block, Petrov had assigned seven of their most experienced men to a team to be led by Pavel. With four men including himself in each of two vehicles, Pavel was confident that the long search for the two Englishmen would soon be over.

He had contemplated waiting for them in the car park itself but the entrance and exit procedures for the car park were both fairly slow and with no fob for the car park, he did not want to break in or somehow bypass the security system when they may have had a lengthy wait. Further, having checked out the car park on foot, he had seen that it was only half full and there was no knowing where the Englishmen would park. The time taken for them to reach the Englishmen from where they were waiting, even if only seconds, would take away the element of surprise and enable the Englishmen to arm themselves. Pavel did not want a prolonged gun battle in the car park. He was well aware of the Englishmen's capability and he wanted a quick, clean hit with no casualties on his side.

Just as Dan had put on his indicator in preparation for turning into the car park, a black Chevrolet SUV with blacked out windows cut in front of him, forcing him into the kerb with a squeal of his tyres. A glance in his mirror revealed a similar vehicle hemming him in from behind.

Dan could see the doors of both vehicles opening and took the only course open to him. Neither able to go backwards or forwards, he wrenched the steering wheel even further to the right and mounted the pavement and drove the car through the outside terrace of a restaurant. Customers and waiters jumped aside screaming as the Range Rover ploughed through, smashing and scattering tables and chairs and sending bottles and plates of food flying through the air. Within seconds the car emerged through the carnage on to the pavement on the other side of the terrace but not before it had been hit by several bullets and the rear window had been shot out.

'Are you ok?' Dan shouted at Jimmy.

'Never better,' Jimmy replied as he checked his Glock and twisted in his seat to return fire through the now glassless rear window.

Pavel cursed. He might have known that it would not have been as easy as he had planned.

'Back in the cars! After them!' he screamed.

His car was at a similar angle to the pavement as the Range Rover had been after they had cut in front of it so the driver simply followed the same path that Dan had, wreaking more destruction on the restaurant as it crushed and broke more furniture on its way through. The other car managed to do a U turn in the road and tucked in behind the Range Rover and soon both cars were on its tail. One of Jimmy's bullets hit the windscreen of the lead car and caused the glass to star. The front seat passenger punched out the glass and the driver dropped back a bit.

'Just keep them in sight. When you get a chance, try to overtake them and force them off the road.' Pavel's voice came through on the walkie talkie fitted in the lead car.

Dan drove as fast as he dared through Nueva Andalucia and headed north towards the Ronda road. He was swerving from side to side to avoid the gunfire coming from the car behind and to prevent it from overtaking, a manoeuvre it attempted every time there was a reasonably straight bit of road.

Meanwhile, Jimmy had climbed into the back and removed one of the AK 47s from the canvas bag on the floor.

'We'll soon be on the Ronda road,' Dan shouted. 'Try not to open fire with that thing till we're out of the residential area.'

'So says a man who's just destroyed a restaurant full of diners!' Jimmy replied.

When they reached the Ronda road, Dan accelerated through the flat part surrounded by golf courses, large villas and upmarket urbanisations and soon reached the climb into the mountains. He kept his head down as much as he could as he was conscious of the almost continuous gunfire from the car behind. He then heard Jimmy firing the AK 47 in response. The car behind dropped back again but as the bends became tighter, it closed up quickly and at one bend rammed the Range Rover from behind.

'Shit! There's so much firepower coming from the car behind, I can't really get my head up to aim the AK!' Jimmy shouted from the back seat. 'I'm better off with the Glock.'

'Hold on tight!' Dan replied. 'I'm going to try something!'

Dan knew that the car behind was going to take any opportunity to try to drive them off the road and over the side of the cliff. The road was winding its way up the mountains with a sheer drop on the outside. He also knew that the driver would be unwilling to try to overtake on the outside for fear of being pushed over the side himself. However, he would surely take any opportunity to force his way up Dan's inside and then ram the Range Rover from the side to try to push it over.

After a few more bends, Dan saw an opportunity to try what he had planned. In taking a sharp right hand bend, Dan deliberately took it wide giving the impression that he had slightly misjudged the bend at that speed. The driver of the car behind saw his opportunity and needed no second invitation. As soon as Dan drifted wide, he shot up Dan's inside so that that Dan was on the outside with the sheer drop to his left.

The driver then pulled his steering wheel to the left broadsiding the Range Rover and, as Dan had anticipated, trying to push it over the edge.

'Jesus, Dan! What the fuck are you doing?' Jimmy shouted, as the wheels of the Range Rover veered dangerously close to the drop.

'Hang on!' Dan shouted. He wrenched the wheel to the right to try to counter the manoeuvre of the other car and for about a hundred yards, the cars shot forward at high speed locked together with the Range Rover's wheels on the left inches from the drop. Then, as another right hand bend appeared ahead, Dan suddenly applied his brakes. The car on his inside shot ahead and before the car following behind ran into them, Dan slammed down his accelerator and the powerful Range Rover surged forward.

The driver of the car ahead had had to slow down for the bend and as he began to turn, he glanced to his right and realised with horror what was about to happen. The Range Rover smashed into the side of his car spinning the back round so that the Range Rover was pushing it sideways towards the drop ahead on the bend. The four occupants of the Chevrolet desperately tried to get of the car but were unable to do so before the left wheels of the car dropped over the edge and the whole car then toppled into the void, smashing into rocks on its way down and eventually bursting into flames.

Jimmy whooped with delight. 'I knew you had it covered!' he said.

'One down, one to go!' Dan replied. 'Now for the other one!'

'The odds have tilted our way now.'

'That's what I thought.'

Pavel watched with horror as his lead car plummeted over the edge. He realised now why the two men ahead were so dangerous.

'What now?' his driver asked.

'Keep going!' Pavel shouted back. 'There's four of us and only two of them. But keep back. We'll blast them off the road!'

He turned to the two men in the back, but they had already wound their windows down and were preparing to rake the Range Rover with automatic weapons.

They then reached a stretch of road where the bends were tighter and more frequent as the road wound deeper into the mountains. The opportunities to exchange fire became less as the Range Rover would disappear around a bend and by the time the Chevrolet was around it, the Range Rover was negotiating the next bend. Pavel had a Uzi on his lap but he knew that there was no point in firing it until they were much closer.

Chapter Fifty Five

Up ahead, Dan and Jimmy knew that when the road straightened out, the car behind could keep up a relentless barrage of fire which would pin Jimmy down and sooner or later, one or both of them would be hit.

'Why are we running?' Jimmy asked.

'My thoughts exactly,' Dan replied, as he flung the big car around another bend. 'They're expecting us to keep going and just waiting for their chance to blast us. Why don't we do what they're not expecting?'

Jimmy removed the other AK 47 from the bag and checked it was ready to fire.

'Ok. All ready. We just need to find a suitable location,' he said.

Dan accelerated as fast as he dared on such a treacherous road to put some distance between them and the car behind. After a few minutes, they came to a straighter stretch and it appeared that there would now be slightly longer distances between the bends.

Back in the Chevrolet, Pavel was conscious of this too.

'Get ready,' he said. 'We'll soon have them in our sights.'

Dan saw a bend ahead and took the car around almost on two wheels. There was a straight stretch ahead but more importantly, the rock face on their inside ended halfway down the stretch and there was a kind of run off into scrub. Dan slammed on his brakes and span into the run off across gravel bringing the vehicle to a halt almost broadside to the traffic following behind. Almost before the car had come to a halt, he and Jimmy flung open their doors and dived behind the the other side of the car. Jimmy threw an AK over to Dan just as the Chevrolet was rounding the bend.

Pavel saw immediately what the situation was.

'Stop!' he screamed.

The driver slammed on his brakes and turned the Chevrolet towards the rock face. It was the last thing he did. A hail of bullets smashed into the vehicle and one of them went through the windscreen and caught him right between the eyes.

Pavel and the two men in the back were luckier. Pavel had seen the stationary Range Rover ahead and the two AK 47s aimed at them from behind the vehicle. Before the bullets hit the car, he ducked down and threw his door open. He then rolled out of the car and took cover behind the vehicle as did the men in the back.

Bullets smacked into the car. One of Pavel's men tried to return fire but as he lifted his head slightly to take aim, a bullet took the top off it and his lifeless body slumped down next to Pavel. Pavel sat there with his back pressed against one of the wheels, clutching his Uzi, not daring to move. All hope of returning to the villa triumphant had gone. He knew that he and the other man, Vasily, were no match for the Englishmen. Surprisingly, he did not feel particularly afraid. Maybe this was what he deserved.

'Pavel, Pavel!' Vasily shouted across from the other end of the vehicle. 'Are you OK?'

This seemed to wake Pavel up.

'Yes, yes, I'm OK,' Pavel replied. 'Can you see them?'

'Yes. I have a good position here protected by the rock on one side and the car on the other.'

Vasily started shooting and the barrage of fire from the Range Rover slowed down. Pavel put his hand around the wheel and let off, one handed, a volley from his Uzi in the general direction of the Range Rover. He knew that there was little chance of hitting anything at that range with a Uzi even if he had been aiming properly but at least it gave the Englishmen something to think about.

Maybe there was hope after all. The shooting stopped for a moment and he ventured a quick look over towards the Range Rover.

'It's a stand off,' Vasily said.

'Until someone runs out of ammunition,' Pavel replied. 'How much have you got?'

'Another two magazines. I reckon we may have more than them!'

Pavel had two spare magazines too and wondered if Vasily was right. What he did not know was that Dan and Jimmy had their whole supply of equipment in their car and enough ammunition to fight a small war. Pavel inched his way over to Vasily and realised that Vasily had been right. They were fairly secure there and maybe, just maybe, they could prevail.

After the initial burst, Dan and Jimmy decided that they had made the right move.

'There's only two of them left now,' Jimmy said, 'but they're holed up between the rock and the car. They'll be difficult to dislodge.'

'Maybe,' Dan replied, 'but I used to be a pretty good cricketer.'

'What the hell's that got to do with it?'

'Just wait and see!'

Dan opened the rear door of the Range Rover and, keeping low, crawled across to their kit bag on the floor.

'How far would you say they are away from us?' he asked.

'I don't know, maybe fifty yards or a bit less.'

'I used to field on the boundary in my day.'

'Are you feeling all right?'

Dan crawled back out of the car and showed Jimmy the two grenades he had taken from the bag.

'Oh, I get what you're on about now!' Jimmy said.

'I was pretty good at pinging the ball into the keeper's hand from the boundary so this is my distance!'

A burst of gunfire came from the other car and Jimmy returned the fire.

'I thought I'd lob one over them to explode on the other side and underarm the other one to explode either just before or under the car.'

'Ok, I'll keep them pinned down while you do it.'

Dan moved to the end of the car as Jimmy changed his magazine. He gave Jimmy the thumbs up and Jimmy fired a long raking burst at the area where the two Russians were holed up. Dan removed the pin from the first grenade and lobbed it up and over the Chevrolet. He figured that that one would probably not do much damage but would certainly attract their attention. He then moved out from behind the cover of the Range Rover, removed the pin from the other grenade and with a firm underarm delivery propelled it towards the Chevrolet. It bounced a few yards away from the car then bounced a few more times and although it did not roll under the car as he had hoped, it hit the car and then exploded.

Pavel and Vasily ducked down as a long burst of fire came from the Range Rover. No sooner had it stopped than a huge explosion took place from further behind them. They turned round to see what had happened and then there was another explosion, this time much closer.

It felt to Pavel as if the whole world was exploding. Their car was lifted off the ground and in the deafening roar was driven back towards him. He was lifted off his feet and must have lost consciousness for a moment. When he woke up, he was on his back. He looked over and saw that Vasily had been crushed beneath the car. Pavel tried to move but couldn't. There was dust everywhere and it was strangely silent. He then heard the sound of boots approaching on the gravel. He looked around desperately for his Uzi but it was nowhere to be seen.

Then out of the dust a figure appeared carrying an AK 47. Pavel looked up at him. The man just stared down at him.

'Who are you?' Pavel croaked.

The man smiled and raised his gun.

'The last person you'll ever see,' he replied.

He fired the gun but Pavel was already dead before the sound reverberated around the mountains.

Chapter Fifty Six

As Jimmy was walking back to the Range Rover, he could hear the sound of sirens approaching from the direction from which they had come. Dan jumped into the driver's seat and reversed the car back on to the road. The car was in a bad way. It was riddled with bullet holes and all the windows had been shot out. However, despite some ominous rattles, it was still driveable.

'Hurry up!' Dan shouted. 'The police will be here in a couple of minutes!'

Jimmy got in the passenger side and Dan set off as fast as he could in the direction of Ronda.

'We're going to have to ditch the car,' Jimmy said. 'It's a wreck and when we get back to a populated area, it'll attract a lot of attention.'

'Let's worry about that when we've put some distance between ourselves and the police,' Dan replied.

'They'll stop when they reach the Chevrolet. They'll have to as it's blocking the road!'

'Maybe. But don't you think they'll have radioed ahead?'

After a few minutes the road became less mountainous as they approached the outskirts of Ronda. Dan had studied a road map before, when they had used the mountain road to dispose of the bodies of Alexei and his two bodyguards. He knew that before Ronda, he could avoid the town by turning right and doubling back to Marbella on the Ojen road.

Unfortunately, as they approached the roundabout which led to that road, they saw that Dan had been right about the police radioing ahead. The road was completely blocked by two police cars with their blue lights flashing. As they got nearer they could see that behind the two cars were four policemen with their guns trained on the approaching Range Rover.

'Shit!' Jimmy said. 'What do we do now?' He could see that there was no way that Dan could drive around them and reached for his Glock.

'No!' Dan said. 'No guns! They're not the enemy.'

'So what do we do?'

'We give ourselves up. Or appear to. Then we disarm them without hurting them too much.'

'You make it sound easy.'

'Let's hope it is.'

Dan brought the vehicle to a halt about twenty feet from the police cars. The two of them just sat in the car. The police officers all looked fairly young and very nervous. They started jabbering away in Spanish and seemed reluctant to come out from behind their cars.

'Ok, let's take the initiative,' Dan said. 'We get out and walk towards them, hands in the air, keeping a distance between us so the two on the left are yours and the two on the right mine.'

They slowly got out of the car. This produced some frantic gun waving from the policemen which only ceased when they saw that Dan and Jimmy were unarmed and had their hands in the air. Dan and Jimmy walked to about five feet from the police cars and stopped.

The policemen looked at each other and the one who appeared to be the oldest said something to the others. As Dan had anticipated, the two on the right approached him and the two on the left Jimmy. They shuffled around the end of their vehicles keeping their guns trained on Dan and Jimmy the whole time.

Dan and Jimmy stepped forward and leant towards the two police cars, putting their hands out in front of them on to the roof of each car, inviting the policemen to frisk them.

The two policemen approaching Dan had what sounded like a fairly nervous conversation before one stood to one side a few feet away and kept his gun trained on Dan while the other holstered his weapon and produced some handcuffs. He came up behind Dan and Dan allowed the man to search him. The man then reached up for Dan's wrist to apply the handcuffs. For a split second, it seemed that Dan was cooperating. Dan allowed the man to reach for left forearm but before the man could get any sort of grip on it, Dan moved with lightning speed. His left elbow came round and crushed the man's windpipe, not enough to kill him but enough to put him down gasping for breath.

Although the other man was a few feet away, it wasn't enough. As Dan's body swung to the left taking out the first man with his elbow, in a continuation of the movement, Dan closed the gap on the other man and seized the gun with his right hand and wrenched it out of the man's grasp before he knew what was happening and had time to react even to the extent of just pulling the trigger. Dan then used his left hand to press down on the pressure points between the second policeman's neck and shoulder and the man sank gently to the ground unconscious.

Dan immediately looked over to see what Jimmy was doing. He need not have worried. Jimmy was leaning on the other car grinning, with two unconscious policemen at his feet.

'What kept you?' he said.

'I hope you haven't killed them!'

'Nah, they'll be fine in a while.'

By this time, the first policeman that Dan had dealt with appeared to be recovering and breathing more easily. Dan hauled him to his feet and put the man's own handcuffs on one of his wrists. He attached the other end to one of the rear window frames of one of the police cars, then removed the man's gun from its holster and threw it into the field at the side of the road. He and Jimmy then applied handcuffs in a similar fashion to the other three men who were still unconscious, attaching one end to a convenient part of the car.

'The other police will be here soon,' Dan said, 'so they won't have to wait long. And we've managed to acquire some replacement wheels. I'm not sure how much life the Range Rover has in it.'

He walked over to it and removed their kit bag. He put it in the back of the other police car. Jimmy laughed.

'Come on! What are you waiting for?' Dan said. 'We can cut back on to the Ojen road now. We've got a reliable fast car and no one is going to stop us or pay much attention to us!'

'Hang on,' Jimmy said. 'Let's make it look even more realistic.'

He bent down and picked up two of the police caps which had come off in the struggle. He tossed one over to Dan and put the other on his head. Dan did likewise and they got in the police car and drove off.

'Can't we put on the blue light and siren?' Jimmy asked.

'I think that would be going a bit far!' Dan replied.

He drove as fast as he could but they only encountered a handful of cars before they reached Ojen.

'Time to ditch the police car,' Dan said. 'We can't drive into Marbella in this. We may be OK up here but not in a built up area.'

Instead of bypassing Ojen, Dan drove into the village and after removing their kit bag, they abandoned the police car and their hats in a side street. Even though the action would barely have been getting going down in Puerto Banus, the village was very quiet. It took them about ten minutes before they found a suitable car on the outskirts of the village some way from the nearest street light. It took Jimmy less than a minute to break into the VW Passat and start the engine.

'What now?' he asked as they drove out of the village.

'Has it occurred to you how they managed to find us?'

Jimmy thought for a while before replying.

'I haven't really had time to think about it till now but they were definitely waiting for us. You don't have two carloads of heavily armed men sitting in the middle of a town's main square on the off chance.'

'I'm worried about Dana. I hope they didn't trace us through her.'

'I shouldn't think so. Someone probably saw us when we left this morning. We haven't been out together for a week.'

'I hope so. But even so, I think we should try to find somewhere else to stay. That area will be swarming with them from now on. And it's too risky for her.'

'Where though?'

'I don't know. The hotels are out. We can't risk trying to rent another apartment.'

'Maybe Raoul knows somewhere.'

'Maybe. But we can't stay with Dana tonight. With a bit of luck, news of what's happened tonight won't have got back to the family yet. I suggest we check Dana's OK, get our stuff and leave the area. We may have to sleep in the car tonight.'

Chapter Fifty Seven

In sharp contrast to Ojen, Puerto Banus was busy. Although the main action was down on the port and road that runs just behind the port, there were lots of people milling around in the area behind the port, eating in restaurants and drinking in bars.

Dan managed to find a space in the road that led down to the port on the right with the beach on the left. He did not want to use the car park under the apartment block just in case the family already knew what had happened and the area was staked out. The car park could turn out to be a trap.

They tried to blend in with the crowds and made their way back to the main square. The area outside the restaurant which Dan had destroyed earlier had been partially cleared up. The restaurant was closed and the terrace had been cordoned off with police tape. There were two uniformed police officers moving on the passers by who stopped to have a look at the damage.

Dan and Jimmy did two circuits of the square and having satisfied themselves that the area was not under observation, entered the foyer of the apartment block and took the lift up to Dana's floor.

Dan unlocked the door to Dana's apartment and immediately sensed that something was wrong when he opened the door. If you had asked him, he would not have been able to say why. He could not hear anything but perhaps it was something he smelt, perhaps it was the temperature but the feeling was strong enough for him to remove the Glock from his waistband. Jimmy did the same. Dan held the gun in his right hand but tucked it inside his jacket in case Dana came out of the living room to meet them.

They entered the living room and everything seemed normal. Dan relaxed a little but carefully opened the door leading to Dana's bedroom. The room was dark and the decor did not exactly aid visibility. For a moment Dan was confused. He thought that Dana was asleep on the bed but he soon realised that that was not the case. He drew his gun, threw open the door and switched on the lights.

Dan was not easily shocked. He had seen things that most people cannot even imagine but what he saw in that room ranked with the very worst and he knew at once that it would remain with him for the rest of his life.

It appeared to him that Dana was staring at him pleading with him to help her. Her eyes were open but there was no life in them. She was lying naked and spread-eagled on the bed. Her hands were handcuffed to the bedframe behind her and her feet were tied to the bottom of the bedframe. There was blood everywhere. Only her face was untouched though it was streaked with dried tears and make up. It was as if someone had deliberately arranged her to be looking at whoever came into the room next.

The rest of her body had been mutilated. The torture had gone far further than whatever had been necessary to extract information from her. Whoever had done this had enjoyed it. Dan had no doubt that before the mutilation had taken place, she would have been raped as well.

Dan walked over to the bed and stared down at Dana's face. He was overcome with feelings of rage and guilt. By deceiving her as to the reasons for their need for accommodation and concealing from her the real reason for their presence in the area, he had brought this on her. She had endured an agonising and slow death because of him.

'I know what you're thinking,' Jimmy said in a voice which was surprisingly gentle for him, 'but you mustn't blame yourself.'

'Who else should I blame?' Dan replied harshly. 'It was my idea to contact her, deceive her, use her, put her in danger.'

'You couldn't have anticipated this. It's easy to be wise after the event.'

'Why not? We knew the sort of people we were dealing with, what they're capable of. They did something similar to Ortega's wife. I could have anticipated something like this!'

'No. We were very careful. There must be fifty or sixty flats in this block. How could we possibly have known that they would trace us to this one?'

'Maybe we couldn't have *known* but it was always a possibility. She wasn't exactly inconspicuous. Her neighbours will have spotted she had two men staying with her. People gossip and the Russians have ears everywhere.'

'At least the men who did this are dead now.'

'At the moment, that doesn't make me feel any better.'

'I should have made that bastard suffer. I made it too easy for him with a bullet to the head!'

Dan leant over and closed Dana's eyes.

'I'm going to kill every last one of them,' he said.

'That's more like it. What are we going to do now?'

'It's time we finished this once and for all.'

'What now?'

'Why not? Now's as good a time as any. They've just lost eight men. Why not hit them before they can bring in reinforcements?'

'What about Raoul and his men?'

'I'll phone him now.'

'He might not be able to get them together now.'

'Well, we'll soon find out, won't we?'

Chapter Fifty Eight

The mood in the nondescript white van was sombre as it made its way towards the agreed meeting place. The four men all knew the risk that they were taking and that some if not all of them might not be making the journey back. But having been driven from their homes in the more affluent areas of the Costa del Sol to the back streets of Malaga to scrape a living however they could, they realised that this was their best and possibly only opportunity for revenge and to rid themselves of the foreign invaders. After the brutal killing of Fernando Ortega, they also knew that they were still vulnerable.

For some weeks now, they had been waiting for their opportunity to strike back as news of the rising Russian body count had filtered back to them. Raoul's three companions had therefore needed little persuasion to join him when he had told them of the Englishmen's plan to attack the Russians in their own fortress. They had all agreed to be ready at a moment's notice and now that moment had arrived. The great Russian bear had been wounded. Raoul had told them that the Englishmen had killed another eight men that very evening and were now planning to attack the villa before the Russians had a chance to react.

Dressed in black and holding automatic weapons, they could feel the tension rising as Raoul turned off the main road on to the uphill climb towards the meeting place.

Raoul slowed down after about half a mile and soon the headlights picked out the cutting to the right between the rocks that Dan had described on the telephone.

'I think this is it,' he said.

He turned the van slowly into the cutting. The headlights illuminated a VW parked about fifty yards in.

'That's their car,' Raoul continued. He brought the vehicle to a halt just behind the VW and switched off the lights. It was pitch black outside. No one moved.

'Where are they then?' one of the other men asked.

'I don't know,' Raoul replied. 'Let's just wait.'

They waited for about five minutes but nothing happened.

'I don't like it,' one of the others said. 'It could be a trap.'

'If it was a trap, we'd be dead by now,' Raoul replied. 'Let's get out of the van and have a look round.'

No sooner had they left the vehicle than two dark figures jumped down from the rocks, one on each side of the van. Each one shone a powerful flashlight at the four Spaniards, temporarily blinding them.

'Sorry,' Dan said, 'but we needed to confirm who you are.'

Raoul grunted. 'You nearly gave us a heart attack!'

'Ok, let's get back in your van and we'll go over the plan,' Dan said.

Dan and Jimmy got into the front seats and Raoul and his men occupied the rear two rows of seats. They could see from the light briefly shed from the interior light before the doors were shut that Dan and Jimmy were not only dressed in black with woollen hats pulled down over their foreheads but had streaked their faces with boot polish or some other similar substance.

'How's their English?' Dan asked.

'Not so good,' Raoul replied. 'I'll have to interpret for them.' He introduced the men and they all nodded at Dan and Jimmy who proceeded to go over the plan in detail.

'Any questions?' Dan said when they had finished.

The men looked at each other but said nothing.

'So is everyone happy with the plan?' Dan asked.

'You're the ones with the military expertise,' Raoul said. 'If we get to the house before we are killed, we won't let you down.'

'Good. Shall we go then?'

'Why not? Let's do it!'

Dan and Jimmy led Raoul's men across the scrub and up the hill to the vantage point that they had used to watch the villa previously, while Raoul, as agreed, stayed with the VW watching for Dan's signal on his mobile phone.

Dan looked at the entrance to the villa through the night vision binoculars provided by Ortega.

'It looks all quiet at the moment,' he said. 'OK, let's go.'

They divided into two groups with Jimmy leading two of Raoul's men to the left and Dan leading the third man to the right. Both groups crawled into position just before the road with the gates about a hundred yards to the left and right of each group respectively. Dan and Jimmy had synchronised their watches and at the same time, both groups hurried across the road and pressed themselves against the wall. They then edged quietly towards the gates and paused when they were about fifty yards away from the gates. Dan and Jimmy knew that in this position, they were not visible from the gatehouse but there was sufficient light shining through the gates to enable them to see each other.

Dan gave the signal to Jimmy and they slowly edged their way towards the gates, leaving the three Spaniards where they were. Dan and Jimmy had debated long and hard as to the best way to mount an assault on the villa. The easiest way to gain access to the grounds would have been to climb over the wall some distance from the gates. However, they would have triggered the alarm as soon as they did so. There was simply no way of approaching the villa without alerting the occupants and if they gained access by climbing the wall, they would then be vulnerable as they approached the villa from behind. It was therefore essential that the guards at the gate be dealt with. Thus, they had eventually agreed on a full frontal assault with a diversion to draw the defenders' fire.

When they reached the gates, they pressed their backs against the wall and waited for a minute to see if they had been detected. When there was no movement from the gatehouse, both men reached into their pockets and removed the pre-prepared lumps of plastic explosive and carefully reached out with their black gloved hands and applied the explosive to the gates' hinges. They then placed detonators in the explosive attached to wires and retreated to about halfway from where the Spaniards were waiting.

Dan then took out his mobile phone and sent the pre-agreed message to Raoul. There was no other traffic on the main road up the hill at that time and within seconds, Dan heard the straining engine of the VW as Raoul drove up the hill as fast as he could.

Dan looked across at Jimmy and gave him the thumbs up signal. Both men detonated their charges at the same time.

Chapter Fifty Nine

The silence was shattered by two almost simultaneous explosions. Dan and Jimmy had probably used more explosive than was necessary but they had wanted to make sure. The gates did not just come off their hinges but half the gateposts holding them in place were blown away. Dan and Jimmy crouched down to avoid any falling masonry and then hurried to the yawning gap where the gates had been. They could see the headlights of the VW as Raoul drove it down the road towards them after turning off the main road.

They entered the grounds with their AK 47s trained on the gatehouse. One man staggered out the door, seemingly disorientated by the explosions, and was immediately cut down. Jimmy was the first to the door and a long burst took out the other two men who had been in the gatehouse. Jimmy changed magazines and ran over to the VW which Raoul had driven into the entrance facing towards the villa. Raoul leapt out of the driving seat and let Jimmy get to work. The other Spaniards had by now arrived.

It took Jimmy only seconds to fit the device that he had made to jam the accelerator. By now they could hear the sound of an alarm emanating from the villa and floodlights came on illuminating the approach to the villa.

'This will only give a few seconds at best,' Dan said to Raoul. 'You know what to do.'

Raoul and his men divided into two teams of two which fanned out to the left and right so as to approach the villa from a wider angle. Jimmy jumped out of the car slamming the door as he did so and the driverless car lurched across the ground towards the villa.

The villa had a wide staircase leading up to a terrace and the front door. The terrace had a balustrade consisting of a stone top and ornate columns. As Dan and Jimmy had anticipated, at least half a dozen men had rushed out of the front door with automatic weapons to defend the villa. Dan, Jimmy and the Spaniards had the difficult task of getting to the staircase, a distance of about a hundred yards, before being cut down. The floodlights made their task even more dangerous but did come to their rescue in one respect. They were able to see the four Dobermen that appeared from around the sides of the villa, two from each side, running towards them.

The VW gave them valuable seconds. The defenders on the terrace, panicked by the explosions and the sudden attack, saw the vehicle coming and trained their fire on it. It was riddled with bullets and eventually came to a halt about halfway to the villa. Dan and Jimmy used the time gained by the diversion to shoot the dogs. But by the time the defenders had stopped shooting at the car, Dan and Jimmy had covered only just over half the distance to the steps with each of them about fifty yards either side of the car.

It was not enough. Dan and Jimmy were running as fast as they could zigzagging towards the relative safety of the wall beneath the terrace but it was virtually impossible for them to return fire in any meaningful manner running like that. Bullets began to tear up the ground around them and it was only a matter of time before they were hit.

Then the firing from the terrace eased off. Dan could see that the terrace was now being sprayed with bullets. One of the Russians went down and the rest retreated. With the Russians concentrating on the car and then Dan and Jimmy, the Spaniards had managed to reach the villa and had circled around until they had a line of sight on the defenders above them.

Dan and Jimmy flung themselves the last few yards, rolling over as they reached the base of the wall. There was now an impasse as the defenders did not want to lean over the balustrade for fear of being picked off from below and the attackers were pinned down at the base of the wall.

Dan and Jimmy, who were now on opposite sides of the staircase, had planned for this. They removed grenades from their pockets and one by one removed the pins and tossed them up on to the terraces. As soon as the first grenade exploded, they charged up the staircase firing to their left and right in case there were still men by the balustrade. They were closely followed by Raoul and his men.

When they reached the top, they saw that the terrace was littered with bodies. There were only two survivors. One tried to defend himself but did not get a shot off before he was cut down. The other tried to retreat to the open front door but did not reach it before he too was shot.

Dan, Jimmy and the Spaniards ran over to the front door but stopped on either side of it as shots were fired through it from inside the house.

'The second line of defence?' Raoul asked.

Dan looked carefully around the door producing another burst of fire from inside.

'There's a central staircase leading up to the first floor,' he said. 'There are men on the landing firing down similar to the situation out here. There are also men downstairs crouching in various doorways.'

'Have you more grenades?' Raoul asked.

'Only a couple and we couldn't possibly get them up on the landing from here. The staircase is on the other side of a large hall.'

'What about the smokebombs we provided you with?'

'That's what we'll use,' Dan replied, nodding. 'I'll throw one towards the staircase. Jimmy, you throw the other just inside the hall. Jimmy and I will head straight for the staircase which is directly ahead. I reckon the family will be up there. The rest of you divide up, two going one way and two the other. Stay close to each other and keep firing. Try to clear the ground floor and then join us upstairs.'

Raoul translated Dan's instructions for the benefit of his men and they all nodded and changed their magazines.

Dan tossed his smoke bomb as far as he could towards the staircase and Jimmy rolled his into the hall. As soon as they went off, Dan and Jimmy ran towards the stairs and the two pairs of Spaniards followed close behind, one pair moving to the left and one to the right.

All hell broke loose. Everyone started firing. Dan was first to reach the stairs and took them two at a time, firing in an arc towards the banisters on the landing. He felt a searing pain in his left arm and knew that he had had been hit. At the top of the stairs, he turned left and continued firing until he ran out of ammunition. As the smoke cleared, he tossed the AK 47 aside. He could barely hold it anyway as his left arm was virtually useless and he was bleeding heavily. He pulled out his Glock. There were two bodies on the landing ahead of him. A third man was lying wounded. Dan shot him in the head and proceeded towards a corridor down which two other men were retreating.

Chapter Sixty

Unaware that Dan had been hit, Jimmy turned right at the top of the stairs. There were two bodies ahead of him. He hurried over to the first door and kicked it open.

A man had retreated to the other side of the room, holding a struggling, partially dressed girl in front of him with one arm and a Russian made Makarov pistol in his other hand. Jimmy immediately recognised him as Petrov.

Petrov grinned malevolently as he raised the pistol. In that split second, a number of thoughts went through Jimmy's brain. First, he had no time to try an accurate shot which might miss the girl but hit the man behind her. Secondly, he knew that if he did not act immediately, he was a dead man. Lastly, Petrov was assuming that his human shield would cause Jimmy to hesitate.

Jimmy didn't hesitate. He fired a burst of three bullets before Petrov could get off a shot. Petrov's gun clattered to the floor. He relaxed his hold on the now dead girl and she slid to the floor. Petrov looked down at his stomach and clutched it in a vain attempt to stop the bleeding from holes caused by the bullets which had passed right through the girl. He sank to his knees with a look of surprise on his face. He looked up at Jimmy and as he pitched forward and died, Jimmy could have sworn that his expression changed to one of admiration.

For a moment, Jimmy was stunned that he had had to kill the girl even though he knew that there were always innocent casualties in any war and that this girl had almost certainly been a hooker prepared to sell herself to the Russians. In that moment of reflection, Jimmy failed to react quickly enough to the sound behind him. He swung his weapon round a fraction of a second too late. Two bullets hit him in the chest and he fell over on to his back, dropping his AK 47. The pain was excruciating. He knew that there was no time to pull out the Glock as a mad eyed Irina Durchenko walked over to him. She raised her pistol but then her head exploded. Raoul stood in the doorway holding a pump action shotgun, a weapon that he had liberated from one of the Russians downstairs.

Dan could hear the sound of gunfire from elsewhere in the house as he charged down the corridor after the two retreating men who had gone into a room off to the right. Dan burst into the room and dived to one side, taking in the scene as he fell. The two men appeared to be protecting a third man behind them. Dan shot one of them as he rolled over just managing to avoid the bullets fired by the other. While still rolling, and oblivious to the pain from his left arm, he managed to fire two shots over his shoulder. He heard a scream and as he got to his feet, saw that the other man had been shot in the leg. Dan finished him off with two shots and turned his attention to the other man in the room.

Sergei Durchenko was a gibbering wreck. He was the family's money man, not a man of action. Dan knew that from Luis Mendez's file.

'Where is your father?' Dan demanded, pointing his gun at Sergei's head.

'In...in.. in the room at the end. With Georgy,' Sergei stammered.

Dan pulled the trigger, released the near empty magazine of the Glock and with some difficulty, given the state of his left arm, replaced it with another.

The gunfire from the rest of the house had died down. Dan hoped that that was a good sign. He approached the room at the end of the corridor cautiously. He tried the door handle. Locked. Dan ducked to one side, which proved to be a good decision as several bullets were fired through the door from the other side.

Dan calmly removed his last grenade and removed the pin. He placed it at the base of the door and quickly retreated to the room where Sergei and his two minders lay dead.

As soon as the door blew in, Dan charged into the room firing at the two figures squatting behind a sofa on the other side of the room. Dan dived behind a large antique desk and surfaced in time to see Viktor Durchenko's large frame heading for a door just behind the sofa. Dan managed to fire two shots before he had to duck down to shelter from bullets fired at him by Georgy. Dan fired back and when Georgy ducked behind the sofa, Dan leapt across the room and jumped at the sofa. His leading foot hit the back of the sofa causing it to tip over backwards. As soon as a surprised Georgy was visible, Dan opened fire. Georgy was dead before the back of the sofa hit the floor.

Dan walked over to the door through which Viktor had escaped. Careful to avoid any firing through the door, Dan leant across and tried the handle. He need not have worried. Viktor was sprawled on the floor of what turned out to be a bathroom. He was lying with his back against the bath, sitting in a pool of blood. Dan had thought that he had hit Viktor with at least one of his shots as he had fled from the previous room and he had been right.

Viktor had a pistol in his right hand but did not have the strength to lift it. Dan kicked it out of his hand.

'I can make you a rich man,' Viktor croaked.

'You think I want your money?'

'I didn't kill your son. Alexei did. I was furious with him.'

'And then you did whatever it took to protect him.'

'He was my son.'

'Not good enough.'

Dan raised his gun and fired.

'So it's over then?'

Dan looked back and saw Jimmy leaning against the door frame in obvious pain.

'Seems like it. How are you?'

'I'll live. The Kevlar vest did its job but I think I've got a couple of broken ribs.'

Raoul appeared behind Jimmy with his arm around one of his men, holding him up. The man appeared to have wounds to his shoulder and thigh.

'What about the other two?' Dan asked.

Raoul shook his head.

In the distance they could hear the sound of sirens.

'We must go,' Dan said.

'We can't go downhill or the police will intercept us,' Raoul said. 'We will have to go up the mountain to one of the villages or urbanisations higher up and try to find some transport.'

'OK,' Dan replied. He was beginning to feel a bit light headed after all the blood he had lost. He removed his belt and with Jimmy's help tied it tightly around his upper arm.

'I'll look after Juan,' Raoul said. 'Can you two make it?'

'You bet!' Jimmy said. 'We've made it back before in a much worse state than this!'

Chapter Sixty One

The journey up the mountain proved to be arduous. Raoul had to carry Juan most of the way and Dan and Jimmy both struggled, Dan due his increasing weakness and Jimmy due to pain. They eventually reached an urbanisation comprising some expensive villas and a block of apartments. The other three waited while Raoul went to find transport.

He returned fairly quickly in an impressive looking BMW.

'I've phoned ahead. The doctor we visited before is expecting us,' Raoul said.

They got in the car and Raoul took them on a circuitous route so that they did not have to go anywhere near the Durchenko villa.

'What about your van?' Dan asked. 'The police will find it.'

'It can't be traced to us,' Raoul said. 'It won't help them.'

'Can we go via Puerto Banus? There's something I need to pick up,' Dan said.

'You are joking? We've just been involved in the biggest battle down here since the civil war, we have three wounded men and you want to go to Malaga via Puerto Banus?'

'Our drunken doctor friend is going to want paying. The money we took from the casino is in Puerto Banus.'

Raoul chuckled.

'I guess that's a detour worth taking then!'

It seemed an age since Dan had discovered Dana but in fact it had only been a matter of hours. While the others remained in the car, he went up to her flat and retrieved the bag of money which he had left in her living room. As he was leaving the flat, he paused and although he had not intended to do so, he went back and took one last look at her. She was of course just as he had found her. He resolved to phone the police and leave an anonymous report of her death. The rage had gone but as soon as he felt himself welling up, he closed her door and left the apartment.

Inspector Valdez surveyed the scene. He could hardly believe what he was looking at. Reports had come through of gunfire at the Durchenko villa but he hadn't expected anything like this. His deputy interrupted his thoughts.

'Are there any survivors?' Valdez asked.

'We found some local domestic staff locked in the cellar. Two of them have bullet wounds but they'll survive.'

'What have they said?'

'Nothing of any help. Most of them were in bed when they heard an explosion and then gunfire which lasted for ages. Some of them were foolish enough to go and see what was happening and two of them got caught in the crossfire. When it was all over, a big man ushered them down to the cellar at gunpoint and locked them in.'

'Nationality?'

'Spanish. But apart from the fact that he was big, we've nothing else to go on. They hardly dared to look at him. There is one thing of interest though.'

'Yes?' Valdez said, impatiently.

'Most of the dead are Russians but we have identified two men who look as if they are Spanish.'

'Show me.'

Valdez followed his deputy to a room on the ground floor where a body lay beside two others. Valdez studied the man's face.

'And the other?'

His deputy led him to another room.

'Interesting,' Valdez said.

'You know them, sir?'

'They are known associates of Fernando Ortega.'

'The arms dealer who was murdered by the Russians in Malaga?'

Valdez nodded.

'So you think that this was some sort of revenge attack by his friends?'

'Possibly. But I find it hard to believe that a gang that fled from the Russians to the back streets of Malaga could have mounted this attack without their leader. Or even with him.'

'So you think they had help?'

'I'm damn sure they had help!'

The doctor, or rather ex-doctor, was waiting for them as he opened the door before they knocked. He ushered them through to the same room where Jimmy had been treated previously. Once again, he stank of drink and the first thing he did was to get five glasses out and a bottle of liquor. On this occasion, even Dan took a glass.

As Juan was in the worst state, the doctor treated him first. He injected Juan in the vicinity of his wounds and, after much clucking from the doctor and screaming from Juan, extracted bullets from his shoulder and thigh. He then stitched him up and bandaged him. Dan had to admit that once again, he did a pretty good job.

Dan was next. The bullet had passed through his arm so the doctor cleaned the entry and exit wounds, stitched Dan up and bandaged him too.

He then diagnosed that Jimmy did indeed have broken ribs but since there was no sign of a punctured lung, he simply bandaged him up tightly and gave him a jar of painkillers.

When the doctor had finished, Dan asked how much he wanted. Through Raoul, he asked for five thousand euros. Dan nodded, reached into his bag and gave him ten thousand, much to the doctor's delight.

'What are you going to do now?' Raoul asked, when they were back in the car.

'Go home, I suppose,' Dan replied. 'It's highly likely the Spanish police will be looking for us so we will avoid airports and railway stations as we did before and drive.'

'You'll need a car,' Raoul said.

'We could take this one,' Jimmy said, 'or nick another.'

'No,' Raoul replied, 'a stolen car is too risky. You can take my car.'

'That would be great. We'll tell you where we've left it,' Dan said.

'Don't worry about that. I'd rather claim the insurance!'

'What will you do?'

'When the police find Carlos and Rafa's bodies, they will come looking for me and Juan,' Raoul said. 'We will disappear for a few weeks while Juan recovers.'

'Where will you go?'

'Fernando had a villa on Mallorca registered in the name of an offshore company. Juan and I will go there and our wives will tell the police that we've gone on a fishing trip. You can take my car and we will take Juan's and head for Valencia, where we can get a ferry. The police will never find us there and when we return, we will just deny all knowledge of what happened tonight.'

They abandoned the stolen BMW a few streets from where Raoul lived and walked the rest of the way to his house. Raoul had phoned ahead and his wife was waiting at the door. Much to his embarrassment, she flung her arms around Raoul's neck. Dan wondered if she'd thought that when he had left home earlier that that would be the last time she would see him.

Raoul quickly packed a small case and they all got into his Jeep Cherokee car and drove the short distance to Juan's house. Juan's wife, an attractive woman in her forties, was upset when she saw her husband's condition but he told her not to worry and that he would be fine. Or at least, that was what he appeared to Dan to be saying as he hobbled into the house and packed a bag for himself. As he was a similar size to Dan and Jimmy, he also provided them with a change of clothes and explained through Raoul that his wife would burn their own clothes.

Raoul and Juan then put their bags in Juan's Opel.

'We will lead you to the main road,' Raoul said. 'Then you will head north and we will head east to Valencia.'

Dan reached into his bag and handed two bundles of notes, each comprising about fifty thousand euros, to Raoul and Juan.

Raoul hesitated.

'We didn't do it for the money,' he said.

'I know you didn't,' Dan replied. 'But we couldn't have done it without you. And it's not as if we're paying you. We took this money from the Durchenkos so you might as well share in it.'

'Thank you,' Raoul said, taking one of the bundles while Juan took the other. 'We will give some of this to the Carlos and Rafa's families.'

'Of course,' Dan said, reaching into the bag again. 'Here's some more for them.'

The four men embraced and then set off on their long journeys.

Chapter Sixty Two

The battle at the Durchenkos' villa had happened too late to make the morning papers and the whole area was blocked off while the police carried out their investigation. There were some short reports on the local television channel of an incident involving gunfire at a villa in the mountains behind Marbella but nothing that gave any details.

Inspector Valdez therefore studied his friend carefully after he had explained what had happened, as he sat with him on his balcony. However, there was nothing in Luis Mendez's demeanour which suggested that he had known anything about the incident before being told about it. Indeed, he appeared to be stunned by the news.

Luis took a sip of his coffee and looked out to sea.

'So the only clue you have is the bodies of two of Ortega's men?' he said.

'We've recovered a lot of weapons left by the attackers but there are no prints on them. We have also found an abandoned van which we believe conveyed the men to the location but it had been stolen earlier in the day.'

'What about the link to Ortega?'

'We've rounded up a number of his old associates but they all deny any knowledge of the incident. But we couldn't trace Raoul Perez or Juan Navarro. Their wives say they have gone on a fishing trip.'

'Fishing? Those two? That hardly seems likely.'

'And I can't imagine any action being taken by Ortega's gang without Perez being involved.'

'So what will you do?'

'Wait till they get back and take them in. But they won't say anything. Anyway, I'm more interested in who helped them.'

'You don't think they acted alone, then?'

'Come on, Luis. You're not telling me that a ragbag gang of criminals was capable of launching a successful assault on a heavily guarded villa. This had all the hallmarks of a military operation. Just like a number of other incidents down here in recent weeks.'

Luis remained silent.

'Any idea who might be responsible?' Valdez asked.

'None whatsoever,' Luis replied. 'But whoever it was has done this area and the country as a whole a great service.'

'I thought you might say that.'

'Don't you agree?'

This time it was Valdez who remained silent.

'You do, don't you?' Luis persisted.

'I guess so,' Valdez admitted. 'And the demise of the Durchenkos is already having huge consequences. News like this travels fast even if the media don't have the full story. Now that the threat from the Durchenkos has been lifted, we have already had a couple of phone calls from people willing to expose corruption at the highest level. There will be a lot of worried people who have made fortunes by cooperating with the Durchenkos.'

'Including police officers?'

'Regrettably, yes.'

'It sounds like you are going to be very busy cleaning up the mess then, even if you don't get to the bottom of who else was involved in the assault on the villa.'

Dan and Jimmy took their time getting home. They crossed over into France and spent a week recuperating at a small hotel on the beach at Le Lavandou, and eventually arrived back in London about a week after that.

Back at Dan's flat, they divided up the rest of the euros between them.

'What will you do now?' Jimmy asked.

'Go back to work and try to get on with my life without Tom. What about you?'

'I guess I'll have to find a job.'

'I can't promise you adventures like the one we've just been on, but we can always use someone like you. Why don't you come and work for us?'

'I thought you'd never ask!'

Sandra Wilson was sitting with the curtains still closed, only half concentrating on daytime television when the doorbell rang. After a couple of minutes, her mother came in with a package.

'I've just signed for this for you,' she said. 'Have you ordered something on the internet?'

'No, of course not,' Sandra replied. 'Give it here. Let's see what it is.'

She removed the brown paper and found something wrapped up in a plastic bag. To her astonishment, she saw that the bag contained a huge wad of euros. There was also a note. 'You don't need to worry about Alexei or any of his associates any more. Use this to get your face fixed.'

8003224R00226

Printed in Great Britain
by Amazon.co.uk, Ltd.,
Marston Gate.